THE MUMMY'S CURSE

M.A. BENNETT

WELBECK
FLAME

Published in 2022 by Welbeck Flame
An imprint of Welbeck Children's Limited,
Part of Welbeck Publishing Group.
Based in London and Sydney.

ISBN: 978 1 80130 023 0

Printed and bound by CPI Group (UK)

10 9 8 7 6 5 4 3 2 1

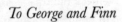

To George and Finn

who had an amazing papa too

Dear Reader,

If you are reading this you are already a time traveller, because this is the year 1894 and Queen Victoria is on the throne.

And if you are reading this you must be a friend, so I feel all right about sharing with you the secrets of The Butterfly Club.

Let me begin at the beginning. My name is Luna and I suppose you would call me a time-thief. I live in a rather smart part of London with my Aunt Grace, who's been looking after me ever since my father disappeared. One Thursday Aunt Grace took me with her to her secret society, The Butterfly Club.

The Butterfly Club meets every Thursday afternoon in Greenwich, at the famous Royal Observatory, which is the Home of Time. It's called that because there is a long brass line running through the courtyard of the observatory called the Prime Meridien, the point from which all time is measured.

Deep in the belly of the observatory is the Butterfly Room, a twelve-sided secret chamber where the Butterfly Club meet. It's called the Butterfly Room because there are butterflies on the walls - those dead ones pinned to little cards - in all the colours of the rainbow. The members of the Butterfly Club are the finest minds of Victorian society - people you might have heard of even in your time, people like Charles Dickens, Charles Darwin and Florence Nightingale.

And that's where I met my fellow time thieves. You see, there are three of us.

Konstantin is from Prussia, he has loads of brothers who are all soldiers, and his father, Dr Tanius Kass, is a very clever inventor. Konstantin loves everything military, but because he was so ill when he was little, he couldn't be a soldier himself. But Konstantin is special in his own way, because he has a mechanical heart. His own heart didn't work so his father replaced it with a clockwork one.

The third time-thief is Aidan. Aidan is Irish, and he is a navigational engineer (or 'navvy') who's been working on the railways ever since he was ten. Aidan knows everything there is to know about machines, and sometimes I think he loves them better than people. And, like Konstantin, Aidan has a secret too; which he also keeps his very close to his chest.

The three of us are called time-thieves because we've been travelling in time, carrying out missions for the Butterfly Club. We use a contraption called the Time Train, which was designed by HG Wells, one of the club's members. We travel forward in time to collect inventions and treasures from the future. We never go backwards. The whole point is to bring back things which our age doesn't have yet, to speed up progress. Aunt Grace says our thieving is for 'the betterment of society'. I hope she's right. The Butterfly Club certainly seem to get a lot of money and prizes out of it.

Well, dear reader, Aidan, Konstantin and me have had quite a few journeys through the decades since the day we met, and faced many dangers, and you can read all about them.

I hope you enjoy our adventures!

Yours until the end of time,
Luna Goodhart x

PS: I'll write again, but always look out for the ink butterfly (above) when I do. It's called a Rorschach blot, every one is different, and that's how you'll know the letter is from me.

LONDON

25 JANUARY 1894

25 JANUARY 1894
11.55 a.m.

Thursday found Luna Goodhart curled up in a window seat, staring out at the snowy London street.

She couldn't wait for the hansom cab to come to take them to the Butterfly Club, and this time she was ready well before her aunt. She'd chosen her dress carefully – it was the vivid indigo of the Great Purple Emperor butterfly, a specimen of which was pinned to the hallway wall in the midst of all its brightly coloured brothers and sisters. She'd also put on a warm carriage cloak and a fur muff in readiness. It was important that she dressed in her best, for that afternoon, she fervently hoped, she would be seeing her fellow time-thieves again.

It was odd, after spending every waking minute with Konstantin and Aidan, to adjust to not seeing them at all.

Konstantin, so far as she knew, was living with his father in Whitehall, somewhere near Horse Guards Parade, which seemed a fittingly military place for him to be. Aidan was living with his father in lodgings in Kilburn – nice and handy for working on the railway tracks for a brand-new line at King's Cross.

It had only been ten days, but she missed them terribly. She missed Konstantin's Prussian accent, his old-world courtesy and his tin-soldier bravery. She missed Aidan's machine-mad passion and his crazy clothes cobbled together with cogs. She even missed his insolent grin. Being back in the tall, skinny house in Kensington, with nothing but the butterflies on the wall for company, was a poor substitute for the two brothers she had found.

She had wondered too, in the past week, if she could expect the return of her father. So convinced was she that he'd been the enterprising fellow who'd managed to post himself off the *Titanic* in a mail bag, that she'd almost expected him to walk back into her life. At the very least she'd expected a letter, and she'd shaken out the pages of every boring book in the library, hoping to find a letter with a Rorschach blot, but there was nothing in them but long scientific words affixed firmly to the pages. Life seemed to pick up where she'd left it off, and however many times she thought she'd seen a lock of auburn hair in a crowd, peeping from a stovepipe hat or a bowler, it wasn't Papa.

The casement clock in the hall chimed noon, and Aunt Grace came to stand behind her, laying a pale hand on her purple shoulder. Aunt Grace had also dressed in her best – the acid orange of a Banded Orange Tiger butterfly, a hue which clashed beautifully with her auburn hair. Aunt Grace had been an angel all week – much kinder than she'd ever been, so delighted was she with Luna's success aboard the *Titanic*. It had taken the Butterfly Club a matter of days to make Guglielmo Marconi's continuous spark wireless radio from the notes Luna had taken from the physicist's dictation, and now the secret society was on course to win the Gabriel Medal and the thousand gold sovereigns that were in the gift of Queen Victoria. So Aunt Grace had spent the week practically purring.

Taking advantage of this good mood, Luna felt she could be a little more forthright than she had been before. 'Hurry up, Aunt! The hansom cab will be here any moment.'

Aunt Grace smiled, the way she'd been smiling all week – like the cat who'd got the cream. 'Actually, my dear, you are going on a little expedition first. I will meet you at the Butterfly Club later.'

'On my own?' Luna, who had been to the future and back, still didn't relish the thought of a solo cab ride around London.

'No, no,' said her aunt. 'You will have a very special chaperone.'

At that moment there was the clamour of horseshoes on the street. A very grand carriage, pulled by four black horses instead of the single nag which usually pulled a hansom cab, stopped in front of the house in a flurry of snow and a spark of hooves. The four were perfectly matched and stood tossing their heads, as if they knew how handsome they were. Their coats were so shiny they looked like they were made of patent leather. The black coach was just as shiny, and through the falling snow Luna could just make out the golden monogram on the carriage door. It read:

A C D

A gloved hand opened the door from the inside and a gentleman in a top hat leant forward. Luna recognised the moustaches first. They belonged to the famous author, Mr Arthur Conan Doyle.

25 JANUARY 1894
Noon

'Well,' said Aunt Grace fondly, 'go on then.'

'I am to go with Mr Conan Doyle?' said Luna, wide-eyed.

'Yes. He is taking you for a treat. By way of a thank you for your successful mission.'

Luna got up and smoothed down her purple skirts. 'What manner of treat?'

Aunt Grace's smile widened. 'You'll see.'

Luna trod carefully through the falling snow, pulling her carriage cloak close over her purple dress.

As she approached the coach a gloved hand reached out to help her up. On the pale inches of skin between glove and sleeve she could clearly see the black stamp of a butterfly tattoo. As she took the proffered hand she recalled that this whole thing had started with Aunt Grace's hand in a glove – when her aunt had come to collect her from Papa's house in Greenwich. What manner of adventure was she embarking on this time?

Luna clambered into the carriage and settled herself across from the author. She had experienced some strange things in the past days and this was certainly one of them. But she needn't have worried. She found herself on the receiving end of the most sincere and heartfelt thank-you speech she had ever heard, all delivered in Conan Doyle's soft Scottish accent.

'Really,' finished Mr Conan Doyle, 'I and the other members of the Butterfly Club are most indebted to you, and your fellow time travellers. With your mission to the *Titanic*, and your recruitment of Signor Guglielmo Marconi, you have done an incalculable service and certainly secured our funding for our next venture.'

Luna felt emboldened to ask, 'Which is what?'

Conan Doyle's answer was the very same as the one Aunt Grace had given that first day at the Royal Observatory. 'All in good time.' He rapped his cane on the roof of the carriage and, with a jolt, it pulled away.

The carriage was beautifully warm and the wheels well sprung, not at all like the tooth-rattling hansom cabs. She enjoyed looking from the window at the snowy scenes of London; the snowbones made by the carriage wheels on the roads; the white expanses of Kensington Gardens and Hyde Park, their trees and fountains now blunted and lumpy with snow. Since it was the dead of winter the lamplighters were already placing their ladders on the lanterns, climbing up with bright tapers to light the wicks.

Luna could only gaze from the window for so long – the silence stretched and soon there must be conversation. But, as it turned out, she didn't have to worry about what to say. People began to shout at the carriage, recognising the gilded monogram as it went by.

'Why d'you kill 'im off, Mr Doyle?'

'It's a bleedin' crime, sir!'

'How could you do it to 'im?'

Some were friendly, some were plaintive, but some shook their fists.

Luna pulled her head in and sat back in her seat, staring at Mr Conan Doyle in surprise. 'Who are they talking about?'

His mouth twisted. 'Sherlock Holmes, naturally.'

Of *course*. It was the talk of London. Mr Conan Doyle's enormously popular Sherlock Holmes stories, in which the Great Detective solved crimes with his sidekick

Dr Watson, were published weekly in *The Strand Magazine* to great acclaim. But in the most recent instalment, Sherlock Holmes had been killed when his nemesis Moriarty had thrown him from a waterfall, and the nation was in shock. Mr Conan Doyle smiled ruefully. 'Anyone would think I murdered the blighter.'

'Well,' said Luna, encouraged by his friendliness. 'In a way, you did.'

'Don't they understand?' cried Mr Conan Doyle. 'I just want to be a historical novelist. The present holds no joy for me. My new passion is the past. And sometimes to reach the past, one has to travel by way of the future.'

Luna didn't even attempt to understand this. 'Where are we going?'

'We are going to see someone who is dead.'

This sounded like a very odd treat to Luna, but she was slightly reassured when the carriage pulled up at the vast and noble frontage of the British Museum. She loved the British Museum and Papa had taken her there many times as a little girl. To her it was a treasure box and a treat indeed.

But as the driver handed her down from the carriage, the shouted remarks addressed to Mr Conan Doyle began again. Luna began to appreciate just how hard it must be for that gentleman to go about town at the moment. Even the coachman had to add his tuppenny-worth. 'When you bringing 'im back, mister?'

'I'm not,' said Conan Doyle shortly as he slammed the carriage door. 'I promise you: Sherlock Holmes is dead and gone. And I always keep my promises.'

The British Museum had never looked more impressive. In the low winter sun the wide stone steps, the mighty pillars and the triangular portico were turned to rose gold – the very building was a treasure in itself. Mr Conan Doyle gave Luna his arm and they began to mount the stone stairs, and it was then a curious thing happened.

A lone black dog trotted across the museum steps. His muzzle was long, his coat was short and sleek and two long ears stood straight up from his head like a jackal's. He turned to look directly at them with almond eyes, then slunk away. 'He's a long way from home,' said Mr Conan Doyle. 'Some stray, doubtless.'

Mr Conan Doyle led her through the crowds of people in the public halls, enduring yet more shouted enquiries about his deceased character, this time a bit more genteel than the cries on the street.

'Oh, Mr Doyle, why did you do it?'

'Mr Doyle, we are *quite* devastated.'

'We are positively in *mourning*, Mr Doyle.'

The object of their disapproval lowered his head and ploughed on. 'I swear, I will shave these moustaches off if this continues,' he said bitterly.

They passed huge stone lions from Assyria, golden sarcophagi from Egypt and winged marble horses from ancient Greece. Mr Conan Doyle spared them not a glance. He hurried up the grand staircase and then took Luna through a little door all but hidden in the shadows. The crowds, abruptly, disappeared.

They walked along a passageway lined with blank-eyed statues, and into an intimate lecture theatre. The auditorium, with dark wood seats steeply raked down to a little stage in the middle, was like an old operating theatre in the great medical hospitals like St Bart's. There was no natural light, no reassuring evidence that it was still daylight outside. This was a gathering of the night. The place was lit by thousands of candles, set upon the wooden pews, which gave the whole proceeding the air of an ancient ritual.

The theatre was packed with people, but they seemed to be a more learned crowd than the general public in the rest of the museum. There were very many distinguished-looking ladies and gentlemen, and lots of them had notepads or sketchbooks with them. In the buzz of learned chatter Luna was reminded of the Butterfly Club.

We're going to see someone who is dead. From all the comments and catcalls on the way there, she had a dark fantasy that Mr Sherlock Holmes himself would be appearing on the little stage. But for one thing, Mr Sherlock Holmes was a fictional character and for another, this was a lecture, not a séance. Luna gave up trying to guess, and shuffled along the row to two empty seats set in a prime position to see the stage. Two familiar figures were already seated in their row. Luna turned to Mr Conan Doyle, beaming with delight.

He smiled below the impressive moustaches. 'I neglected to say,' he said, 'when I said we were going to see someone who is dead, that we would also be seeing two someones who are very much alive.'

Both of the boys leapt to their feet. 'It is very good to see you, *Fräulein*,' said Konstantin, kissing her hand in a courtly way.

Aidan took the same hand and pumped it up and down like a piston. 'Jesus, Mary and Joseph, you're a sight for sore eyes, Duch,' he said, grinning all over his face.

So were they. Konstantin was wearing a suit of Prussian Blue cloth, and although it wasn't strictly a uniform, the brass buttons gave it a military air. His blonde hair and grey eyes shone – the clockwork heart must be doing its work well. Aidan looked as outlandish as ever, in a way that entirely suited him. His clothes, as iron grey and steam white as his beloved engines, were embellished with cogs and chains and buckles. His black hair, crammed under a cap and goggles, had still not seen a comb, and his startling blue eyes shone out from his tanned face.

'How've you been, me old duch?' he enquired, with his usual disregard for manners.

'Bored,' she said honestly.

'Same here,' said Konstantin. 'How about you, Aidan?'

'No time for that,' he said. 'I've been building a little thing called the Great Northern Railway. You're welcome, by the way.' The trademark grin widened. 'What are we all doing here, do we know?'

'No idea,' whispered Luna.

Mr Conan Doyle leant across to them. 'It's something called an Unwrapping.'

'An Unwrapping?' repeated Luna. 'An Unwrapping of what?'

'Shhh,' said Mr Conan Doyle, placing his forefinger below his moustaches and over his mouth. 'It begins.'

25 JANUARY 1894
1 p.m.

A middle-aged man walked into the very centre of the little stage below and the whole place hushed. He had intense dark eyes, a bushy black beard, wavy black hair parted severely on one side and an air of authority. Notebooks rustled in readiness and a young man seated in front of them with a sketchbook on his lap opened it to find a blank space. On the pages he turned, Luna saw wonders and marvels – incredible drawings of dog-headed gods and bird-headed goddesses, golden tombs and silver caskets and turquoise scarabs, all rendered in glorious colour. The young man was clearly a formidable artist.

Then the middle-aged man on the stage began to speak and Luna's attention was all for him.

'My name, as some of you know,' he said, 'is Professor Flinders Petrie, associate director of the British Museum.'

He got no further than this before he was interrupted by a sputter of applause.

'Thank you, thank you,' he said, bowing humbly. 'You are most kind. As those of you who were good enough to applaud are doubtless aware, I also have the honour to be a professor of Egyptian Archaeology at University College London. I have spent these past many years in Egypt uncovering the lost city of Tanis, and now our sphere of exploration has moved to a portion of the Nile Delta called the Valley of the Kings. This valley is so named because under its sands lie great wonders – the tombs of the long-dead pharaohs, chambers lined with gold and unimaginable treasures, palaces of the dead,' he said importantly. 'We are only just beginning to uncover these works, and are at the most exciting era of Egyptology to date. Recently, a major site, most unromantically called tomb KV35, was discovered in the Valley of the Kings, containing no less than three royal coffins, or sarcophagi as we call them. The first of these sarcophagi contained the mummified body of Tiye, Great Royal Wife of Pharaoh Amenhotep III. She has become known to us as 'The Elder Lady'. The signs and hieroglyphs in the tomb lead us to believe that the second sarcophagus will contain her daughter, The Younger Lady. And tonight' – he paused dramatically like an actor – '*we will find out.*'

Just then, eight men in dark suits entered the stage, buckling under the weight of a golden sarcophagus. Three further men placed a wheeled table in the middle of the stage, covered it with a white cloth, and the sarcophagus was placed carefully upon it.

The eleven men, with Professor Petrie making the twelfth, ringed the sarcophagus like the hours of a clock. 'Behold,' said Flinders Petrie, throwing out his arms like a magician. 'The sarcophagus of The Younger Lady. Tonight, before your very eyes, myself and my assistants will unwrap her body from its ancient bandages and you ladies and gentlemen will be the first to look upon her countenance for *three thousand years.*'

A murmur rippled about the crowd, and Luna, Konstantin and Aidan exchanged glances of delicious anticipation. At the centre of it all, unmoved, lay the image on the top of the sarcophagus. A stylised queen, hands crossed on her breast, almond eyes staring from heavy make-up. Her hair, in a hundred black braids, was half-hidden by a glorious headdress of golden feathers, and her gown was an enamelled wonder of turquoise and lapis lazuli. The candlelight kindled the golden coffer as if it was aflame, and the queen stared haughtily ahead, even when the twelve men laid their hands on her, and began to lift the lid of the sarcophagus.

The audience were utterly silent – scribbling and drawing hands were stilled, and every eye was trained on the ornate box and what lay inside. But at the moment the lid of the sarcophagus was opened, with a small puff of three-thousand-year-old dust, the howl of a dog rent the air. Luna had the strangest feeling the howl belonged to the jackal she and Mr Conan Doyle had seen on the museum steps, the one who had looked at them so oddly. His cry chilled the blood. And at that moment, Luna had a terrible feeling of foreboding. She felt that something had been released from that coffin, something nameless and numberless that would not easily be contained.

She realised she'd been squeezing the life out of Konstantin's hand. Shyly, without looking at him, she released it and leant forward as far as she could to see inside the sarcophagus. For a moment she thought there was nothing there, and feared the humiliation that awaited Professor Petrie if that were true. But with the lid lifted entirely she and all those gathered could see a shrunken, shrivelled thing, wrapped in dirty and discoloured bands.

All of the men in dark suits faded away, leaving Flinders Petrie alone on the stage with The Younger Lady. He took off his frock coat and rolled up the sleeves of his shirt. Luna noted that his wrists were bare – no butterflies, no tattoos.

Professor Petrie got to work, quickly and brutally. Luna was shocked at the speed of the Unwrapping. She had expected something slow and reverent, each bandage laid by and numbered or even each stage to be punctuated by prayer. But no. Professor Petrie tore at the wrappings like a child at Christmastide, impatient to get to the prize inside.

He pulled off the cerecloths and bandages, tossing them in a stained heap at his feet. He tore at crackling rolls of linen, which emitted more clouds of ancient dust as they were ripped apart. A strong aromatic odour rose to Luna's nose, which she assumed must come from the dried and blackened leaves that had been lovingly layered between the cloths, only to be scattered on the stage and kicked aside by the professor's boot. At last, Professor Petrie had uncovered what lay at the heart of all those bandages – something dark and shrunken. 'My friend,' said Professor Petrie to one of his accomplices. 'The knives.'

He took two of the implements out of the wooden box that was offered to him, choosing his weapons as carefully as a man about to fight a duel. He then brandished the chosen knives at his audience, clashing them together like a sword-swallower to show that they were sharp and real. 'These blades are heated,' he confided, 'to better prise the ancient flesh from the wood of the sarcophagus. Various sacred oils and resins are used in the mummification process, and regrettably, they act like a rather strong glue.' Professor Petrie then proceeded to dig at the dark mass, scraping and shovelling, as if some stubborn potato had burned on to the bottom of his favourite pan. Under such attack the poor lady quickly came loose, rising and shrugging in a most alarming way, as if she was waking from a deep sleep.

'And now for the *pièce de résistance*,' he declared. Luna didn't understand the French but could tell by the way he said it that they were about to see the climax of this strange performance. 'I and my helpers will assist The Younger Lady to stand erect for the first time in three millennia.'

He pulled the mummy to a sitting position, and in his impatience he tore the right arm clean off, just below the shoulder. 'Oops,' he said, waving the limb, and the crowd tittered in a shocked and sickened way. 'Unfortunately, the flesh is so desiccated by this point that such things are bound to happen. No matter.'

It took just one of his assistants to help Professor Petrie to lift the broken thing right out of the sarcophagus, as the body seemed as light as a bird.

They set her on her feet, standing between her two living sentinels, like some obscene arrest of the dead, and the audience clapped and clapped.

The Younger Lady seemed small, much smaller than Luna, perhaps five feet in height. Her clothes were no more than shreds, leaving her shoe-leather skin cruelly exposed. The skull was bald, the eyes closed and there was a gaping hole in her left cheek. The young man sitting in front of Luna began sketching with rapid strokes, transferring the scene in front of them to the page.

The mummy made a pathetic sight, a dreadful contrast to the proud queen on the lid of the sarcophagus, who watched from where she was propped against the wall, seemingly unmoved by the fate of her mortal flesh. 'Jesus, Mary and Joseph,' breathed Aidan. 'She's nothing but a bag o' bones.'

Mr Conan Doyle's response was somewhat different. He craned forward. 'Hmm,' he mused in an undertone. 'The cause of death looks like a large defect involving her left cheek, left maxillary sinus, alveolar process, and part of her left mandible. Perhaps an axe wound, or else a good kick from a horse. Poor soul.'

The accomplished young man with the sketchbook looked round with interest.

'Ah, perhaps you do not know,' said Mr Conan Doyle in Luna's ear. 'Before I became a writer I was a medical doctor.'

'So you are more of a Dr Watson than a Sherlock Holmes?' whispered Luna.

'Most assuredly,' said Mr Conan Doyle. 'I've never detected anything in my life.'

Luna's eyes travelled back to the shrunken figure on the stage. The mummy's remaining hand was clasped as if in a fury. There was something eerie, and strangely powerful, about her. Tiny and shrivelled, naked and incomplete, she still looked as if she could reach out her twig-brittle arms to the audience and claim them for her own dark realm. Luna's palms began to dampen with fear, but before the skeleton could do anything of the sort, the sarcophagus was cleared away and the mummy laid on the white cloth that covered the table.

'Now I will cut away a section of the skull, and show you all a wondrous thing.'

Professor Flinders Petrie set to work once more, this time with a small serrated blade, and as he sawed energetically there was a strong acrid smell like burning hair. At length he lifted a circle of bone like a lid. He turned the wheeled table round so that the audience was staring directly into The Younger Lady's skull.

'As you can see,' he said, 'empty. Hollow as a drum. And this is because after death the ancients actually pushed burning hot hooks into the cranium, scrambled the brain like a panful of eggs, and then pulled the grey matter out through the nostrils.'

At this he got a satisfactory reaction from the ladies, who gasped and swooned. Aidan chuckled happily.

'And there may be yet another secret.' Petrie lifted the mummy's remaining arm, and attempted to open the clasped hand. A couple of the dry finger joints cracked off in his hand, so he tossed them into the sarcophagus. At last he achieved his object, prising the fingers open. He took something small from the hand and held out what he had found to the audience on an open palm. Everyone leant forward as one, but instead of a priceless jewel or a magic ring, there just lay a few mud-coloured grains.

'Mummy wheat,' the professor declared. 'A variety of grain which has not been seen for three thousand years.

And the wonder of it is, my friends, that if I were to plant this it would grow as if it was cultivated yesterday.' The crowd's disappointment transformed to wonder, and Professor Petrie was careful to say, 'If you visit this very museum in the coming months, you will see these very seeds transformed into green shoots.' The audience made satisfying *oo* and *ah* noises. 'And now,' said Professor Petrie, as his assistants imprecisely tucked The Younger Lady back in her box, 'are there any questions from the floor?'

A forest of hands shot up.

'Are these bones to be given a Christian burial, once they have answered the questions of science?' asked one lady. Luna gazed at the back of her head with fierce approval. The lady had put into words what Luna herself had been feeling – that this didn't seem the right way to treat a person's remains.

'Dear lady, no,' said Petrie with a little laugh. 'Once we have completed our researches The Younger Lady will be on display in this very museum, with the other finds from her tomb. You must remember,' he slapped the sarcophagus smartly with his hand and the bones jumped a little, 'these were heathen peoples – ignorant souls who worshipped snakes and dogs and hawks.' There was a ripple of laughter from the crowd. 'There is no need to afford them the godly rites we Christians deserve.'

Luna's insides felt a bit squirmy at this answer and she missed the next few questions as she stared at the broken queen – now no more, as Aidan had said, than a bag o' bones. Or rather, a box of bones.

Then the young artist sitting in front of Luna put up his hand. 'You mentioned a third sarcophagus,' he said in bright and eager tones. 'Who was in that one?'

'Ah, good evening, Howard,' exclaimed the professor. 'Nice to see you.' Flinders Petrie lowered his voice to a dramatic whisper. 'We had a very strong reason to believe that the third sarcophagus would contain the mummy of The Younger Lady's son, and The Elder Lady's grandson. It was a juvenile male skeleton, so we allowed ourselves to hope that it was the mummy of a pharaoh whose name is legendary among Egyptologists, but who seems as far out of reach as the ancient precincts of Atlantis. It is a name you may know...' He paused for effect. 'It is Tutankhamun.'

The word echoed around the lecture theatre like an ancient incantation. The crowd gasped, and the candles flickered in the breeze of a hundred exhalations.

Luna felt a shiver travel up her spine. She had, of course, heard of the fabled boy king, but like most people, thought him about as real, and about as likely to be found, as the Holy Grail. Was it possible that he had, at last, been traced? But in another moment she knew that it couldn't be true. If Tutankhamun *had* been found, he would have been the subject of this horrid unravelling. It would be his arm that was wrested from its socket, his head that was sliced open like a melon.

'Sadly,' Professor Petrie went on, 'it was not he. So the search continues.'

There was a small silence and it seemed that the spectacle was at an end. But then Mr Conan Doyle raised his hand. Professor Petrie stepped to the edge of the stage and shaded his eyes against the candlelight. 'Ah, my old friend Mr Conan Doyle! I am delighted to see you, sir.'

There was a murmur and a rustle and the audience turned as one to gawk at the famous author. Mr Conan Doyle, who clearly hadn't wished to be identified, growled a little beneath his moustaches. But he asked his question all the same. 'Is there no clue as to Tutankhamun's whereabouts?'

'Not a single one,' said the Egyptologist. 'We could certainly do with the assistance of Mr Holmes himself, were he not so recently deceased.'

A little ripple of laughter shivered the audience and Luna looked sharply at the professor. People didn't usually make jokes about their greatest disappointment. But he didn't sound as downcast as he might have done; indeed, Luna thought she could see a tiny sparkle in his eye besides the candle flames. *He knows something*, she thought.

As Professor Petrie thanked the crowd, and the ladies and gentlemen rose and left the auditorium, Luna took a last peek at the sketchbook of the young man in front of her. There, beautifully rendered, was The Younger Lady, just as she had stood before them. She was still broken and incomplete, but, even in the drawing, she seemed to possess a formidable power.

25 JANUARY 1894
3 p.m.

As the auditorium emptied and Professor Petrie's assistants went about extinguishing candles, Mr Conan Doyle leant across to address the time-thieves. 'Come,' he said, 'I want you to meet Flinders. As he already revealed, he is a friend of mine.'

It was lucky Professor Petrie had spoken up, because Luna was about to indignantly share with her friends the opinion that the eminent Egyptologist seemed to have little respect for the young woman in the sarcophagus. But when Mr Conan Doyle said that, she contented herself with rolling her eyes at the other two and grimacing in a way Aunt Grace would think most unladylike. The others seemed to share her view, because when they followed the author down to the stage Konstantin bowed his head in respect before the now-closed sarcophagus, and Aidan crossed himself.

'Ah, Arthur, my friend!' The professor held out his hand. 'You are goodness itself to come.'

'As I promised,' said Mr Conan Doyle, warmly shaking the hand that was offered. 'And I always keep my promises.'

The Egyptologist smiled pleasantly at the time-thieves. 'Won't you introduce me to your young friends?'

Mr Conan Doyle spoke all of their names, which he seemed to know as well as his own, and Professor Petrie nodded at them politely until his friend mentioned the Butterfly Club, at which point the Egyptologist regarded them with a new interest.

'Well, and what did you think of our little performance?' he asked. 'Not strictly scientific, of course, but you have to give the crowd something.'

'It was,' said Luna carefully, because Papa had raised her not to lie, 'most diverting.'

'Yes, yes,' said the Egyptologist fretfully. 'I suppose it was. They seemed to like the brain bit, but I'm not sure if they fell for the seeds.'

'You mean,' said Aidan, 'those seeds *weren't* mummy wheat?'

'No, no,' said Professor Petrie sadly, 'just ordinary barley from the brewers on the Mile End Road. I put them in her hand myself. In the game we call it a "fool's harvest".'

'How fortunate, then, that you broke the lady's fingers in the course of the deception,' said Konstantin. Luna, who knew him well, knew that his courtly politeness masked a strong disapproval.

Professor Petrie seemed not to notice. 'Well, you have to sell it,' he said. 'And we do grow a bit to show them at the museum, which always causes a bit of a sensation. But the public are easily bored; they won't pay their two pence to see a measly bit of wheat forever. Museums are a business, you know,' he said, shrugging his square shoulders. 'No museum entrance fees mean no profits. And no profits mean no more expeditions to Egypt. What we need,' he said, driving his fist into his palm with determination, 'is to put on a show. We need a *celebrity*. We need *Tutankhamun*.'

Again, the fabled name seemed to have a strange power to it.

'But I think you said that the third body in KV35 was not his?' said Conan Doyle.

'It was not, my friend,' said Professor Petrie. 'Sadly, the third body was Webensenu, son of The Elder Lady and

The Younger Lady's brother. He was a boy of ten, not even a pharaoh. A worthless child.'

Again Luna got that squirmy feeling beneath her bodice. She was almost sure that you shouldn't talk about a dead child like this, however many thousands of years had passed since his demise.

'Well, I have been acquainted with you many years, Flinders,' said Mr Conan Doyle, 'and I divine that you are not defeated yet.'

Professor Petrie looked at his friend and half-smiled. 'You do know me well, my friend. There is yet hope. We found something that may be, as your Mr Holmes might call it, a clue.' He looked about him as the last candles were snuffed. 'It is damnably dark in here. Why don't you come to my private office? I have something to show you.'

Professor Petrie led them through the quiet courts of the museum, where the public clearly never trod. As they walked among these vast and ancient giants, footsteps echoing down the marble halls, it seemed to Luna that the almond-eyed deities fixed their vengeful gaze upon the figure of Flinders Petrie for what he had done to one of their own, and the golden statues shimmered with rage. Professor Petrie, immune to the stares, led them to a dark wood door, with a little brass plaque bearing his name. Excitingly, he looked left and right before opening the door with a key from his pocket. And even more excitingly, once his quartet of visitors were safely in his office, Flinders Petrie locked the door firmly behind him.

25 JANUARY 1894
3.15 p.m.

The Egyptologist's office was rather dark and untidy and dominated by a big mahogany desk. Professor Petrie lit an ancient-looking oil lamp on the desk and the light warmed the room. Luna could see that the office was stuffed with antiquities, which looked like bits that had fallen off other things. There was a big gold toe, the scroll of a stone ear and a nose carved of ebony. Luna might almost have believed that Professor Petrie was attempting to make his own ancient deity by stitching a creature together like Mr Frankenstein.

'I am afraid there is not room for all of you to sit,' said Professor Petrie. 'But what I have to show you will not take long.'

He unlocked a drawer in the mahogany desk and, as he did so, he did that thing again where he looked over each shoulder to make sure he was not observed, even though the only people in the room were those he'd invited. He took something from the drawer which flashed gilt, and placed it on the desk.

It was a little figure, the golden colour of a Gatekeeper butterfly, and about as tall as a wine bottle. It had heavily made-up eyes in the Egyptian style, an elaborate headdress, and its hands were crossed on its breast.

'Is it a mummy?' asked Luna.

'It'd have to be a tiny little fella to fit in there, to be sure,' said Aidan.

'Actually, babies were often mummified,' said Professor Petrie. 'But that is not the case here. This is a *shabti*, a representation of a servant who was placed in a pharaoh's grave to do his bidding in the afterlife.'

Konstantin peered closer. 'What's he holding? Weapons?'

'No,' said Petrie. 'One hand holds a hoe and the other a pick, so that the shabti might carry out tasks for his master even in the beyond.'

'And who was this chap's master?' asked Conan Doyle.

'Well, he was found in a storm drain in the Valley of the Kings, very near the tomb where The Elder Lady, The Younger Lady and the child Webensenu were found. But this chap did not belong to them. His hieroglyphics tell a different story.'

He pointed to a series of little pictures painted on the side of the shabti, enclosed in a little oval. All his guests leant in.

'How can you read that?' asked Luna

'Ah well, for that we must thank our friend the Rosetta Stone, a stone artefact that featured the same passages in three different languages. All it took was for our archivists to understand *one* of the languages, to understand all of the others. They understood the Classical Greek, and that gave them a starting point. It took twenty years to translate the stone, but we now have a good understanding of all of these hieroglyphic symbols. So,' Professor Petrie went on, 'we may read the following: a sun disc, a basket, a scarab and three strokes.'

The time-thieves and Mr Conan Doyle leant in to better see the markings.

'All are enclosed within an oval, or cartouche, which means "royal".' Flinders Petrie looked up, his eyes aflame. 'These four humble little symbols are the throne name of *Tutankhamun*.'

There was an awed silence. Then Mr Conan Doyle whispered, 'My dear fellow. Are you sure?'

Professor Petrie nodded. 'Wherever you see these markings, you know they relate to the boy king. And there's more.' He turned the little figure round, to show more hieroglyphics, smaller this time, written down the back of the figure like a spine. 'This is a message from the *Book of the Dead*, Ancient Egypt's most sacred text. It says: "Verily I am here when thou callest". Now,' he said. 'That could be a simple servant's vow – "master, I am here when you want me". But there is another interpretation. The shabti was a creature of his master and spoke with his master's voice. I think this inscription is a message from Tutankhamun. *Verily I am here when thou callest.*'

Luna shivered a little at the thought of the young king speaking across the centuries.

'His tomb is out there. We just have to find it.' His eyes took on a faraway look, and the time-thieves could tell that he was lost in an antique land of pyramids and level sands. 'This shabti means King Tut's tomb exists and was entered at some point. Now, it might have been robbed recently, or it might have been entered thousands of years ago.'

'Then will the treasure be gone?' asked Conan Doyle.

Professor Petrie shrugged. 'We cannot know. But I can tell you one thing.' He turned to Luna. 'My dear. Will you pick the shabti up for me?'

Luna looked at Konstantin and Aidan. This seemed like an odd request. But she placed her hand on the gilded figure and lifted. It didn't move. Glancing at Professor Petrie, she added her other hand – the little figure was still incredibly heavy but she could just about lift it.

'It's jolly heavy,' she said.

'Precisely. Shabtis are usually made of clay, wood or stone. This one is made of solid gold.'

Luna and the boys goggled at the figure. Solid gold!

'Jesus, Mary and Joseph,' exclaimed Aidan. 'That little man could buy a palace and a coach and four to drive you to it, and still give you pocket change.'

'Indeed,' said Professor Petrie, his eyes glittering with greed and gold. 'And remember that a pharaoh can have *hundreds* of shabtis in his tomb. So if even Tut's *shabtis* are made of gold, then we are talking about…' He lowered his voice to a hoarse whisper. '… *unimaginable* treasure.'

Mr Conan Doyle said drily, 'Am I to assume that you have not shared this find with the trustees of the museum?'

'Not a chance,' said Professor Petrie. 'There are too many Egyptologists among their number, and they are just as keen to find King Tut as I am. No, my friend. Archaeology is a race.'

Luna was reminded of her conversations with Signor Marconi, who told her that science was a race. Was *everything* a race?

'I feel it in my bones that in the next few years Tutankhamun will be found,' said the Egyptologist. 'If I could only be given some intelligence as to the precise location of his tomb!' Professor Petrie looked at Mr Conan Doyle. 'You remember, my friend, when you came to dine at my club? Over our third pipe of tobacco you told me of a wondrous chance you had discovered – a way to ask questions of the future. Were you serious that night? Might you be able to help?'

Mr Conan Doyle glanced at the children and started to smile. 'Yes. I think we may be able to assist you.'

'It hardly seems possible,' said the professor. 'How is such a thing to be achieved?'

'It would be easier just to show you,' said Conan Doyle. 'Come along, old chap. And bring your little golden friend.'

Flinders Petrie extinguished the lamp on his desk. 'Where are we going?'

Mr Conan Doyle smoothed his moustaches. 'Well, my dear fellow. It is time to visit *my* club.'

25 JANUARY 1894
7 p.m.

'Welcome to our regular Thursday meeting of the Butterfly Club.'

Aunt Grace stood astride the Greenwich meridian line, the copper home of time itself. The distinguished Butterfly Club members stood in the shadows of the twelve-sided room. In the bright orange dress she looked like the golden hands at the centre of a clock; every eye gazed at her, every ear listened. Even the dead butterflies on the walls seemed to be attending.

For Professor Petrie, Aunt Grace was only the latest of the many surprises of the night – the ease of their entry into the fabled Greenwich Observatory, the hidden door within the clock which could only be opened by setting the hands to 4.45, and the secret Butterfly Room set directly on the meridian line.

'In the usual way, as you know, we meet at noon on Thursdays, but today some of our number had an important engagement.' Aunt Grace smiled at the latecomers. 'More of that to come. But the first item on our agenda must be to congratulate Signor Marconi.' Luna saw her old friend Guglielmo Marconi standing at her aunt's elbow. He closed one soft brown eye at Luna in a conspiratorial wink. 'This very afternoon he was at Buckingham Palace, where our beloved sovereign Queen Victoria awarded him the Gabriel Medal for Communication for his continuous spark radio, together with a cash prize.'

The Butterfly Club burst into that funny kind of muted applause that happens when people are wearing gloves, while their old friend Marconi waved delightedly.

But as the applause heightened, Aidan spotted another old acquaintance among the crowd. Arthur John Priest, indistinguishable from the other gentlemen but for the golden watch nestling in one eye socket, was clapping too. He was standing between Konstantin's father on one side and Aidan's father on the other. Aidan gave a snort.

'There's that one-eyed fiend,' he said, with a curl of his lip.

'Are we just supposed to call a truce with him now?' whispered Konstantin out of the side of his mouth.

'Well,' said Luna, who always strove to be fair. 'If both your fathers and my aunt have accepted him into the Butterfly Club, then yes, I suppose so.'

As if he'd heard them from across the room, Arthur John Priest stared right at the time-thieves with his single eye. He sketched an ironic salute at them with his left hand, and they could clearly see the butterfly tattoo on his wrist. The matter seemed settled. Their former enemy was now their friend.

'Thanks to Signor Marconi and our intrepid young time travellers,' Aunt Grace spoke again as the applause dwindled, 'we have both the reputation and the funding to embark upon further ventures. And to that end, I will now hand over to one of our most distinguished members, Mr Arthur Conan Doyle, and his guest.'

Mr Conan Doyle and Professor Petrie stepped forward to give the presentation they had hurriedly decided upon on the coach ride. As the grand finale, Professor Petrie produced the golden shabti. 'We know that Tutankhamun's tomb is out there. We know it is in the Valley of the Kings. We just don't know precisely where. What I need is to locate the tomb, so I may take my own dig out there and uncover the treasures.'

'Ah yes,' said Aunt Grace, 'the treasures. We can undoubtedly assist you, but first we must – how can I put this? – negotiate a reward for our troubles.'

Professor Petrie nodded. 'Agreed.'

'And,' added Aunt Grace almost casually, 'since Tutankhamun would undoubtedly create the most popular exhibition the British Museum has ever seen, the Butterfly Club would expect a fifty per cent cut of all the entrance fees.' She smiled sweetly. 'For our own expenses, of course.'

Professor Petrie gritted his teeth. 'Of course. Now, my dear madam, having given so much, it is time for you to fulfil your side of the bargain. Mr Conan Doyle said there might be someone in your company who would know where Tutankhamun is.'

'Indeed,' said Aunt Grace, inclining her auburn head. 'That person is not among us yet. But in an instant, he will be. Dr Kass, bring the bird.'

Just as before, Konstantin's father placed a small twelve-sided table in the very centre of the large twelve-sided room, on the meridian itself. The table had a lumpy shape on it, obscured by a midnight-blue silk. Konstantin's father removed the cloth with a magician's flourish to reveal the brass bird beneath.

'Chronos!' exclaimed the three time-thieves in unison. It was like seeing an old friend.

Dr Kass turned the little brass key until the filigree feathers began to twitch and the ruby eyes to sparkle. Chronos's beak opened wide, and a long, tall beam of light shone forth into the room. The beam changed and morphed into a figure, then into a man, and Professor Lorenz, the inventor of the Butterfly Effect, was in the room.

Flinders Petrie started backwards at the sight. 'It does take a bit of getting used to,' said Luna kindly.

'It's a hologram,' said Aidan helpfully. 'A sound and light show, such as you might see at the fairground.'

'There's nothing to be afraid of,' said Konstantin the Brave. 'You may attempt to shake his hand. I've tried myself.'

'Professor Flinders Petrie,' said Doctor Kass, 'meet Professor Edward Norton Lorenz. He is speaking to you from the year 1969.'

'Glad to know you, Flinders,' said the professor affably, holding out his hand. Professor Petrie, automatically propelled by good manners, stepped forward as if in a dream, and of course his hand passed right through the other professor's. Professor Lorenz, used to such greetings, seemed not to notice – but he did notice the time-thieves. 'Oh, hey kids! How ya doin'? Luna, I gotta break it to you that *Yesterday* isn't number one any more. It's now *I'm Gonna Make You Love Me* by Diana Ross and the Supremes. Aidan, those crazy folks at NASA are on course to fly to the moon in the summer. And Konstantin, the US army are still fighting in Vietnam, I'm afraid.'

Professor Petrie had gone almost the same bluish white as the professor. His ran his hand through his neat black hair until it stood on end. He stumbled backward until he was half-hiding behind his friend. Luna heard their whispered conversation. 'I don't believe it, Arthur,' he said to Conan Doyle's shoulder. 'This is one of your spiritualism nonsenses – séances and vibrations from the beyond and all that rot.'

'Not a bit of it,' retorted Conan Doyle. 'The professor lives and breathes, but he does it far in the future. Look.' He invited Professor Petrie to look about him at the other members of the Butterfly Club. 'You know Mr Oscar Wilde, I think? Mr Joseph Conrad? Mr Bram Stoker? Are they all fantasists like myself?'

'They are writers, which comes to the same thing.'

'Then what of Signor Marconi? You will own that he, at least, is a man of science? Look at the medal he holds. The hand that placed it in his belongs to our queen.'

Professor Petrie stepped out of Conan Doyle's shadow and addressed Signor Marconi directly. 'You believe in this, Signor?'

'I do,' said Marconi. 'I cannot explain it, but I believe it.'

'Professor,' said Aunt Grace, interrupting these pleasantries. 'Might we ask you to turn your attention to the matter of Tutankhamun's tomb?'

At the mention of that sacred name, Professor Petrie seemed to prick up his ears, like the jackal on the museum steps.

'Ah, that's the next thing, is it?' said Professor Lorenz with a dry chuckle. 'Well, a certain amount I can tell you from memory. The tomb was found by a fella called Howard Carter in 1922. King Tutankhamun was taken to the British Museum, and you can still see him there to this day, so far as I know.'

'Good gracious,' exclaimed Professor Petrie. 'Howard Carter is one of my students. I'll be damned if I let that young whippersnapper get ahead of me. And was it complete? The tomb, I mean?' His voice was hoarse with greed and hope.

'That it was, Flinders, that it was,' said the hologram. 'It was the richest find ever in the Valley of the Kings, and is still thought to be the most significant archaeological discovery of all time.'

Professor Petrie positively licked his lips.

'Hold on, I've got an encyclopaedia somewhere. I'm guessing what you really need is the exact whereabouts of the tomb.' He stooped as if at a low shelf and a large book appeared in his hands. He leafed through it. 'Golly, I wish they'd put all this stuff on the computer. Guess they'll get around to it one day.'

'What's a computer?' said Aidan, curious.

'Long story, sport. Ah, here we go: "George Herbert, the fifth Earl of Carnarvon, a collector of antiquities, sought out Egyptologist Howard Carter to supervise excavations in the Valley of the Kings. On November 4, 1922, Carter found the first sign of what proved to be Tutankhamun's tomb". That's not a lot of detail. Now we have a date, let me try the microfiche.'

Of course, the time-thieves knew by now that the microfiche was the name for the magic lantern that held all the newspapers of the twentieth century, but Luna imagined that to Professor Petrie it looked jolly odd to see the professor sitting down and scrolling away, his face backlit by the unseen screen. 'Hmm. Just give me a second.'

As he scrolled through his machine, Luna plucked at her aunt's orange sleeve. 'Aunt. Why do the Butterfly Club want to do this? Besides the money, of course.'

Aunt Grace looked a little surprised. 'Why, we want to make sure that Tutankhamun's remains come to the British Museum for safekeeping. We know nothing of this Carter fellow – he is working with a nobleman of means, this Lord Carnarvon person – and he may keep the treasure or, even worse, sell it to a foreign power. I'm sure Egyptians are a very good sort of people but I highly doubt if they could be trusted to look after their artefacts properly.'

Luna strongly disagreed with her aunt and hoped that didn't show on her face. It didn't seem to her that the British Museum was taking very good care of King Tut's mother, The Younger Lady. But she didn't get to question further because Professor Lorenz was talking again.

'Okay, we have *The Times* of London, November 30, 1922: "What is claimed to be the most sensational Egyptological discovery of the century is announced in a Cairo dispatch to *The Times* from the Valley of the Kings on the site of ancient Thebes, near Luxor—"'

'My God,' broke in Professor Petrie, 'that's the very place where I myself was lately digging.'

'There you go, sport,' said Professor Lorenz with a smile. 'It goes on: "A series of subterranean chambers has been explored and so far has disclosed the funeral paraphernalia of the Egyptian king Tutankhamun, one of the kings of the eighteenth dynasty, reigning about 1350 BC. The discovery is announced by Lord Carnarvon, specially summoned from England by the explorer Howard Carter, who has been excavating at this place with Lord Carnarvon for several years, but until the 4th of November, with little success."'

Professor Petrie moved forward until he almost touched the hologram, his fear forgotten. 'Is there an exact location of the tomb?'

'There's no more detail than that, I'm afraid,' said the professor. 'Folks, I think you're gonna have to play the man, not the ball.'

'What do you mean?' asked Mr Conan Doyle.

'Sorry, baseball analogy. I mean find Howard Carter, not the tomb.' He stood up purposefully. 'Here's what you do. You go to the Valley of the Kings *a day early*, on November 3rd, 1922. You find out where Carnarvon and Carter are digging. You find out where they're planning to dig the next day, and you get there first.'

Now Professor Petrie took a step back. 'What do you mean, "go to the Valley of the Kings a day early"?'

'What he means,' said Aunt Grace, 'is our agents will travel to the future and harvest the information for you.' As Professor Petrie's mouth dropped open, she turned to the time-thieves. She clasped her hands together, suddenly as girlish as Luna. 'Well, my dears, how about it?'

'*Us?*' said Luna.

Aunt Grace smiled upon them. 'We thought that, since you were so successful in the previous mission, you might like to travel again. I do know,' she said, almost fondly, 'how tiresome you have found it being cooped up in the house this past ten days.'

'Oh *yes!*' said Luna, eyes shining. Go on an adventure in time with her two best friends instead of going back to dull old Kensington? 'I'd *love* to.' She looked left and right at the boys, but their expressions told her she didn't even need to ask. 'That is, we'd *all* love to.'

Professor Lorenz broke in on the joy. 'I do have a bit of a warning, though, and this one's for young Konstantin.'

Konstantin stepped forward, clockwork heart ticking faster.

'Just to let you know, sport, that you'll find a very different world from the one you experienced in 1912.

I want to warn you, and especially you, about something very dark that happened. It happened from the years 1914 to 1918. Son, the fact is that…'

And, as ever, just at the crucial moment, Chronos ran down.

Konstantin drove his fist into his other hand. '*Verdammt!*' he said. 'Always when he tries to give a warning!'

'Don't worry,' said Luna soothingly. 'I'm sure it was nothing.'

'I dunno, Duch,' said Aidan doubtfully. 'Last time the prof tried to warn us of something, it was that the ship we were heading to was going to sink.' He pushed back his cap and goggles and scratched his head. 'And why just you, Konnie? Why not us too?'

Konstantin raised his chin. 'Well, whatever it was I'm not going to let it stop me. He said the dark thing ended in 1918, and we're going to 1922. So it can't affect us, can it?'

'We do think, though, that this time you will need an adult with you,' said Aunt Grace. 'Whereas on board ship we believed it would be to your advantage to be lone children, in this case we think your presence would not be so easily explained.'

'That is true,' said Professor Petrie. 'The only children on the digs in the Valley of the Kings are the waterboys, and they are all Egyptians.'

'Therefore,' said Dr Kass, 'we think you may need to pose as the relatives or servants to a grown-up.'

This time Luna exchanged a less than enthusiastic glance with the boys. A *grown-up?* Did that mean they had to take the director of the British Museum with them? She was sure Professor Petrie was a jolly nice chap, but she was still a little disturbed by the Unwrapping. 'I'm sure, that is, I mean to say...' she stammered, 'Professor Petrie would be most welcome of course.'

'Professor Petrie is not, for the moment' – Aunt Grace inclined her handsome head – 'a member of our club. No, we had someone else in mind. Someone with an excuse to be in the Valley of the Kings for the purposes of research for a historical story. Someone whose name and reputation, even thirty years hence, we would confidently expect to open doors.'

Mr Conan Doyle stepped forward. 'The game's afoot,' he said. 'Shall we?'

Luna felt a rush of relief. She had warmed to Mr Conan Doyle throughout the day, with his dry humour and gentle Scottish tones, and was confident he wouldn't be one of those interfering grown-ups.

'Messrs O'Connell, senior and junior,' called Aunt Grace. 'May I trouble you to bring the Time Train?'

Aidan and his father went to the wine-coloured curtain at the far side of the room and drew it back. The two navvies brought forward the Time Train, all brass and ivory and velvet, with its crystal columns glowing gently at the rear with their strange power. Forks of blue lightning gathered around the wheels and the chimney gently steamed as the machine moved smoothly along the meridian line. Professor Petrie's mouth dropped open.

Konstantin and Luna climbed into the back of the train as Dr Kass picked up Chronos and placed him gently inside the clock face of the console, closing the little doors on the mechanical cuckoo. Aidan set the dials and threw the levers, and the Time Train shot forward along the meridian. A blur of faces streamed past as they rushed toward the double clock, faster and faster. Luna was left with a lasting impression of Professor Petrie clutching his golden shabti, a look of utter surprise stamped on his face. She remembered this feeling – that they were going to crash into the clock – but just as before, the Observatory, Professor Petrie, Arthur John Priest and all the other members of the Butterfly Club fractured, atomised and fell away like dust in a sickening lurch forward through time.

THE VALLEY OF THE KINGS EGYPT

3 NOVEMBER 1922

3 NOVEMBER 1922
11 a.m.

The first thing that hit the travellers when they clambered out of the Time Train was the heat.

Aidan was reminded of the furnaces on the *Titanic*, and the blast of searing air from the stoke-holes. Luna's button boots sank into the white-gold desert sand, and she looked up to a limitless sky as blue as a Blue Adonis butterfly.

'Good Lord,' exclaimed Mr Conan Doyle, unfolding himself from the front seat. 'It worked! I'd heard tell from other travellers, but my word, it's a different proposition doing it oneself.' He stumbled a little on the sand and put his hand on the canopy of the Time Train.

'Steady on, sir,' warned Konstantin. 'It takes you a bit oddly at first, but you'll be all right in a minute.'

Aidan, recovering quickly, clambered up a nearby dune and shaded his eyes to scan the terrain. 'There seems to be some activity over yonder. And a fair bit of sand rising up – I reckon they're digging.'

'That'll do,' said Mr Conan Doyle. 'Now, what shall we do about this contraption?'

'Shall we bury it?' Luna suggested. 'We can't risk someone taking it.'

Aidan sucked his teeth. 'That should be all right,' he called down to them. 'If we cover it with the tarpaulin first. I wouldn't want any of this sand to get in the works.'

'Hang on,' said Konstantin. 'Let's take Chronos. You never know when we might need him.'

Carefully, he turned the hands on the dashboard clock until they read 4.45, the little doors popped open and Konstantin extracted the clockwork cuckoo. Since Chronos was his father's invention, Konstantin always looked out for him, and now he wrapped the bird carefully in his greatcoat. It was much too hot to wear anyway. 'I hope the locals are friendly,' he said.

'Er, I don't think so,' said Aidan, from the top of his dune. 'The welcoming party are on the way.' From the direction of the diggings came a group of men in white robes, running towards them and shouting. 'We must have kicked up some dust when we landed, or else they've spotted me.' He leapt back down to the others, half-stumbling, half-slithering through the dry sand. 'Let's hide this thing before they get here.'

They worked frantically to bury the Time Train, Aidan stripping off his jacket and Luna abandoning her carriage cloak and fur muff. They half-expected Mr Conan Doyle to stand by and watch, but he felt the urgency and joined in too. Like the others, he shed as many layers of clothing as he could against the searing heat and helped to cover the Time Train with the strong waxy cloth, then scooped up armfuls of sand to completely cover the machine until it looked like a small extension of the larger dune.

'There,' gasped Mr Conan Doyle, stumbling back from the mound. 'I defy anyone to find it now.'

'Still, let's get away from it before those men get here.'

They all climbed to the top of the dune and watched the men come closer. They were wearing long white robes and wore white turbans of twisted white cloth on their heads. They were all shouting at once. Petrified, Luna slid her hand into Aidan's, and Konstantin said quietly, 'If this is the end, it has been a privilege to travel through time with you all.'

The men were upon them, still shouting in their language. Konstantin did not see any weapons in their hands but he was still convinced that they were about to be captured and imprisoned. And then, who knew what their fate would be?

Conan Doyle straightened up, puce in the face. 'Stand back! We are Englishmen, and will not be taken without a fight.'

One of the men stepped forward, holding the others back with outstretched arms. 'English sirs? English lady?'

'Yes,' confirmed Mr Conan Doyle. 'English.'

The man bared his teeth, and the time-thieves braced themselves. Here it came. But the man's mouth widened, and after a few very tense seconds they realised he was *smiling*. The man's smile was missing a number of teeth but that made it no less of a relief. The man pointed to his chest. 'I am Sallah. You want tent?'

'I *beg* your pardon?' Mr Conan Doyle was clearly struggling with the adjustment between expecting a prison cell and being offered more comfortable accommodation.

'Want tent?' the man said again. 'Sallah get you a very nice tent. Luxury tent for English gentlemens. Very nice beds. Very nice cushions. English tea.'

Mr Conan Doyle considered the offer. 'As it happens, we *do* need a tent.'

The other men in the pack, grumbling, turned and strode away across the sand. Clearly, they all been rushing to offer their services to the newcomers to the valley, and Sallah had been the one to close the deal first.

'I would need room for all of my associates here.'

Sallah smiled and bowed at each of the time-thieves. 'Oh yes, sir. Room for everybody. I have big family. Brothers and cousins. We all make big tent together.'

'You and your... er... family will find British sovereigns acceptable, I suppose?'

Mr Conan Doyle took out a purse of money and handed a gold coin to the man.

The man carried it to his mouth and bit it before replying. 'Oh yes, sir. That will do very nicely.' He beckoned the time travellers to follow him, and set off at a sprightly pace across the sand.

'I never understand why people do that,' said Luna, as she stumbled across the dunes.

'Nor I,' said Konstantin.

'It's easy to see you two have always had money,' said Aidan, but not unkindly. 'Real gold is soft – if you bite it your teeth leave marks. If the coin is counterfeit you won't see your bite.'

'I suppose those are real then,' said Luna.

'Indeed they are,' said Conan Doyle, overhearing. 'All of them.' He stopped, opened the purse and held it under their noses. There were at least a hundred sovereigns in there, tiny cousins of the sun, glinting in greeting at their kinsman in the sky.

'I *say*,' exclaimed Luna.

'Writing must pay well,' remarked Aidan drily.

'Oh, but they are not mine,' said Mr Conan Doyle. 'They are really yours by rights.'

'Ours?' echoed Luna.

'Yes. This was the bounty that came with the Gabriel Medal for Communication.'

'Is that the thousand English sovereigns?' asked Konstantin.

'It's some of them, yes,' said Mr Conan Doyle. 'I did wonder if they would be acceptable currency in the future. But gold is always acceptable, and British gold even more so.'

They were just walking across the sand in the direction of the diggings when Luna called, 'Stop!'

They all obeyed, surprised.

Luna said, low-voiced, 'If no one can see the Time Train now, shouldn't we make sure that *we* can find it again?'

They looked at each other, round-eyed with horror at what they'd been about to do. What if the Time Train had been lost in these infinite sands, and they never found their way home again? Quickly, the boys ran back and made a pile of rocks on top of the Time Train, building the stones into a little cairn which could be clearly seen from a long way off.

They'd just finished this crucial task when their guide, waiting patiently, joined the conversation. 'You dig?' Sallah made a shovelling motion. 'Find King Tut? Need spades? Picks? Shovels?'

The newcomers scanned the horizon. Now they'd come closer, the time-thieves could see that there were many tents, and many separate archaeological digs. The Valley of the Kings, far from being a barren desert, was a hive of activity.

As far as the eye could see, workmen dressed like Sallah crawled over the dunes like ants. Tents, plentiful as mushrooms in a meadow, were dotted all over the valley, and between them tufts of brave green bushes grew in the arid rock. Wooden scaffolds had been constructed around various diggings, and measuring strings taut as piano wire were stretched between wooden pegs thrust into the sand. Mules laden with water skins traversed the valley, led by boys who would fill earthenware amphorae and stick their pointy ends into the ground, and haughty-looking camels carried planks and baskets, planting feet on the sand that were as big as dinner plates. The blacksmiths' music of things being hit with hammers and picks filled the air, as workmen chiselled at rock that had gone untouched for millennia, clouds of sand rose into the blue sky and the choking smell of stone dust filled the air. Wooden walkways connected the various digs, and were crowded with the constant traffic of people. Everyone had a task, everyone held equipment – measuring instruments, shovels, hoes and barrows. Chains of men formed over the rocks, passing baskets of earth and singing a rhythmic and beautiful song. The earth was tipped into buckets on pulleys and, ultimately, into little trucks on a mini railway snaking through the valley, to clear away the dirt from the diggings. Snooty camels regarded this innovation with disdain, and planted their slow footsteps in the sand as they'd done for centuries, carrying canvas and scaffold.

Mr Conan Doyle's mouth dropped open beneath his moustaches. 'Are… are *all* of these people trying to find Tutankhamun?' he asked Sallah.

'Oh yes, sir.'

The time-thieves regarded the scene with dismay. All of these people represented their competition – it was crucial, in order to complete their Butterfly Mission, that they found Tutankhamun first.

'Archaeology really *is* a race,' murmured Luna.

Their guide nodded enthusiastically. 'Oh, yes, English miss. The whole world wants to find King Tut. Americans. French. Germans.'

Konstantin looked up, interested to hear that some of his countrymen were here. 'Germans?' he repeated.

'Yes, yes, even Germans,' said Sallah, his expression darkening. 'I spit on them.' And, to Konstantin's surprise, he did exactly that, spitting in the general direction of the tents, his effort falling on the sand a few feet away.

Konstantin straightened up. He was a proud Prussian, and although that empire stretched all the way to Russia, his beloved home town of Konigsberg was actually in Germany. 'Now look here…' he began hotly.

Aidan put a hand on his chest. 'Steady,' he murmured. 'We want this fella to help us. So he doesn't like Germans, so what? He's only one bloke. A lot of people don't like the Irish, but you don't see me starting any bar fights.'

Konstantin saw the sense in this. He held his tongue with an effort but he followed the others with clenched fists.

'This way, honoured Englishes,' said Sallah. 'Almost there.'

Conan Doyle motioned at the time-thieves to hang back a little. 'Before we meet our fellow countrymen,' he whispered, 'we need a cover story. A disguise, if you will.'

'Such as Sherlock Holmes might use?' said Luna.

Mr Conan Doyle raised his eyes to the vivid blue sky. 'Good Lord. I *had* hoped that by exchanging one continent for another, and one century for the next, I might leave that blighter behind.' But he smiled. 'Yes, such as Sherlock Holmes might use. And now, let that be the last time we mention that infernal name all the time we are out here.' He seemed to be joking, but half-serious too. 'Now. I was thinking you could be my niece, Miss Goodhart, foisted upon me for the Christmas holidays to enjoy the benefits of travel and perhaps a little sketching.' Luna nodded happily. 'Mr Kass, you will be my secretary, a young man hoping to become an undergraduate at Oxford or

Cambridge, and placed with me to gain experience. And Mr O'Connell…'

'I know, I know,' said Aidan resignedly. 'I'll be your servant.'

'Actually,' said Conan Doyle, 'I was thinking you could be more of a factotum.'

'A fact-what-um?' asked Aidan.

'A factotum is an assistant with many diverse responsibilities. Chief of which, for you, shall be to oversee our friend Sallah and the construction and maintenance of our living quarters. I thought that would appeal to your engineering sensibilities.'

Aidan grinned his trademark grin, pleased with this new title. 'Aye *aye*, sir.'

'And that is the last time I will address you so formally,' said Conan Doyle. 'For the purposes of our deception you will be Luna, Konstantin and Aidan. You boys will address me as sir, and Luna will call me uncle. Agreed?' The three nodded, eyes shining. 'And we must not, for one second, lose sight of our mission, which is to find Tutankhamun before all these people, take him home to the British Museum for Professor Flinders Petrie, and stage the exhibition of a lifetime to further enrich the Butterfly

Club for future missions. We are not here to make friends. Everyone is a rival, no one is an ally. That clear?'

The time-thieves nodded again, with a little less certainty, but no less determination.

'I say! My good man!' Mr Conan Doyle called ahead to Sallah, who turned back. 'An extra sovereign if you pitch our tent next to Lord Carnarvon's.'

'All Englishes together,' said the guide, nodding. 'Yes, sir.'

3 NOVEMBER 1922
Noon

The travellers followed Sallah down the dunes to the village of residential tents, some tiny, some large and luxurious. Next to the biggest one in the valley, a palace of creamy canvas, their guide began to make marks in the dunes with his sandal. He called over a number of similarly dressed friends, and they began to place sticks where the markings were made, and produce, as if from a magic lamp, rolls of canvas and divans and chests and silver tea things and rugs and cushions and china cups. In a very short time the team had constructed a canvas dwelling as big as a house, with walls and a roof of taut canvas, and proceeded to fill it with all the comfortable things. Aidan, who had quickly become firm friends with Sallah, marvelled at how efficiently the construction was done. He sensed they'd done this many times for stupid Europeans with lots of money but very little sense.

Beyond all this activity, in the shade of the neighbouring tent, a man in a cream flannel suit and a panama hat was furiously hitting golf balls into the distant dunes. Several white-clad Egyptian boys ran after them, whooping, to bring them back to their master. The man was perhaps fifty years of age and of middling height, with rather intense pale blue eyes and a neat grey moustache.

Another man with a moustache, stocky and dark and wearing a permanent frown, sprawled in a lawn chair in the shadow of the tent, moodily leafing through a sketchbook. He looked vaguely familiar.

'Well,' said Conan Doyle, surveying the pair from a distance. 'No time like the present.' Some instinct made him, despite the heat, put his jacket back on and twitch his tie into place. Then he strode right up to the first man, only stopping when he was in danger from the swinging golf club. The author watched in silence for a moment and then said, 'Are you winning?'

'Not in any sense,' said the man. He thwacked another ball as far as he could, with targeted aggression, and the giggling boys gave chase. Then, as if suddenly exhausted by the effort, he stopped and leant on his club. He squinted at Conan Doyle suspiciously from beneath the brim of his hat. 'May I help you?'

'Not at all, not at all,' said Mr Conan Doyle. 'Just thought I'd pass the time of day, don't you know, while my man puts my tent up. You carry on.'

Then he turned away, and headed back towards the time-thieves. Luna thought this clever. She thought walking away like that would make the men curious, and it did. The one in the chair sprang to his feet and marched up to Conan Doyle aggressively. 'I say. If you're coming to sniff around for Tutankhamun you can bugger off. I haven't been here for five years just for some Johnny-come-lately to swoop in and snake my find.'

'For God's sake, Carter,' said the man with the club. 'Sorry about him.' This to Conan Doyle. 'He's a bit defensive.'

'You just don't think I'm ever going to find him,' said Carter moodily.

'*No one* thinks you're ever going to find him.'

'Well, don't worry,' said Conan Doyle. 'I'm not here for King Tut.'

'You're not an archaeologist?' said the golfing man.

'Writer.'

'Not a bally *reporter*?'

'Short stories.'

'Thank *God*.'

The gentleman looked Conan Doyle up and down, and evidently judged that he passed some kind of test. 'You seem to come from another age,' he said, looking beyond the author to the time-thieves. 'All of you. A more elegant age, when people actually knew how to dress.' He looked at Luna approvingly. 'Not all this bobbed hair and white faces and red lips, and girls who think they are young men.'

Aidan looked up with interest.

'I say. While you're waiting, why not come and have a spot of luncheon with us?'

The golfer's palatial tent looked as if it too had been constructed by their friendly guide and his expert team. There were patterned rugs on the floor, comfy divans, even pot plants. A yellow canary sat in a gilded birdcage which hung from a tall stand, chirruping happily away. A table was set in an anteroom for lunch with cutlery, linen and crystal, just as if they were in an English country house. In the corner was a machine which Aidan recognised as a gramophone. It had an enormous golden bell like a trumpet, and a black disc revolving scratchily around as if on its own accord, playing loud music. The music was fast and jolly with blaring brass and clashing cymbals and it hurt the ears. Next to the machine, dancing as energetically as the heat would allow, was a fascinating creature.

She had her hair bluntly shorn off at the level of her chin, in a razor-sharp cut all around. Her face was covered with some sort of white pancake make-up, with a little circle of red high on each cheek like a doll, and her lips were painted a bright scarlet. She wore a mannish tailored shirt, tucked into trousers. *Trousers*. And on her feet she wore golfing brogues, just like the man they'd met in the dunes. She looked wonderfully strange, and strangely wonderful.

This then, must be what the golfing man had been talking about. The girl was a few years older than Luna, perhaps sixteen, but the differences between them were much greater than age. A fascinating creature without sex, without species, she could have been from another planet, let alone another century. She might have been one of the aliens from Mr H. G. Wells's books, who came to make war on the world. And perhaps she would defeat the extra-terrestrials with her terrible music – it was certainly ear-splitting enough.

The creature smiled at them and said breathily, 'Wouldn't you just *die* without jazz?'

Konstantin, presuming that 'jazz' was the name of the strange cacophony coming from the gramophone, searched for a polite reply. 'It is certainly… most invigorating,' he said in his halting English. 'Although I might myself express a preference for Wagner.'

He was trying not to give offence, but evidently ended up doing it anyway. The needle made a scratching noise as it travelled across the record, and the two men and the girl stared at him.

Konstantin was just wondering what he'd said that was so dreadful, when the older man said, with narrowed and hostile eyes, 'Where are you from, young man?'

'Königsberg. I'm Prussian,' said Konstantin, slightly surprised.

'Ah yes,' said the man with a curl of his lip. 'That's what they all say *now*. I've met so many of your kind who now say they are Hungarian, or Austrian – anything to lessen the stain. But I knew what you were the minute you opened your mouth.'

It slowly dawned on Konstantin that it was not what he said, but how he'd said it, that was the problem.

'You are what you are: a German. And some of us will never forget what you *did*.'

The final word was uttered with such venom that Konstantin actually took a step back.

'Father!' exclaimed the exotic girl.

'No, Evelyn,' he snapped. 'Can you have forgotten that Porchester, your own brother, was almost killed in the war? Can you have forgotten that our own dear home, Highclere Castle, was a field hospital for injured troops?'

'Yes, but that's not *this* chap's fault,' said the girl reasonably. 'Look at his age. He must have been too young to fight with Porchey or anyone else.'

'It is his race with which I find fault, not his person. I'm sorry, Evelyn, but I will *not* share my table with a German.'

'Well, in that case—' began Luna furiously.

'No…' said Konstantin, laying a hand on her purple sleeve. 'No. I will go. I must…' – he remembered their cover story – 'set up Mr Conan Doyle's office, make sure he has sufficient ink and paper, *et cetera*.'

He bowed to the young lady who had defended him so spiritedly, clicking his boots smartly together. 'If *you* will excuse me,' he said to her, studiously ignoring her father. And, turning on his heel, Konstantin left the tent.

Luna looked at Mr Conan Doyle. She could understand him enough, even on so short an acquaintance, to know that he was furious that Konstantin had been thrown out. His moustaches were working up and down with irritation, but the mouth below them remained firmly closed. It was obvious that, despite his anger, the author was determined not to ruin all their plans by showing it.

With Konstantin's departure their host calmed down a little. 'I am sorry, I meant no offence to your man. I know there are those who think that after the Treaty of Versailles we should all let bygones be bygones, but when one has had a loved one in combat, one finds it difficult not to hold a grudge.' He turned to Conan Doyle confidentially. 'My son Lord Porchester was in the 7th Hussars regiment, you know. Fought in Mesopotamia.'

'Ah,' said Mr Conan Doyle, nodding sagely, although Luna could tell he was as much in the dark as she and Aidan were. What was the Treaty of Versailles? Which bygones should be bygones? And where on earth was Mesopotamia?

'Do sit down,' said their host. 'And let us have some proper introductions. I am George Herbert, fifth Earl of Carnarvon. This is my daughter, Lady Evelyn Herbert. And this,' said the nobleman, indicating the frowning man with the black moustache who had kept so quiet during the whole exchange, 'is Mr Howard Carter, the man who is leading us all on this wild-goose chase.'

It was time. 'This is my niece, Luna,' said the author. 'This is my general factotum, Mr Aidan O'Connell. You briefly,' he said wryly, 'met my secretary, Mr Kass. And I...'

Luna noticed he took a breath, for this was the true test.

'I am Arthur Conan Doyle.'

3 NOVEMBER 1922
12.10 p.m.

Konstantin wandered about aimlessly for a time, furiously kicking sand. He honestly didn't know why he'd been thrown out of the tent, and that somehow made things worse. He couldn't protest, or explain. He looked around for something to do. He thought about going for a walk, but the midday heat was uncomfortably warm, and he didn't fancy getting lost in the future. He considered going to see how Sallah and his team were getting on with the tent, but from the sounds of clanging and banging coming from next door he would only be in the way.

Then he saw a boy about his own age sitting in the shade, on a low wall of golden stone, which could have been thousands of years old. He was wearing a loose white robe and a knotted turban of the same cloth on his head, and his feet were bare.

The boy regarded Konstantin with curious eyes, black as olives, and then patted the wall beside him. Konstantin, without a moment's hesitation, went to sit on the warm stone. After what had just happened, it felt good to be invited somewhere, even if it was just to sit on an old piece of wall.

He jerked his head at Lord Carnarvon's tent, and, by way of explanation, said, 'They wouldn't let me eat with them.' He spoke in English, not really expecting the boy to understand.

'They won't let me eat with them either,' said the boy, in English as good as Konstantin's own.

'I'm Konstantin. Konstantin Kass.'

'Kon-stan-tin-kass,' repeated the boy carefully. 'I'm Hussein Abdel Rassoul, but everybody calls me Abdel.'

They shook hands solemnly.

'You speak very good English, Abdel,' said Konstantin.

'I have been working for the Englishes for five years. Since I was eight.'

'For Mr Carter and Lord Carnarvon?'

'Yes.'

Konstantin began to think it might not have been such a bad thing to be thrown out of the tent after all.

He was mindful of his mission to find out anything he could about the whereabouts of Tutankhamun, and this friendly boy might have some good intelligence for him. 'And what do you do in the English camp?' he asked innocently, hoping Abdel might have some sort of crucial role.

'I provide the most vital part of this English expedition,' Abdel declared proudly, pounding his chest with his fist.

This was very promising. Konstantin expected to hear an amazing tale about digging for Tut and decoding ancient hieroglyphics.

'I make the tea.' The boy laughed and Konstantin's hopes vanished. 'The English cannot function without it. It is their fuel. Coffee too. I fetch and carry the water for all their drinks. Me and Cleopatra there.' He pointed to a white mule calmly tethered in the shade. Abdel stretched out his legs in front of him and wiggled his toes in the sand.

'And... do you enjoy it?'

Abdel looked surprised. 'I love it. I wasn't joking when I said that it was an important role. My dream is to open my own coffee shop one day.' He tapped a grimy finger to his temple, just below the turban. 'Mark my words – one day, coffee shops will be big business.'

Konstantin doubted it, but he wanted to get Abdel back to the point. 'I expect you don't know much about the expedition, then?' asked Konstantin casually.

'Actually I hear all sorts of things,' said Abdel. 'All *sorts* of things. Great secrets.'

'Like what?'

Abdel looked about him, as if to check that no one was listening. 'Like Tutankhamun was murdered.'

Konstantin turned to him, wide-eyed. 'You think King Tutankhamun was *murdered*?'

'Shh,' said Abdel, as if even the mule might overhear them. 'It is not *me* who says it. It is Mr Carter.'

'Go on.'

Abdel bit his lip. 'I am not really supposed to say it. No one knows but Mr Carter and Lord Carnarvon. Not even Lady Evelyn.'

'Then how do *you* know?'

'I overheard while I was serving the tea. The gentlemen ignore me – I don't matter because I am an Egyptian, and a servant. I'm invisible. I don't think they even know my name.' He said this without resentment, so Konstantin felt it for him. 'The secret is something Mr Carter found out when he was making his tomb drawings. He pieced the story together...' Abdel stopped, and looked at

Konstantin. 'He would be angry if I told you. He was very excited. He says no one else alive today knows this secret.'

'But we are friends, are we not?' urged Konstantin. He remembered what Mr Conan Doyle had said about not being in Egypt to make friends, but it was too late. He already liked Abdel.

Abdel hesitated, then said, 'Yes, Konstantinkass. We are friends.'

'Well then.'

Abdel looked around again and then said, 'Tutankhamun was young and healthy. He was nineteen years old, with no reason to die. But what Mr Carter found out was that King Tutankhamun had a very young and beautiful wife called Ankhesenamun. Very lucky, yes? But he also had a vizier who was jealous of their love. Very *un*lucky, no?'

'What's a vizier?'

'Like your Mr Lloyd George.'

'Who?'

'Your prime minister.'

As far as Konstantin knew, the British prime minister in 1894 was Mr Gladstone, but of course that would have changed by 1922, which it now was.

'Mr Carter thinks Tutankhamun's vizier – his prime minister – killed King Tutankhamun for his wife. The vizier Ay and the wife Ankhesenamun married within a year of Tutankhamun's death.' Abdel tapped his finger to his lower eyelid. 'Very suspicious.'

Konstantin thought about this. That did seem awfully fast to marry again. Could Ankhesenamun have actually loved King Tut if she had done that? He smiled at Abdel. He wasn't sure exactly how knowing Tutankhamun was murdered would help them find the tomb, but he was grateful to the boy for trusting him.

'So, we know why I am not at the lunch table,' said Abdel. 'I am just a waterboy. But you are a gentleman. Why are *you* not at the table?'

'Because I am a German,' said Konstantin.

'Ah.' Abdel nodded, seeming to understand at once, so Konstantin judged it was worth asking. 'Do *you* know why they threw me out?'

'Yes, of course,' said Abdel, slightly surprised. 'Because of the Great War. 1914 to 1918. It ended four years ago but it will take them a lot longer than that to forget.'

The Great War. That did sound serious. 'Who were the belligerents?'

'I do not know this word.'

'Sorry. Who started it?'

'Oh. Germany invaded Belgium, then England declared war on Germany.'

That explained the atmosphere in the tent. 'How bad was it?'

'*Very* bad,' said Abdel. 'Four years. Millions dead. The whole world joined in.'

Konstantin was silent for a moment, absorbing this information. '*Gott in Himmel*,' he breathed.

'How did you not know any of this?' said Abdel, curiously.

Konstantin thought quickly. 'I was ill. For many years. In bed,' he said quite truthfully. 'My brothers are all soldiers.'

'My brother too. He fought for the Allies.'

'He went to Germany?'

'I don't think any of it was fought in Germany,' said Abdel. 'France and Belgium mostly but the east too. My brother, he fought in Mesopotamia. I'll bet you didn't know that Egyptian soldiers fought in the war.'

'I didn't even know there was a war.'

'They were conscripted into a war they had nothing to do with. My brother's name was Karim. He was killed.' Abdel stated this devastating fact very casually, as if he was talking of the weather. 'He was nineteen. Same age as Tutankhamun.'

'It's very young to die,' said Konstantin gently.

'Yes,' said Abdel soberly. 'It was in Ancient Egypt, and it is now.' He looked down at the sand and folded his lips into a tight line, an expression that spoke more than his words.

Konstantin didn't know what else to say. He felt, as a German, somehow *guilty* about Karim's death, but that was ridiculous, and he wouldn't even begin to know how to say it out loud. And besides, Abdel didn't seem to bear him any grudge. So the two of them sat in a sympathetic silence until a little bell tinkled.

Abdel got up. 'That's me.'

'Tea time?'

'Tea is at four o'clock in the afternoon. After lunch it's coffee,' said Abdel. 'And it isn't even proper Egyptian coffee. It is weak and European and they put the milk of cows in it.' He made realistic sick noises. 'I wouldn't give it to Cleopatra.'

The mule, recognising her name, looked round and whinnied. Konstantin laughed. He watched Abdel disappear into the flap of Lord Carnarvon's tent, and felt a bit more cheerful than he had before.

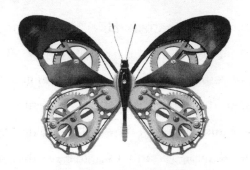

3 NOVEMBER 1922
12.10 p.m.

'Arthur Conan Doyle? *Sir* Arthur Conan Doyle?'

'Well, I don't know about the "Sir" part,' said the author modestly, looking around the Carnarvons' luxurious tent.

Lord Carnarvon frowned slightly. 'You were given a knighthood in 1902.'

'Well, how very nice,' said Mr Conan Doyle, clearly delighted. 'I mean, yes, yes, of course I know. But you know, one hardly ever uses it. Takes a bit of getting used to.'

'You've had twenty years to get used to it,' said Carter suspiciously, narrowing his eyes.

Luna found Howard Carter quite grumpy, and thought how cheered he would be if he knew what was to happen tomorrow, the 4th of November 1922, when he would uncover the greatest archaeological find of all time. But of course that wasn't the kind of thing you could just tell someone.

'Carter, don't be rude,' said the Earl of Carnarvon. 'Sorry, he's a bit blunt. But I could have sworn that… I mean, one heard… well, not to put too fine a point on it, that you were… ahem… *dead*.'

Mr Conan Doyle looked amused. 'Well, I can assure you, reports of my death have been much exaggerated.'

'Of course,' spluttered Carnarvon hurriedly. 'Some old story – got whiskers on it now, of course – some sort of explosion. But I must have been mistaken. Getting old, you know.'

Luna looked at him sharply. Did the earl know something about Mr Conan Doyle that they didn't?

'Why don't you *prove* who you are?' asked Lady Evelyn, playfully. The yellow canary, who had been freed from its cage to fly around the tent, settled on her shoulder like a pirate's parrot.

'A very good idea,' said Howard Carter harshly. 'All manner of charlatans come to our door, pretending to be any number of people, for the merest sniff of Tutankhamun. But I can expose you at once, with the evidence of my own eyes. If you are who you claim to be, I saw you many years ago, at the British Museum, when I was just a young man with a sketchbook.'

'That was you!' exclaimed Luna before she could stop herself.

Luckily the gentlemen were too intent on each other to hear her. 'What were we there to see?' asked Mr Carter.

'An Unwrapping,' said Mr Conan Doyle. 'Performed by Professor Flinders Petrie of the British Museum. He revealed the mummy of The Younger Lady, the mother of the king you seek.'

Lady Evelyn looked at Mr Carter, and the canary on her shoulder cocked its little head too, copying her. 'Is he right?'

'Yes,' grumbled Howard Carter, grudgingly. 'Yes, he is.'

'That's enough,' said Lord Carnarvon. 'We cannot question a peer of the realm and a literary genius like a common criminal. Let's eat.'

Lunch looked glorious, and the time-thieves were starving, having not eaten since 1894. The large table was set with an array of dishes in earthenware pots – chicken broth with white rice, leafy vegetables stewed with fragrant meats, beans with bright wedges of lemon and warm flatbreads. There was a gorgeous smell of unfamiliar but enticing spices which set the travellers' stomachs rumbling. They tucked in as politely as their appetites allowed.

'You are welcome to our table,' said Mr Carter, with a fraction more warmth. 'And our... I was going to say home, but it's a tent.'

'You've been living in a tent for five years?' asked Aidan in surprise.

'No,' said Carter, 'I have a house in Luxor. But tomorrow we dig, so I wanted Lord Carnarvon to be on the spot, in case tomorrow is the day. Although he doesn't think I'm ever going to find King Tut.'

'*No one* thinks you're ever going to find him,' said Lord Carnarvon, but Carter was intent on studying Mr Conan Doyle.

'The years have been kind to you,' said Mr Carter, examining Mr Conan Doyle's face through narrowed eyes. 'Good God, man! You haven't aged a day. You don't look any older than myself.'

There was nothing Mr Conan Doyle could say to this, because of course he *hadn't* aged a day. But luckily Howard Carter changed the subject. 'What are you doing out here anyway?' he asked, somewhat ungraciously.

'I assure you, my interest is purely literary,' said Mr Conan Doyle. 'I intend to write a short story or two about Egypt, and it does seem to be all the rage.'

'Egyptomania,' said Carter bitterly. 'Every man-jack from every tin-pot country is here with a shovel to try and find King Tut. Amateurs, I tell you, rank amateurs.'

'Well,' said Conan Doyle. 'I bring only my pen rather than a shovel. I am a mere writer.'

'Only the greatest writer in the *world*,' blurted Lady Evelyn.

'*Evelyn*.' Lord Carnarvon pressed the heels of his palms into his eye sockets. '*Manners*. Young ladies don't just charge in like baby elephants when gentlemen are speaking.'

'Oh, excuse my butting in, Mr Conan Doyle,' said that young lady, 'but I'm the most *enormous* fan.'

'I don't mind a bit,' said the author. 'It's a foolish man that cannot accept a compliment.'

'I do have one question about Sherlock Holmes,' said Lady Evelyn eagerly.

Mr Conan Doyle managed not to roll his eyes. 'Go on.'

'Why on *earth* did you kill him off?'

Mr Conan Doyle sighed and his gaze took on a faraway look. 'Sometimes you just have to let someone go.'

'That's *exactly* what I've been telling Carter!' exclaimed Lord Carnarvon. 'It's time for this King Tut pipe dream to die.'

'I will continue,' said Carter through gritted teeth, 'until I find him.'

'Well, not on my shilling,' said the earl. 'I've told you, tomorrow is the last day. Finish. Kaput. So if I were you, I would choose where you dig very carefully.'

Aidan saw an opportunity. 'Where exactly *are* you planning to dig tomorrow?'

Lord Carnarvon rang a little bell. 'I need some coffee to fortify me before Carter tells you where he's going to spend the rest of my money.'

3 NOVEMBER 1922
12.30 p.m.

At the sound of the bell a servant came into the tent, a good-looking boy in white robes, and began, quietly and competently, to heat the water for coffee.

Just as Luna was thinking how handsome he was, Lady Evelyn moved her chair close and whispered, 'He's rather a dish, isn't he?'

'I have no idea what you just said.'

'He's very handsome.'

'The waterboy?' asked Luna.

'No not the *waterboy*,' giggled Lady Evelyn. 'Your engineer. Mr O'Connell. He's jolly good-looking.'

Luna looked at Aidan bending over a map that Carter was unfurling among the remains of the lunch things, his dark hair falling in his eyes as it always did. She felt a sudden jag of irritation at what Lady Evelyn had said. She felt stupidly possessive of Aidan. He was *her* friend. What right had this entitled young lady to goggle at him like that? But in another instant she realised how ridiculous that was. She didn't own Aidan, no one did.

So she smiled in an extra-friendly way at Lady Evelyn to make up for the feeling. 'Yes, he is. And he's a lovely person too. But highly annoying.'

'You talk of him like I talk of my brother,' said Lady Evelyn.

Luna thought about that. She supposed she did think of Aidan as her brother, and Konstantin too. And yet – that didn't seem quite the right description.

'Was your brother the one who was in the country with the funny name?'

'Mesopotamia. Yes.'

'And he was almost killed?'

'Yes. He lived to annoy me another day.' Lady Evelyn's lipsticked mouth curled into a mischievous smile. 'I'm joking. I love him to bits. But he is a dodo-head sometimes.'

The waterboy came round with the coffee, which was poured from an ornate silver pot into little jewel-coloured glasses, not at all like the china cups Luna was used to at home. As the delicious, bitter smell of the coffee rose to her nose Luna watched Carter chatting to Aidan over a map of the Valley of the Kings. The Egyptologist seemed much friendlier to Aidan than to the others, so she hoped that he would be able to get some information about Tutankhamun's whereabouts.

Luckily, Aidan was able to be extremely knowledgeable about digging and making safe tunnels with joists and supports and walkways, because that was exactly what he had been doing at home in the course of his work on the Great Northern Railway. Carter talked Aidan through the map, which was divided into quadrants. Every quadrant was cross-hatched with pencil, to show it had already been explored. Every quadrant except one. But looking at the scale of the map, Aidan could see that even the section that was left was quite a few miles square. He needed a more specific location, but had to be subtle about how he questioned Carter.

'Five years,' he said, with a low whistle. 'It's a long old time to look for one tomb.'

'It is an important mission,' said Carter defensively. 'On the manifest of eighteenth-dynasty pharaohs, Tutankhamun is the only one whose mummy or tomb has not been found. So he is out there somewhere.'

'How do you know for sure?' asked Aidan.

'Thirty years ago, my old tutor – the very same Flinders Petrie your employer mentioned – found a golden shabti bearing the hieroglyphics of Tutankhamun. Do you know what a shabti is?'

'Yes,' said Aidan truthfully. 'An image of a grave servant.'

'That's it,' said Carter, grudgingly impressed. 'The shabti was found in the valley, near the tomb that held Tut's mother and grandmother. So we know he's here somewhere. And it's imperative that the British find him first. He belongs in the British Museum where he can be properly preserved for posterity. And where the most people can see him.'

'You mean where the most *British* people can see him.'

'Who else matters?'

Aidan did have an answer to this, but swallowed it. 'So you have one quadrant left. But that's still a hell of a lot of ground to cover. If you've only got one more roll of the dice, where exactly are you going to dig tomorrow?'

He'd gone too far. Carter's friendliness evaporated and he let the map roll up again with a sharp snap. 'I'm sorry,' he said, not impolitely. 'I mean no disrespect but I simply can't say.' He nodded to Conan Doyle. 'He may be an author, but you are clearly an engineer, not just a factotum. I can't take the risk.'

'I understand,' said Aidan, inwardly cursing. 'I'd be the same.'

'I say,' said Lady Evelyn to Luna, her eyes never leaving Aidan. 'Would you like to see a tomb this afternoon? You *and* your... factotum?' Her eyes sparkled. 'It will give you an idea of the sort of thing Carter's looking for. I can take you to the Temple of Hatshepsut. I think you'll like it.'

'Can we bring my uncle's secretary?' said Luna, immediately thinking of Konstantin.

'Of course,' said Lady Evelyn. 'Why do you ask?'

'Well, your father didn't seem to like him very much,' Luna replied, hoping Lady Evelyn would explain why.

She did and she didn't. 'Well, it's because of the war. The older generation do keep things up so. The young are not the problem. We want to move forward, not to forget, but to forgive. We want to make sure it was the war to end all wars and that it will never happen again. How terrible if in the future it was only known as the First World War.'

'Oh, quite,' said Luna faintly. She still didn't really know what had happened. There had clearly been some sort of conflict, but she couldn't really ask for any details without giving herself away.

After this it became clear that Carter wanted them to go – he was clearly anxious to return to his treasure hunt – so Mr Conan Doyle, taking the hint, finished his coffee. As he rose from his chair, he said politely, 'Thank you for a wonderful luncheon. Most illuminating.' His eyes twinkled with inspiration. 'Perhaps you will allow me to return your hospitality tonight? Would you do the honour of joining me for dinner? I'm confident that my man will have everything in readiness by then.'

Carter's trademark scowl returned at this – Luna could see that he didn't particularly want to. He clearly had no desire to be up late dining the night before his final and crucial dig. But Lady Evelyn clapped her hands in delight and squealed excitedly, as the yellow canary joined in. The girl was obviously keen to spend more time with these exotic strangers. And that was enough for Lord Carnarvon – as a fond father, he readily agreed. 'We'd be delighted.'

3 NOVEMBER 1922
2.30 p.m.

They went outside to look for Konstantin and Mr Conan Doyle was cock-a-hoop as they walked across the hot sand. 'I think that went rather well,' he declared.

'*Do* you?' said Aidan in surprise. 'They seemed pretty reluctant to tell us anything about where they're digging. That Carter is a cagey old cove.'

'Oh, I don't know.' Mr Conan Doyle sang a little tune to himself, a small smile curling beneath his moustaches.

Luna was beginning to recognise this mood. 'Uncle?'

'Niece?'

'What are you planning?'

He twinkled at her. 'I have the germ of a notion. But I need a couple of hours to think about it.

Sometimes I find the best ideas blossom if I just have a bit of peace and quiet to smoke a pipe or two. I have a feeling that this will be a three-pipe problem. What will you young people do with your afternoon?'

'Lady Evelyn has invited us to a temple,' said Luna. 'Do you think that's a good idea?'

'I think that's a capital idea. And, niece?'

'Yes, uncle?'

'Find out as much as you can about Tut, won't you?'

Back at Lord Carnarvon's tent, Konstantin was relieved to see the two gentlemen had gone and Lady Evelyn was alone with her yellow canary.

'Hello again, chaps.' She marched right up to Konstantin and held out her hand. 'We never met properly. I'm Evelyn.'

'I'm Konstantin.'

Lady Evelyn shook his hand in a masculine way then turned to Luna. 'I say, Miss Conan Doyle. Do you want something a little more comfortable to wear? No offence but my mother wore dresses like that when she was a little girl.'

Luna was too hot and uncomfortable to be offended. 'Do call me Luna. And I'd be very glad to change, if it's not too much trouble.'

'No trouble at all,' Lady Evelyn assured her. 'I could find you some flannel bags.'

'Some... *what?*'

'Some trousers.'

'Oh.' Luna was taken aback. 'I'm not sure my uncle would like it,' she said truthfully.

'Rot,' said Lady Evelyn dismissively. 'If we women can vote, why should men always wear the trousers?'

Aidan looked up, pleased. 'Exactly,' he said.

'Do sit down, chaps,' said Lady Evelyn airily as she dragged Luna away. 'Have a chat to Alexandria.' She indicated the yellow canary. 'Not that you'll have a choice. She never shuts up anyway, do you, angel?'

The yellow canary chirruped in reply. Lady Evelyn blew the bird a kiss, and led Luna through a canvas flap into another part of the tent.

'This is my bedroom.'

There was a rail hung with clothes, a carved chair, a fringed lamp and a dressing table covered in lipsticks and powders and paints. There was also a comfy-looking divan on the floor to sleep on, with a net bunched above it and hooked to the ceiling canvas, to spread about the bed like a skirt. 'Keeps the mosquitoes off,' explained Lady Evelyn. 'They can be deadly out here.'

Luna had no interest in mosquitoes – although she was to remember the remark later – but she was very interested in the decor. 'Why, it's just like a room in a house!'

'Yes, I suppose it is,' said Lady Evelyn. 'Sallah and his Egyptian chappies are awfully good at putting up tents. I'm sure yours will be just as grand. Well, I suppose I'll see tonight at dinner. I'm *so* excited you're all here.' She smiled happily. 'It will be *such* fun.'

'Yes,' agreed Luna, smiling too. Lady Evelyn was so charming and friendly, she had to constantly remind herself that she was on a mission, and she must find out as much as she could about Tut. 'And so exciting that you'll be doing the final dig tomorrow. So much at stake. Do you know where Mr Carter plans to look?'

'Not an earthly idea, darling,' said Lady Evelyn, sorting through her clothes rail. 'Here.' She selected a pair of coffee-coloured trousers and a loose cream shirt and flung them at Luna, with all the happy confidence of an older sister dressing a younger. 'These will do. Try them on.'

Showing the boys her new look was very shy-making. Luna emerged wearing fitted trousers that were gloriously comfortable, and a loose cream shirt with the sleeves rolled up to her elbows. There were supple leather boots on her feet and as a finishing touch Luna's auburn hair was tucked under a trilby hat.

The boys had very different responses. Aidan looked very obviously approving but Konstantin looked a little wary of her, as if Luna herself had changed and not just her clothes. He could barely tear his eyes away and she saw him watching her when he thought she wasn't looking.

Luna laughed at him. 'It's still me,' she said.

'I know, I know,' he said, laughing at himself. 'But you look so…'

'So what?'

'So… *different.*'

'She's dressed exactly right for where we are going,' declared Lady Evelyn. 'You'll see.'

3 NOVEMBER 1922
3 p.m.

In the mid-afternoon it was a little cooler, but the sun was still fierce in the searing blue sky as the little party set off across the valley.

As they walked through the Valley of the Kings the pale sand became rock, and the time-thieves began to see the dark mouths of caves and the more regular shapes of doorways that had been cut into the rock in search of tombs. They passed at least five excavations, with older men dressed like Carter and Carnarvon shouting orders in different languages at younger men like Abdel, who were digging with spades and picks and shovels, desperate to find the elusive boy king first.

After a time, they arrived at a magnificent temple of light-coloured, almost white sandstone. It was carved out of the foot of sheer cliffs fringing the vastness of the desert beyond. It had hundreds of pillars and shady colonnades, and a long central ramp leading the traveller into the dark.

Here again there were crowds of people, but quite a different set of people to the ones digging in the Valley. Here there were tourists – gentlemen in flannel suits; ladies with bobbed hair in silk dresses, carrying parasols against the sun; schoolchildren with sketchbooks. Lady Evelyn stopped at the beginning of the ramp, which was guarded by two enormous stone hawks, and threw out her arm. 'Welcome to the Temple of Deir el-Bahri. Otherwise known as the tomb of Hatshepsut.'

Luna shaded her eyes with her hand and gazed at the glory. 'He must have been a powerful pharaoh indeed.'

'She.'

'She?'

'Yes.' The red lips curled into a smile. 'Told you you'd like this place. Come on.'

Lady Evelyn led them up the vast ramp of golden stone and into the atrium of the temple. She stopped by a huge stone frieze. 'Look,' she said. 'Here she is. Queen Hatshepsut.'

The time-thieves looked up at the image carved into the golden stone. It was taller than all of them, even Aidan, and portrayed in profile, as all the figures were.

'But she has a beard!' Aidan exclaimed.

'Yes,' said Lady Evelyn. 'She wore the headdress, the false beard and the kilt of a pharaoh.'

'So she was a woman,' said Aidan slowly, 'but she dressed and lived as a man.'

'Yes. She felt that her people would respect her power more.'

'And did it work?' asked Aidan, interested.

'Well, look around you. Her priests built this place to be her tomb. She wasn't even supposed to be in line for the throne,' said Lady Evelyn, who obviously knew an awful lot about the subject. 'When her husband, Thutmoses II, died, his direct heir was her stepson Thutmoses III. He was too young to be king at that time, so Hatshepsut was only supposed to rule until he came of age. But she pronounced herself pharaoh instead, and ruled jolly well for fifteen years.' She gazed at the carving with evident admiration.

'And she always wore male clothes?' asked Aidan.

'Yes,' said Lady Evelyn. 'All the time. And I don't blame her. Besides the political message, they're *much* more comfortable.'

'Would you agree?' Aidan asked Luna, grinning his usual grin. 'How do you feel?'

She smiled. 'Free.'

Suddenly Aidan's grin faded as he saw a party of gentlemen walking down the colonnade.

'Jesus, Mary and Joseph,' he exclaimed. 'Come on, quick! Get into this chamber. That man can't see us.'

He pulled them all through a stone doorway into a subterranean tomb which was much cooler than the rest of the temple. The walls were crawling with hieroglyphics and the floor was paved with hexagons like the back of a tortoise. Aidan's secrecy was infectious and they all huddled in the black shadows.

'Who are we hiding from?' asked Lady Evelyn.

'His name is Arthur John Priest,' whispered Aidan, as if he could hardly believe it himself. 'Hopefully he won't see us.'

'Which one is he?' asked Lady Evelyn, peering through the doorway at the group of gentlemen walking towards them.

'It's easy to tell – he's the one with a watch for an eye. He's a thoroughly bad hat.'

Luna craned around the pillar to look at the approaching party. If it wasn't for the golden watch, screwed into his eye socket like a monocle, she would not have known their old acquaintance. Gone were the top hat and tails of the Butterfly Club. Here was a new man, tanned and sporting an exquisitely cut cream suit and panama hat. Only his blunted, broken-nosed face and the fire of his single eye were the same.

The gentlemen he was walking with were dressed even more oddly. They were in khaki uniforms and caps, all the same, with a strange symbol on their sleeves and hats.

'They're from the German dig,' said Lady Evelyn, peering round the corner. 'I've seen them around. They're looking for Tut too. And they all wear that rather strange symbol, but I've no idea why.'

The others looked. And sure enough, each soldier wore an odd design on their sleeve. It was a black cross, with four arms bent at right angles, on a white circle background.

'What is it supposed to be?' asked Luna. 'What do you think, Konstantin? That's your part of the world.'

'No idea,' said Konstantin, peering round the doorway too. 'Back when Prussia was… well… Prussia, we had a double-headed eagle as our symbol. But they're wearing some sort of bent cross thing. I don't recognise it.'

'I've seen it before,' said Lady Evelyn. 'I think they call it a swastika.'

'Swas-ti-ka.' Luna repeated the funny word. 'What does it mean?'

'I don't know exactly,' said Lady Evelyn. 'But I've seen it carved in some Egyptian temples. I think it's a symbol of peace.' She nodded at the soldiers. 'Maybe they're some kind of peacekeeping force, you know, like the League of Nations.'

'Well, that's a relief,' said Luna, stepping forward. 'I suppose we should say hello.'

Aidan, who'd suffered more at the hands of Arthur John Priest than the others, felt as if his veins flowed with ice. 'Are you mad?' he said. 'After what he did on the *Titanic*?'

'Well, but now he's a member of the Butterfly Club,' argued Luna. 'If your da, Konstantin's father and my aunt are all right with him, then surely we can be too? Maybe they sent him after us to help.'

'Don't be a fool,' hissed Aidan scornfully. 'He's obviously working for the Germans now. Get back from that doorway before he sees us.' He yanked Luna back into the tomb a bit harder than he meant to, and she couldn't help letting out a muffled exclamation.

It was fatal. Arthur John Priest turned and looked in their direction, excused himself to the rest of his party and walked down the stone steps towards them on rapid feet.

There was no use trying to hide, but luckily Lady Evelyn was a quick thinker.

'Get back, everyone,' she said. 'I'll deal with this "bad hat" of yours.'

As the time-thieves retreated into the shadows she ran her fingers over the hieroglyphics of the tomb – one of which, Luna saw with surprise, seemed to be a *frog* – and said, as casually as she could, 'Yes, most definitely eighteenth-dynasty sandstone.' Then, pretending to notice the approaching man for the first time, she said casually, 'Oh, good afternoon. How are you today? You're with the German dig, aren't you?'

'That's right,' said Arthur John Priest guardedly. 'My name is Arthur Cruttenden Mace,' he lied. 'I'm acting as a consultant Egyptologist to our German friends.'

'And I am Lady Evelyn Carnarvon,' she replied.

'I know who you are,' he said, bowing politely. 'Your father's reputation as an Egyptologist is unrivalled.' He looked around the walls of the tomb. 'It is inevitable, I suppose, that those with a love of Egyptology will congregate at the same sites. I wanted to show the tomb of Hatshepsut to my colleagues and you wanted to show it to your… friends.' The single eye swept over the time-thieves where they stood huddled in the shadows. The time-thieves could tell that his eye pierced the darkness and saw them at once. They shuffled forward awkwardly.

'Well,' Lady Evelyn said, 'we must be going. *Jolly* big temple. *Loads* to see.'

Arthur John Priest's silver-topped cane shot out and connected sharply with the door jamb, barring their way. And as his wrist emerged from his cuff, the time-thieves could see, as clear as day, the black stamp of a butterfly tattoo. 'Perhaps we will soon have cause to gather at another, even more significant tomb?' he said pleasantly.

'Who knows?' said Lady Evelyn airily, backing away.

'I hope your father and Mr Carter have made good progress in their search?'

'Oh, me too,' she said enthusiastically. 'It would be awfully jolly to be the first to find King Tut, wouldn't it? Thing is, to find the bally tomb. So many places to dig.' Her lipsticked mouth curled into a playful smile. 'Such a lot of... *sand*.'

The one-eyed gentleman smiled back tightly. 'I do hope, Lady Evelyn, that you are not keeping the knowledge of his whereabouts to yourself. Such a pity to be *nationalist* about such a find. I'm sure you would agree that such an important discovery ought to be shared with the world – in the spirit of reconciliation between Britain and Germany after recent...'

– he coughed delicately – '*hostilities*. A joint venture between the two countries would send such a powerful message of friendship. I'm sure *you* agree, Herr Kass?'

Konstantin jumped a little at the shock of being singled out, but quickly recovered his composure. He stood up very straight, in what Luna had come to call his 'tin soldier' stance, and stared coldly at their old enemy.

'Oh, quite, quite,' said Lady Evelyn breezily. 'But as a seasoned archaeologist, you know what it's like. You have to know your *ankh* from your *akhet*, and your Hemetbast from your HemetNetjeret, and your *torque* from your *tura*. Don't you agree?'

There was an awkward silence.

'You have no idea what she just said, do you?' said Konstantin. He had seen enough to come down firmly on Aidan's side – Arthur John Priest was up to no good.

Aidan's senses were tingling. This was all a bit too familiar – standing in a big, echoing chamber, a bit too close to the back wall, with Arthur John Priest a bit too close to the door. 'Konstantin,' he whispered. 'Be careful. Fella's as wily as a whole sack of foxes.'

'What a shame,' said Konstantin pleasantly, as if Aidan hadn't spoken, 'if your new German friends found out that you *weren't* actually an Egyptologist at all.'

Arthur John Priest's face went suddenly still. 'Well, they won't learn it from *you*,' he said. 'I hope you like this tomb, for it will be your own.'

Too late, Aidan remembered when he had been in this position before: on the *Titanic*, when Arthur John Priest had shown him the secret watertight chambers of the ship, before trapping him inside one of them. 'The door!' he cried, and leapt for the exit.

It was too late. In one fluid movement Arthur John Priest had stepped outside and depressed one of the hieroglyphs just outside the door. A circle of ancient stone, as tall as a man, rolled surprisingly quickly into place, closing the portal completely. Aidan only just managed to snatch his fingers back before the circle landed in place with a cloud of dust and a *boom* of finality.

They were trapped.

3 NOVEMBER 1922
3.30 p.m.

'**E**xcellent,' said Aidan into the darkness. 'Well, that's just excellent. I told you to watch it, Luna. But you had to pop out of that doorway like a carriage clock cuckoo, and now we're caught like lobsters in a pot.'

'Oh, so it's *my* fault?' said Luna. 'It was Konstantin who wound him up like a railway watch. And if you hadn't nearly pulled my arm off, I wouldn't have cried out.'

'Hardly *pulled your arm off*,' countered Aidan hotly.

'Shut up, you two,' said Konstantin, who was trying not to let the tide of panic wash over him. 'Instead of arguing, save your breath for calling for help.'

'Konstantin's right,' said Lady Evelyn. 'There are simply oodles of tourists at the tomb. We'll be out of here in a jiffy.'

But they were not out of there in a jiffy. They shouted until they were hoarse, and banged on the stone circle until their fists were raw, but there were no answering voices.

'These walls are made of thick sandstone,' said Aidan sorrowfully. 'And even this door is a foot wide. Sandstone traps sound very effectively. We could shout all night and no one would hear us.'

The horrifying realisation grew in them all that Arthur John Priest could well be right. They could be trapped here until they died. Even if Mr Conan Doyle or the Carnarvons sent a search party, who knew if they would be found in a complex of this size, with all the antechambers? For all they knew, the entrance to this chamber was now entirely hidden from the outside by the stone circle.

'There *must* be a way out,' said Luna, refusing to give up. 'Arthur John Priest pressed something to close the door. One of the hieroglyphs outside the doorway. So there must be something *inside* the doorway to open it again.'

'You'd think so, wouldn't you,' said Lady Evelyn, 'but I'm very much afraid…'

'What are you afraid of?' asked Luna nervously.

'I'm afraid that we're in the Puzzle Chamber of Thutmoses,' Lady Evelyn replied. 'I had heard of it. But I didn't know it was real. No one did. It's a legend really.'

'Which Thutmoses again?' asked Aidan. 'Was that the stepson?'

'Yes,' said their new friend. 'Hatshepsut's stepson, Thutmoses III. He was not a nice character. For one thing, he attempted to erase all memory of his stepmother's reign. And for another, he had a rather horrid way of testing his ministers. He'd trap them in a specially constructed puzzle chamber, and if they could work out ten puzzles to release themselves they would be awarded a place on his council.'

'And if they couldn't?' asked Aidan.

'They'd starve to death.'

'Terrific,' said Aidan. 'That's just terrific. Well done, Duch.'

'I fail to see how it's *my* fault that—' began Luna, when Konstantin broke in.

'Shh, don't you see?' he said. 'If this is Thutmoses' Puzzle Chamber, there *is* a way to get out. We just have to work out the puzzle.'

'Puzzles,' corrected Lady Evelyn. 'There are ten of them, remember?'

'Easy,' grumbled Luna. 'Should be simplicity itself to do that in the pitch dark.'

'Well, this might make things easier.' There was a scrape and flare of a match, and the whole tomb warmed into light. Aidan shook the little box in his hand. 'A tinderbox. A good navvy is never without one. You never know when you'll be in a dark tunnel.'

'How many of those matches do you have left?' asked Luna, a little haughtily. She was still angry with Aidan, and the knowledge that he'd been right and she'd been wrong made her even more cross.

Aidan held the light over the tinderbox and counted. 'Thirteen,' he muttered, crossing himself. 'Unlucky for some.'

'Don't say that,' said Lady Evelyn in an artificially bright voice. 'I'm sure if we put our heads together we can think of a way out of here. And you all seem like educated types.'

'I didn't go to school,' said Luna a little sadly. 'I don't think the British government see the use in educating girls. Everything I know I was taught by my papa.'

'I didn't go to school either,' said Konstantin. 'I was always too ill.'

'You've read practically every book, though,' said Luna comfortingly. 'You must know *something*.'

'Not about Egypt,' said Konstantin sadly. 'You know who we could have done with? Abdel the waterboy. I bet he'd have got us out of here.'

'No use wishing,' said Aidan practically. 'What about you, Me Lady?'

'I had a governess, but she was pretty useless,' said Evelyn. 'I know a good deal from Father, because I've been out here in Egypt for an age. But it's hard to know *what* we need to know. We don't even know the questions, let alone the answers. There are ten riddles in the Puzzle Chamber of Thutmoses, that's all I know. But it could be *any* ten things.'

'Well, *I* won't be any help to you,' admitted Aidan ruefully. 'I wasn't educated at all, unless you count Sunday school – I had to go to that every week, or I'd get a good hiding. But I always wanted to be on the railways helping Da, so I used to avoid *actual* school like the—' He stopped, frozen, mouth agape.

'Like the…?' prompted Luna.

He turned to her, wide-eyed, their quarrel forgotten. 'Like the *plague*.' Just then he jumped and cursed as the match burned his fingers, and the tomb went dark again. That made Aidan's next words all the more spooky. '*The Ten Plagues of Egypt*,' he breathed.

3 NOVEMBER 1922
3.35 p.m.

'What on earth,' asked Konstantin, 'are the Ten Plagues of Egypt? Hang on – why not light another match?'

'Not yet,' said Aidan. 'We should save them. We'll need them to see, but we don't need them to plan. Just listen for a second.' He took a breath. 'The Ten Plagues of Egypt were ten terrible things that God sent to Egypt in Biblical times. We learned about them in Sunday school.'

'He's right,' said Lady Evelyn. 'I've heard of them too.'

'What kind of terrible things?' asked Luna, who was trying to be brave about being in an ancient Egyptian tomb in complete blackness.

'Rivers of blood, locusts, hail,' said Lady Evelyn. 'Can't remember any more.'

'Gnats, flies,' added Aidan. 'A darkness that settled over all the land. Livestock died. People got horrible boils. Oh – and frogs rained from the sky.'

'I saw a frog just inside the door!' exclaimed Luna excitedly, her voice echoing around the tomb, her fear quite forgotten.

'Very well,' said Konstantin. 'Supposing the ten plagues are the key to getting us out of here? Perhaps we just have to find the symbols for each of them on the walls.'

'It's the best idea we've got,' said Lady Evelyn, and they could tell, just by the way she spoke, that she was shrugging her shoulders.

'All right,' said Aidan. 'Let's be smart about this. We have thirteen matches left. When I strike one, Luna, you find your frog as fast as you can. Ready? Go!'

The second match scraped and flared. As soon as the chamber was illuminated, Luna ran to the doorway and sought the frog that she'd seen when Lady Evelyn had pretended to examine the hieroglyphics. Even in the dim golden matchlight she saw the frog at once. There he sat, squat and fat, as if he'd been poised to leap for three thousand years.

'Found him!' shouted Luna, her voice echoing around the ancient stones.

The others gathered around, Aidan shielding the little flame with his hands. They all peered at the frog in the half-light.

'Now what?' said Lady Evelyn.

Luna looked closer. The frog looked almost three-dimensional – more deeply etched than the other designs. Inspired, she laid her fingertips on the plump little body and pushed as hard as she could.

Almost immediately there was a sound – a grating and moving of ancient stone. 'Something's happening!' said Konstantin. 'The door's opening!'

But the door was not opening. The stone circle stayed where it was, tight-fitting as a cork in a bottle. And in the last light of the match, the prisoners saw a terrifying sight.

One of the pavings beneath their feet, a single hexagon, dropped downwards to leave a gaping hole. Collecting around it, the time-thieves could not even see the bottom. When the flame burned his fingers, Aidan cursed and dropped the match down the hole. The little light fell and fell into infinity, and met no floor at all.

It was dreadful enough to stand in complete darkness in an ancient Egyptian chamber. It was doubly horrible to do so when you knew there was a gaping hole in the floor with no bottom. The time-thieves and Lady Evelyn didn't dare move a muscle in case they fell down to the depths of the tomb.

Aidan said a very bad word under his breath, one that he'd learned on the railways. 'I was so *sure* the ten plagues would be the thing.'

'Perhaps they are,' said Lady Evelyn. 'But maybe we have to get them in the right order.'

'You're absolutely right,' said Aidan. 'There was a saying, to help us remember. One of those where the first letter means something.'

'A mnemonic,' said Konstantin, who had indeed learned something from all those books. 'Like *Never Eat Spider Webs* for the points of the compass. North, east, south and west.'

'Oh, what was it, what was it?' In the darkness Aidan pushed back his hat and goggles to scratch his head, something that always helped him think. 'It was about how friendly girls should smile and not frown…'

'*What?*' said Luna.

'Yes,' said Aidan. 'It stuck with me because the priest always pointed at my six sisters and me. And of course, I didn't think it applied to me. Oh, this was it: *Bright Friendly Girls Frown Less By Having Laughing Dimply Faces.*'

'So what did the first B stand for?' asked Konstantin.

'Blood,' said Aidan, and the word sounded particularly grim in that dark chamber. 'A river of blood. The whole of the Nile turned red. I'm pretty sure that was the first plague.'

'I sincerely doubt there's a hieroglyph for a river of blood,' said Luna.

'But there is one for a river,' said Lady Evelyn suddenly. 'It's a wiggly line.'

'All right,' said Aidan. 'This is what we do. As soon as I strike a match, we all scatter to different parts of the chamber and look for a wiggly line. And for God's sake, mind that bleeding great hole in the floor.' He took out his tinderbox.

'Wait!' said Luna suddenly. 'What if we get it wrong again and another piece of the floor drops?'

The others froze. 'She's right,' said Aidan, appalled at what they'd been about to do. 'Everyone stay around the edges of the room. We'll be hugging the walls anyway, looking for the river. But structurally, that'll be where the floor is strongest. Ready?'

He struck the third match, and as soon as the chamber illuminated, the prisoners scattered to each wall, avoiding the yawning hole in the floor. Because there was only one light, the hieroglyphics were very dim, and they all used their fingers as well as their eyes. It was like learning how to read again, an entirely different language, in pictures not words. That might have sounded easy if they were in the schoolroom, but in a dim chamber by the light of a single match with roughly one minute of burn time, it was enormously challenging.

It was Lady Evelyn who shouted, 'I think this is it!'

Shielding the little flame, Aidan carried the match to her part of the wall and held it close to the wiggly line.

'Should we press it?' asked Luna, unsure.

'Whatever we're doing, let's do it fast,' said Aidan. 'For the sake of my fingers.' The precious match was burning low.

'Very well,' said Lady Evelyn. She applied her fingers to the wiggly line and pressed as hard as she could. Everyone braced themselves, looking nervously at the floor, but this time the pavings didn't move. And, unlike the frog, which had popped back out again when the floor fell in, to lie back in line with the rest of the wall, the river stayed pushed in. The time-thieves breathed again.

'I think we got one right,' said Konstantin brightly, as the match went out. This time the darkness was much less scary. 'What next?'

Aidan said the mnemonic again to himself under his breath. '*Bright Friendly Girls Frown Less By Having Laughing Dimply Faces*. It's one of the Fs. Frogs or fleas?'

'I do remember the frogs being quite early on,' said Lady Evelyn, 'and the winged beasts later.'

'Very well,' said Aidan. 'At the next match, Luna, find your frog again. The rest of you – round the edge of the floor.'

Luna did as she was bidden, and pressed the frog's body as hard as she could. This time the little creature's stone body stayed pressed in, and the floor stayed where it was. 'That's two,' said Luna triumphantly. 'Now what?'

'*Bright Friendly Girls*,' said Aidan rapidly. 'G for gnats. A plague of them were sent to cover Egypt, buzzing around all the people and animals. But what on God's green earth would a *gnat* hieroglyph look like?'

'A winged insect,' said Konstantin. 'Let's look quickly, before the match goes out.'

They scattered like cockroaches and searched the walls.

'Found one,' called Konstantin. 'Look, he's just like a fly.'

He put out his hand to press the image.

'Wait!' shouted Lady Evelyn, and Konstantin's hand stopped inches short of the wall. 'Isn't that just the trouble?' said Evelyn. 'Flies are the next on the list after gnats. *Bright Friendly Girls Frown*. Isn't that right, Aidan?'

Aidan nodded just as the match went out.

'So how do we know which is which?' said Luna's voice into the dark.

There was an uncomfortable silence in the blackness. 'But we have to risk it,' said Aidan. 'Otherwise we're just wasting matches.' He struck another light, and Konstantin pressed the winged creature, but then immediately had to quickly sidestep, as the hexagon under his right foot collapsed below him, and the insect carving popped back out to line up with the wall.

Konstantin leant on the cold stone, clutching the wall, clockwork heart hammering. 'So the bad news is,' he said, collecting his breath, 'that wasn't a gnat. But the good news is, we probably found the fly.'

While his match was still lit, Aidan counted the rest. 'Seven left,' he said, just as the flame burned his fingers. 'I'm about to light another. We *have* to find the gnat. Then, if we do, Konnie, press the fly straightaway after. We can save a match that way.' He struck a light and everyone searched desperately for another winged creature. 'Here's one,' said Lady Evelyn suddenly.

'Press it!' shouted Aidan.

Lady Evelyn did as she was bidden. The carving moved in with a grating sound, and stayed where it was. The floor stayed level too.

'Konnie! The fly!'

Konstantin, obeying Aidan's instruction, hit the fly carving as hard as he could. That too sank into the wall and stayed pressed in this time, and no more hexagonal pavings fell from the floor. Then the match ran out, but now the darkness was even less frightening. 'We've done four,' he crowed. 'That's nearly halfway. What's next, Aidan?'

'*Bright Friendly Girls Frown Less*,' Aidan replied. 'L for livestock. All the Egyptians' animals sickened and died.'

'Or locusts,' put in Lady Evelyn. 'That's the one I remember. Plagues of locusts descended like a blizzard and ate all the crops.'

'I feel like locusts came later,' said Aidan. 'I don't remember three insects together.'

'Let's go for livestock then,' said Luna. 'But this is a tricky one. There are loads of different animal hieroglyphs. What would represent livestock in Egypt?'

'Cattle,' said Lady Evelyn. 'There are tons in the Nile Delta. Look for a cow.'

The match scraped on the tinderbox once more, and the time-thieves scattered, avoiding two gaping holes in the floor now, to peruse the walls. This time it was Aidan who found the cow hieroglyph and pressed it at once.

The cow sank into the wall, stayed there, and the floor was still stable.

The next hieroglyphs presented a problem. '*Bright Friendly Girls Frown Less By Having...*' mused Aidan.

'Boils and hail, I think. People fell ill, with these big painful bubbles on their skin. And hail came from the sky – hard ice that falls like rain. Now, they could both look like little round things, so we don't want to get them confused. And we're on our…' – he counted – '… ninth match out of thirteen. We can't afford any more mistakes.'

But as it turned out, the mistake was his own. Having struck a thousand, perhaps a million matches in his work as a navvy, in tunnels and diggings and coal shafts all across the world, this time he struck too hard – the match snapped in two without lighting and fell to the ground. Aidan dropped to his knees to try to rescue the top of the match, but it had disappeared down one of the gaping holes in the floor. He said a terrible curse word once more. 'I'm sorry,' he said. 'I'm *so* sorry. But we only have three matches now. We need to try to get these two in one match.'

With great care he struck one of the remaining matches and held it high. Every eye glued itself to the walls.

'Here's something,' said Luna, almost at once. 'It looks like the river hieroglyph, but lots of them falling from the sky.'

'Grand,' said Aidan rapidly. 'But don't press it yet. We need the boils first.'

This was next to impossible. There were lots of people on the walls, but none of them seemed to have little blisters or even look remotely ill.

'All right,' said Aidan. '*Any* sick-looking person. We have to try.'

'What about this one?' said Konstantin, pointing rather doubtfully. 'This person looks poorly.'

For a split second the prisoners looked at the carving and then at each other. The picture did not look like anything much. Then Aidan shrugged. 'We *have* to try. Or else we're trapped for good.'

Feeling that he needed to redeem himself after the business with the broken match, Aidan pressed the thing himself. They all braced themselves around the wall for the floor to fall from under them, but nothing happened. The hieroglyph of the strange sick person stayed pushed in, the floor stayed where it was, and Lady Evelyn leapt across the hole in the floor and pushed the hail symbol as hard as she could. That worked too, and as the light went out, they felt much more confident.

And their luck continued. The second L, the locust, was easy to find, as it was the only winged insect left.

But the next symbol presented much more of a problem.

'*Bright Friendly Girls Frown Less By Having Laughing Dimply…*' said Aidan. 'D for dimply. D for darkness. A terrible darkness covered the land for three days, and the sun never showed his face.'

'How on earth do you represent *darkness* in a carving?' wondered Konstantin.

'I dunno. But we'd better find out quickly,' said Aidan grimly, striking the eleventh match.

Luna swiftly found a symbol which she thought looked like a cloud.

But she was a little too confident on the back of recent triumphs. She pressed the carving at once, but the paving she was standing on collapsed beneath her, and her stomach lurched to her throat as she fell through the floor.

3 NOVEMBER 1922
3.50 p.m.

Aidan, who was next to Luna, threw out his arms to catch her. Her weight as she fell pulled him to the ground, and his arms were nearly wrenched from their sockets, but he just managed to hold on to her hands with his.

She dangled below him, pleading, '*Don't let go,* Aidan. *Don't let go.*'

With his chin against the pavings and his arms dangling down the hole, Aidan held Luna as tight as he could. Her hands, sweaty with terror, began to slip from his. Jaw jammed tight by the floor, he said her name over and over again through his clenched teeth, like a charm. '*Luna, Luna, Luna.*' Before his eyes, the match he'd dropped in order to catch Luna burned like an ember on the ancient pavings. As he watched, it dwindled and went out.

Of course, Konstantin and Lady Evelyn leapt to help, but as they were plunged into total darkness the two rescuers could not cross the floor rapidly as it was now full of hexagonal holes. They were obliged to crawl, feeling their way on hands and knees towards their friends' voices, avoiding the yawning gaps in the paving.

One of Luna's hands slipped from Aidan's grasp and she let out a piercing scream. She was now dangling by a single hand, her feet kicking out above the infinite dark. Aidan grabbed her wrist with his free hand, but all seemed hopeless – she began to slip from his grip once again. But suddenly Konstantin and then Lady Evelyn were at his side, feeling down his own arms to find Luna's. Together the three of them pulled her up, like a fish from an ice-hole, to lie panting on what was left of the floor.

'Jesus, Mary and Joseph, Duch,' groaned Aidan, as he turned on to his back, every sinew screaming, heart hammering. 'You gave me *such* a fright.'

'You saved my life,' she panted to him in the dark. 'And this time you really did pull my arms out of their sockets. But if you hadn't, I would have died.' She was silent for a moment, and then said, 'I'm so sorry for getting us into this. You were right. It was my fault.'

'Don't worry,' said Aidan's voice from the blackness. 'You're about to get us all out of it.'

'What do you mean?' asked Luna.

'I realised something as I was saying your name.' Aidan's jaw felt like it belonged to someone else. 'You're always telling us that Luna means moon. That your father called you that. Surely for darkness we just have to look for the moon.'

'All right,' said Konstantin. 'This one's on me. You two take a break. Where's the tinderbox?'

There was an awful silence as Aidan realised the terrible truth.

The tinderbox was gone.

Aidan said the worst curse word he knew into the warm darkness. 'I must have dropped it when I went to catch Luna,' he said. 'No one move, but really, really gently feel around yourselves to see if it dropped on to the pavings. Go carefully, because we don't want to push it down one of the holes.'

Each of the captives felt in a circle around themselves where they sat. Sweaty fingertips met ancient dust, but there was no sign of the tinderbox.

'*Verdammt!*' exclaimed Konstantin – a much milder swearword than Aidan's but no less deeply felt. 'It must have dropped down the hole that opened beneath Luna.'

There was another dreadful silence as they faced the truth. They were one carving away from freedom, and trapped in an ancient tomb with no light.

'Maybe we could *feel* for the moon?' said Lady Evelyn.

Aidan said in a shaking voice, 'How long do you think the floor would last if we just took a few shots in the dark?'

No one answered. There was nothing left to say. The four of them sat quietly in the dark, all coming to terms with the fact that this could be the end of their adventures.

Then, 'Wait!' said Luna, her voice full of hope.

They all turned in the direction of the sound. 'There's a match here,' she said. 'And another one! They must have scattered when the box dropped.'

'You're sure they are not the spent ones?' asked Konstantin tensely.

'No,' said Luna. 'There's the little bud of sulphur on the top of each.'

'But there's no tinderbox to strike them on,' said Lady Evelyn.

'Doesn't matter,' said Aidan, his voice suddenly alive. 'You can strike a match on any rough surface. Like a stone wall. I've done it a thousand times in a railway tunnel.' There was a pause, and the darkness suddenly seemed thick with promise. 'Luna,' he said, trying to keep his voice calm, 'pass the matches to me really, really carefully.'

Luna and Aidan felt for each other's hands in the blackness. Their fingers met in the dark to transfer the matches, a last warm touch of a final chance. Aidan held the two precious matches in his teeth as he felt his way to the nearest wall of the chamber. Shaky as a newborn foal, he stood. He took the twelfth match in his right hand, keeping the thirteenth in his left. He'd told the others he'd struck a match on stone a thousand times before, and so he had. But never had there been so much at stake before.

With a trembling hand, he dragged the match head sharply across the rough stone. It flowered at once, but there was no time for relief. Desperately he scanned the budding flame across the hieroglyphics, looking for anything that resembled a moon. His companions saw him pause at a particular symbol.

'Brace yourselves,' he said. 'Make sure you're not standing on just one paving. In fact, lie down across at least three.'

Luna, Konstantin and the young noblewoman did as they were bidden, stretching out across three pavings.

And Aidan pressed the moon.

It was all right. The moon carving pressed in, and stayed in, and no more hexagons fell from the floor. The prisoners had time to smile weakly at each other before the light went out.

'Right,' said Lady Evelyn, sounding positively chipper in the darkness. 'Just one more and we're out of here. The Tenth Plague of Egypt. What is it?'

There was a horrible silence.

'Aidan?' prompted Luna.

'God,' said Aidan, his voice very small. 'I've no idea. My mind has gone completely blank.'

'Well, you just said all of them at the very start, when we were first trapped in here,' said Luna. 'You and Lady Evelyn. You listed them, remember?'

'I said rivers of blood, locusts and hail,' said Lady Evelyn. 'And Aidan said gnats and flies.'

'Also darkness,' Konstantin took up the thread. 'Livestock dying. People getting horrible boils.'

'And frogs,' finished Luna, who'd been counting on her fingers. 'But that's only nine.'

'Use the mnemonic,' urged Konstantin. *'Bright Friendly Girls Frown Less By Having Laughing Dimply Faces.'*

'F!' exclaimed Luna. 'The last plague begins with an F. F… F… F… We've had flies and frogs. What else could it be? Feathers? Fire? Fever?'

'Think,' said Konstantin. He dared not move to Aidan's side, because the floor was now as full of holes as a honeycomb. But he knew that their freedom – and indeed their lives – depended on Aidan remembering his Sunday school lessons. Konstantin made a superhuman effort to make his voice calm and light. He knew a little about the Prussian science of psychology, and knew that, with the right nudges here and there, that marvellous organ, the human brain, could be coaxed into remembering even something long forgotten. 'Take yourself back,' he said, in the same gentle, hypnotic voice. You're sitting in Sunday school. Describe your surroundings to me, exactly as you see them.'

There was a silence and then Aidan's voice flowed, steady and dreamy, out of the dark. 'I'm in the vestry with my sisters, sitting on hard chairs. There's coloured light coming through the stained glass window. The priest is talking. He has a black robe, a white collar and a southern accent. Cork or somewhere like that. I'm fidgeting. Aoife, my oldest sister, kicks me to stop me squirming. She has her Sunday shoes on, so it hurts.'

'Then?' coaxed Konstantin.

'The priest sees her kicking me and gives her a telling-off.'

'What does he say?'

'He says, *you better mind your manners, Aoife O'Connell, or the Lord will send the Tenth Plague of Egypt after you.*'

'And what,' said Konstantin, hardly daring to breathe, 'is the Tenth Plague?'

There was a horrible pause. The darkness was every bit as frightening as it had been before – all the more so because this time it might be forever. But then Aidan said, in a voice that was almost a whisper, '*The death of the firstborn.*'

At any other moment such a horrible pronouncement would be terrifying. But at that moment it was music to the ears of the other prisoners. Very carefully, everyone got to their feet.

'All right,' said Konstantin slowly. 'We should look for a symbol for death. What would that be?'

'I know this one,' said Lady Evelyn. 'Appropriately, it's a mummy lying down.'

'Grand,' said Aidan. 'Then it's all down to you, Me Lady. When I light the thirteenth match, find us that symbol as fast as you can. Ready?'

In the darkness, they could all hear Lady Evelyn swallowing nervously. 'Yes,' she said.

More carefully than he had ever done before, making sure he was on solid ground if the match dropped, Aidan struck the final light on the wall. It did not strike at once. One, two, three attempts, and no light. Aidan was suddenly soaked in the sweat of terror, and he moved his wet fingers back from the sulphur bud – had his perspiration damped the final match? Would it even light? The others hardly dared breathe, as he struck a fourth time.

The match flamed.

Almost before it had kindled, Lady Evelyn hopped over the holey floor, somewhat like a frog herself, and began perusing the walls. The time-thieves watched her, frozen with dread. All except Aidan. He was watching the little flame creeping towards his fingers, each fraction representing the sands of time running out for them.

Just as the heat on his fingers began to be unbearable, Lady Evelyn shouted, 'Got it!'

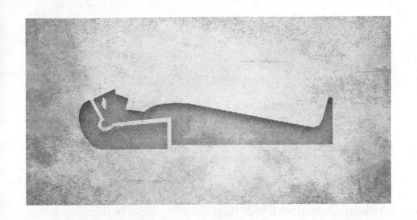

She reached for the symbol of the dead mummy and pressed it as hard as she could.

There was a second of silence that seemed to stretch into infinity. Then a sickening grating sound of stone upon stone, much louder than there had been before. The prisoners clung, cowering, to the walls as three things happened at once.

All the ten carvings that had stayed pressed in, popped back out until they were in exact line with the walls.

The missing hexagon pavings rose back up from the depths of the tomb to fit back in place, completing the floor once more.

And the circle of stone blocking the doorway rolled away, opening the portal completely, offering them sweet freedom.

Daylight streamed in, blinding them, and they all ran for the source of the light. Once safely beyond the doorway of the tomb they turned back. The Puzzle Chamber of Thutmoses looked like a perfectly innocent tomb, with four square walls, a decorative hexagonal floor and hieroglyphics from floor to ceiling. But all the treasure in Tutankhamun's tomb could not have induced any one of them to step inside it again.

3 NOVEMBER 1922
6.15 p.m.

By the time the sightseers returned to camp, dishevelled and exhausted by their adventure, their own enormous tent had been pitched right next to Lord Carnarvon's. Sallah and his friends had clearly done a marvellous job for their gold sovereigns.

Lady Evelyn, who felt much closer to her new friends after their ordeal, went to wash and change for dinner, and Luna, Aidan and Konstantin went inside their new home.

The tent was more of a pavilion, the interior hung about with swags of bright cloth. Brass lamps set with jewel-coloured glass were suspended from the roof, sending reflections of red and blue and green on to the canvas. Wicker furniture was placed elegantly on patterned rugs, and four smaller bedrooms led off from the main room, all with comfortable-looking divans with bed-nets to keep insects away. Mr Conan Doyle emerged from one of them and hurried into the makeshift main room, carrying Chronos in his hands. 'Oh, good. You're back. I was wondering where on earth you'd got to.'

He seemed very concerned, and sat them all down and called for lemonade. Mr Conan Doyle's face grew very serious when he heard of their encounter with Arthur John Priest and their imprisonment in the Puzzle Chamber of Thutmoses.

'That blighter seems determined to get his hands on Tut,' he mused, 'and equally determined to stop us finding him. Well, I've a plan that should put us streets ahead of him.' He seemed agitated and excited, taut with suppressed energy like a coiled spring.

'Did the pipe-smoking work?' asked Luna. The lemonade was very refreshing, and she felt the shock of what had happened to them that afternoon subsiding.

'It did,' said the author. 'It took three pipes, as predicted. But I do now have a plan to find out exactly where Howard Carter is going to dig tomorrow. We all have a part to play. Even Chronos.' He set the clockwork cuckoo down on the table. 'And especially you, Luna.' He seemed to notice the trousers for the first time. 'Although I'm afraid you'll have to put your frock back on.'

She looked down at herself. 'Do you disapprove?'

He smiled. 'Not in the slightest. But the plan depends rather on you having very full skirts.'

Luna looked puzzled.

'All will be explained,' Mr Conan Doyle assured her. 'That's the easy part. On the more difficult part I will now consult you all. Do gather round.'

The time-thieves pulled their wicker chairs around the dining table and listened attentively.

'As I said,' began Mr Conan Doyle, 'I think I have thought of a way to persuade our friend Mr Carter to reveal the exact location of where he plans to dig tomorrow. The answer came to me this afternoon.'

'And what is the answer, sir?' asked Konstantin.

The author leant forward in his chair and uttered one word. 'Spiritualism.'

Luna thought she must have misheard. Spiritualism? That was the current craze taking over Victorian London. It began in private homes, where enthusiasts gathered to hold gatherings called 'séances' in the presence of a 'medium' – someone who was supposed to have the power to contact the dead. And the craze had grown to the point where now audiences packed into West End theatres to watch those same mediums communicate with the beyond and bring back messages from loved ones who had passed to 'the other side'.

Aidan had no such scruples. 'Isn't spiritualism a load of old hogwash though?'

Mr Conan Doyle smiled. 'Well. I'm rather inclined to believe in it all. Much more fun, don't you find, to think of an afterlife and spirits swimming around in the ether, than an eternity of black nothingness?'

Now it was time for Aidan to hold his tongue. He was from a Catholic family and everyone knew that when you died you went through the pearly gates to heaven, where angels sat on clouds and played golden harps. Surely anything else was just nonsense?

Konstantin took up the thread – of the three he was the least sceptical and the most interested. 'Do you really believe people can speak from beyond the grave?'

'Let us just say I am a student of the occult,' replied the author. 'And although I *myself* am inclined to believe, I have become acquainted, in the course of my researches, with the tricks and ruses by which charlatans cheat the unwary.'

Konstantin spoke for them all. 'I'm sorry, sir, but I'm not entirely sure what you mean.'

'I mean,' said Conan Doyle, looking over his shoulder, 'that although I myself think there may be something in it, there are a lot of people who are making a lot of money by *pretending* they can speak to the dead. And we, my fine fellow travellers, are going to employ some of those tricks after dinner tonight, in order to find out the whereabouts of Tutankhamun's tomb.' He tapped his fingers on the table. 'One thing is missing. I need a piece of information that *they can't possibly know that we know*. The amazing piece of knowledge that mediums produce like a rabbit out of a hat, and it leads all the people at the séance to trust them.'

'And why would we need that?' asked Konstantin curiously.

'Because tonight,' said Arthur Conan Doyle, 'we are going to have a séance. And call forth the spirit of Tutankhamun himself.'

3 NOVEMBER 1922
6.30 p.m.

The time-thieves stared at Mr Conan Doyle.

'But... but... we don't have a medium,' stuttered Luna. 'Will you do it?'

'Not I,' said the author. 'I think they would be suspicious of me and my motives. Carter already thinks there's something fishy about me because of my "youthful" looks. Better an innocent child. The medium will be *you*, Luna.'

'*Me?*' Luna's mouth fell open.

'It is often said that women possess more sympathetic and more open characters, and therefore provide better pathways for the spirits,' said Mr Conan Doyle. 'But as I investigated further I realised that one of the main reasons women were employed in this way was a practical, not a spiritual one.'

'And what was the reason?' asked Luna.

'The simple fact of the female costume. I do not refer, of course, to the trousers you are wearing now. I mean the full skirts and voluminous sleeves of Victorian dress which can conceal all manner of tricks. That is why you will see female mediums often dress in Bohemian flowing gowns, and even the men will don the robes of the Orient or Arabia – not only to give them an air of mystery, but so that they can conceal their trickery.'

Konstantin was curious. 'What trickery?'

'Our friend Chronos here,' said Conan Doyle, turning the brass bird's key clockwise until the little ruby eyes shone. 'He is all the trickery we need.'

The brass beak worked indignantly. 'I've been called many things,' said the bird huffily. 'But *trickery*? I am not some sort of sideshow.'

'Oh, do dry up, Chronos,' said Aidan. 'I want to hear.' But what Mr Conan Doyle said next didn't exactly help to clarify things.

'Yes, you boys have a part to play too. You must react in a way that *sells* the trick. When Luna gets a message from Chronos, or the table rocks, it is your *reaction* that will convince our guests as much as Luna's fraud. Now,' he said, 'we are all ready, but what we don't have is that crucial nugget of information. Ideally, we need something that Mr Carter knows but no one else does.'

Konstantin sat up very straight. *Something that Mr Carter knows but no one else does.*

Without saying anything he rose and went out into the sunset. The sky was as scarlet as a Red Admiral butterfly and Abdel was sitting on the low stone wall, in his accustomed place. He was surrounded by his water vessels, talking softly to Cleopatra.

'Abdel.'

The boy looked up and smiled. 'Konstantinkass.'

'We're friends, Abdel, aren't we?'

'Why yes, Konstantinkass.'

'Would you come and tell Mr Conan Doyle what you told me earlier? About how King Tut died?'

Abdel only hesitated for a moment before getting to his feet. 'If my friend asks it of me, I will do it.'

Back inside the tent, Mr Conan Doyle listened to the waterboy tell the tale of Tutankhamun, his beautiful young wife Ankhesenamun, and Ay, the jealous vizier who ended his life. His moustaches began to twitch and his eyes began to sparkle. '*That's it!*' he exclaimed.

He got to his feet and shook Abdel's hand. 'Young man, you have done a great service to the British Empire.'

Konstantin saw a glimmer of misgiving in Abdel's eye. 'Why, sir?' he asked, a little panicked. 'What did I do?'

Arthur Conan Doyle clapped him on the shoulder. 'You, my good fellow, have just given us the key to the puzzle. Now,' he said, 'we are ready.'

3 NOVEMBER 1922
7.30 p.m.

Everything was set for Mr Conan Doyle's dinner for the Carnarvons and Mr Carter.

The main atrium of the tent was set with a dinner table and chairs, just as you might see in a great English house. There the Englishness ended, though, as the table was draped with turquoise silk and set with tumblers of chunky red and blue and yellow glass. The lanterns shone above in their primary colours and the swags of silk that hung about the tent stirred in the warm evening breeze.

Mr Conan Doyle had been busy that afternoon, organising. He'd asked Sallah to arrange a lavish feast in the Egyptian style: flatbreads and curried meats and pomegranate seeds like bright rubies, all laid out at once with no courses.

Lady Evelyn made an entrance, posing as she came into the tent as if she were taking a curtain call. 'Darlings,' she cried, as if she was meeting them all for the first time. 'How lovely!' There was no sign of the trauma of that afternoon. She was wearing what seemed to be a pair of men's silk pyjamas in the striking green of a Brimstone butterfly, and she had a pair of diamond stars clipped into her severely bobbed hair. Her face was white, her lips red and her grey eyes painted with black lines to elongate them, so she looked like an Egyptian queen.

Luna felt frumpy and old-fashioned in her bulky purple dress. She also felt sick to her stomach and sure she would not be able to eat anything. She couldn't wait to sit down, because she had something rather uncomfortable strapped to her leg underneath the skirts of her dress and she was afraid that the something would fall down at any minute. She took a couple of deep breaths but the butterflies that had somehow begun to fly around her stomach continued their persistent fluttering.

Lord Carnarvon and Mr Carter shook Mr Conan Doyle cordially by the hand. 'Good evening, Sir Arthur.'

'I'll never get used to that,' laughed Mr Conan Doyle.

'Abdel has come with us too,' said Lady Evelyn, drawing the waterboy forward, hands on his shoulders.

She'd obviously developed a fondness for him. 'He insisted on joining us – he says no one serves coffee like him.'

Luna exchanged a glance with Abdel and knew the truth – he wasn't there to serve coffee but to see the séance. He looked, in his quiet way, almost as excited as Lady Evelyn. Howard Carter looked twitchy and cross, as if he would rather be anywhere but there. Lord Carnarvon shot a troubled glance at Konstantin but said nothing, and Luna got the feeling that in the intervening hours Lady Evelyn had had a sharp word with her father about being polite to Germans. He held his tongue, but sat as far away as he could from Konstantin.

Dinner seemed to go on for ever, but at last Lord Carnarvon called Abdel to bring the coffee. This, the time-thieves knew, was when the séance was most likely to begin. Carnarvon had a brandy with his cup. 'Might as well, seeing as it might be our last night,' he said gruffly. 'If we don't find Tut tomorrow, we're going home.'

He waved his forefinger in Howard Carter's face. 'One more dig, Carter. I can't put Highclere Castle on the line. One more day. Or else by sundown tomorrow you'll hear the sound of the camel's back breaking.'

Mr Conan Doyle sipped his coffee carefully, so as not to dunk his splendid moustaches. 'If you have just the one card left to play, Mr Carter,' he said, 'I would want to be sure it was the right one.'

'That's impossible,' said Carter scornfully. 'I am confident in the spot I have picked, but I can never be *sure* that I'm digging in the right place. There's not exactly anyone I can ask.'

Arthur Conan Doyle leant forward with an air of mystery which was aided by the fact that at that moment a desert wind lifted the flap of the tent and flickered the lamps, as if some spirit had entered with it. In his soft Scottish voice he said, '*You could ask Tutankhamun himself.*'

Their three guests reacted entirely differently to this. Lord Carnarvon sat back with a laugh that was almost a bark. Lady Evelyn let out a shocked giggle. And Howard Carter's mouth curled into a sneer under his neat black moustache. 'Ah, yes. All that spiritualism nonsense. I forgot you were a champion of such things.'

'Not a champion,' corrected Mr Conan Doyle. 'Merely an interested observer. I just think it is worth a try. But if you do not agree, we will make no further claims on your time.' He dabbed his moustaches with his napkin, and made as if he was getting up from the table. It was the same trick he'd used earlier when he'd walked away from

Lord Carnarvon when he was golfing on the dunes, and it worked again.

The earl stopped the author with one single syllable. 'Wait.'

Mr Conan Doyle stood still.

'Tell us more.'

The author took his seat again. 'It would require all of us to be open, not sceptical. We shall merely ask the question of the ether, and wait and see what comes forth. Probably nothing. But we shall see.'

'Oh, *do* let's, Father,' pleaded Lady Evelyn. 'You remember we used to have séances at Highclere, and it was *such* enormous fun. So we would be very open-minded.'

Lord Carnarvon could not resist such an appeal. 'Very well, my dear. But who shall be our medium?'

'My niece Luna here has shown herself to be a very conductive being for the spirits,' said Mr Conan Doyle, and Luna's heart began to thump.

Everyone looked at the sardonic Mr Carter – he was the one who needed convincing. 'All right,' he said. 'I'll buy it. What do we need?'

'We all need to be gathered about a table,' said Mr Conan Doyle.

'We already are.'

'No – the circle of power must be smaller, we must be closer together so our hands can touch. This one will do.'

He pointed to the small wicker table and the guests obligingly gathered their chairs around it. Just as planned, the two boys sat either side of Luna, so that no one else was close enough to see what she was doing. Lady Evelyn, just as before, made sure she was sitting next to Aidan, and Mr Conan Doyle sat beside Konstantin, since it was clear neither of the gentleman wanted to sit next to a German.

'And now,' said Mr Conan Doyle with an air of ceremony, 'we place our hands lightly on the table and touch our little fingers together.'

Howard Carter let out an impatient exclamation, but he placed his hands on the table like everyone else. Mr Conan Doyle made a little fuss about getting everyone's hands in exactly the right position – palms down on the table, fingers spread, everyone's little fingers touching.

This was Luna's cue. She reached under her dress, felt for Chronos where he was attached by a garter to her knee, and turned his little key anticlockwise. Then, last of all, she placed her own hands on the table and the wire hooks hidden inside her sleeves invisibly slid beneath the light wicker table top. The light was low, the scent of the Nile reeds filled the air, and the desert breeze, the same one that had breathed across the dunes for three thousand years, stirred the silks of the tent.

Luna the Medium gave Mr Conan Doyle a little nod.

She was ready.

3 NOVEMBER 1922
9.45 p.m.

'There are two things that false mediums need in order to carry out a séance at home,' Mr Conan Doyle had said that afternoon. 'A means to move the table, and a means to communicate the messages from the beyond. The wire loops in your sleeves will allow you to lift or at least shake a light wicker table. And Chronos, strapped to your knee and hidden under your skirt, will be the dead's mouthpiece.'

Now, in the warm Egyptian night, Luna took a deep breath of the spicy air. '*King Tutankhamun.*' She made her voice as loud and mysterious as she could, just as she had been instructed. '*We call to you across the millennia. Hear us. We invite you to our sacred circle.*' She could feel Aidan shaking with suppressed laughter next to her, so gave him a swift kick under the table until he stopped.

'*Is there anybody there?*' Luna asked, her voice deep and dramatic.

Mr Carter began to fidget.

'Is anybody there?' Luna repeated.

Nothing but silence followed.

For the third time Luna asked, 'Is there anybody there?'

This was the moment. Luna squeezed her knees together to indicate to Chronos he should speak.

YES.

His silvery voice seemed to have an ethereal other-worldly quality. The sound was even louder than when they'd trialled it that afternoon – probably because it was now dark and the desert winds were swirling about the tent. Luna had been afraid, when they'd rehearsed it, that it would be immediately obvious that the sound was coming from her lap. But by some trick of acoustics, perhaps because of the muffling fabric of Luna's skirt and petticoats, it was impossible to tell.

The effect of the sound was immediate. All the participants broke the circle and jumped about a foot in the air. Lady Evelyn squealed like a steam train. 'What was *that*?'

'There's someone there,' said Konstantin, eyes round with fear, just as he'd practised. 'A spirit is trying to communicate with us.'

'Nonsense,' said Carter. 'The waterboy has cracked one of his jars, that's all.'

'But the waterboy is here,' said Lord Carnarvon, nodding to Abdel where he stood watching by the tent flap.

'Then the wind knocked something over.'

If you're losing them, Conan Doyle had said, *go to the next stage.*

Luna let her head drop on to her chest with a low moan.

'What's happening?' said Aidan, just as planned. 'Is she all right?'

Luna lifted her head suddenly, eyes wide and unseeing.

'Shhh,' said Conan Doyle. 'She's in a state of "fugue". That means the spirits are speaking through her.'

Again as planned, Konstantin lifted his hand and waved it in front of Luna's eyes. She didn't blink.

'She can't see you or hear you,' said Conan Doyle. 'She is now a conduit for the dead. We may ask her questions now.'

'Oo, I have a question!' burst out Lady Evelyn. 'Are you a man?'

Luna squeezed Chronos.

YES.

'Are you Egyptian?'

YES.

Konstantin said, 'Are you a pharaoh?'

YES.

'Yes!' exclaimed Lady Evelyn. 'It's him!'

'Well, let us ask,' said Conan Doyle cautiously. 'Spirit. Are you King Tutankhamun?'

YES.

This time, when Chronos spoke Luna rocked the table with the wires at her wrists. But she actually underestimated the force she would need to move it and it almost lifted up. But that turned out to be a fault on the good side. Everyone at the séance cried out loud.

Mr Carter let out a snort, but this time everybody shushed him.

'Is your mother The Younger Lady?' asked Konstantin.

YES.

'And your grandmother The Elder Lady?' asked Aidan.

YES.

'These are things that any schoolboy could know,' scoffed Carter. 'And you, Sir Arthur, certainly know these particulars, for I saw you at the British Museum myself, at the Unwrapping of The Younger Lady.'

'This yes/no business is hopeless,' said Lady Evelyn, who was turning out to be the time-thieves' greatest ally, even though she had no idea what was going on. 'We need to ask more specific questions. What a shame we can't just let him say what he wants to say.'

'Well,' said Conan Doyle, 'let us ask the spirit. Is there something you would like to tell us?'

Luna let a dramatic pause fall. Then she gave Chronos a little squeeze with her knees.

AY.

'Ay,' repeated Konstantin, furrowing his brow. 'That makes no sense.'

'Perhaps another soul has interrupted,' said Aidan.

'It's possible,' said Mr Conan Doyle. 'Sometimes troublesome spirits do interrupt the channel.'

AY-AY-AY, said the spirit again, getting increasingly agitated. *AY-AY-AY!*

The table rocked perilously.

'I know,' Lady Evelyn sat up very straight, her eyes wide. 'Perhaps the spirit means yes. Aye means yes, doesn't it?'

'Utter nonsense,' scoffed Carter. 'As if a three-thousand-year-old pharaoh would use a Middle English contraction like "Aye".'

'Then it is another word altogether. Or,' said Conan Doyle, shooting Carter a look beneath veiled eyelids, 'a name perhaps?'

Howard Carter visibly started, the colour draining from his face. '*Ay*,' he whispered, almost to himself. 'It is indeed a name, and one I myself know well.'

Through her staring eyes Luna could see that he was now beginning to believe. She felt the grim elation that those fake mediums must feel – the Egyptologist was a fish on her hook.

'Perhaps, Mr Carter,' said Conan Doyle, 'you would like to ask the questions.'

Swallowing, Carter nodded. He licked his lips nervously, then said aloud, 'Great Tutankhamun. Who is Ay to you?'

VIZIER.

'Vizier,' giggled Lady Evelyn. 'What a funny word. Whatever does it mean?'

'Prime minister,' said Howard Carter, not even looking at her. 'Ay was Tutankhamun's prime minister and closest friend.' He spoke to the spirit again. 'Who is your wife?'

ANKHESENAMUN.

'And who was your successor?'

AY-AY-AY. Tutankhamun's spirit became agitated again.

Lord Carnarvon turned to Carter. 'Is that right? Did Tut's prime minister become pharaoh after him?

Carter turned troubled eyes upon the earl. 'Yes, he did. But' – he shook his head – 'it's still something that a scholar might know.'

'But not a young English girl like my niece, surely?' said Conan Doyle.

Carter ran his hands through his black hair, disturbing its precise neatness. 'I don't know. I just don't know.'

Luna, still staring straight ahead, remembered what Mr Conan Doyle had told her that afternoon. *Once he's on the hook, reel him in.* She began to squeeze her poor knees together again and Chronos spoke once more.

MUR-MUR.

'Wait,' said Aidan, playing his part admirably. 'Something else is coming through.'

MURDER! shrieked Chronos, just as they'd rehearsed – an unholy sound that pierced the night air.

Carter sprang up, his face the colour of paper, and Luna was careful to let the table drop. 'But… but… that's *impossible*,' he stammered. 'No one knows this but me. I told only one other man on this earth, and he sits right there.' He pointed to Lord Carnarvon with a wavering finger.

'But this soul to whom we speak is *not* on earth,' said Conan Doyle precisely. 'Sit down, Mr Carter. We are getting somewhere.'

Like a man in a dream, the Egyptologist settled himself back at the table, and carefully placed his hands so that the little fingers touched Lord Carnarvon's on one side and Lady Evelyn's on the other. He fell to questioning the spirit once again.

'Are you saying that someone *killed* you?'

Luna gave Chronos the signal to reply, but there was a problem. She was so sweaty with the effort of representing the spirits of the netherworld that Chronos was slipping from his harness around her knee. Luna would have to secure him again before he fell to the floor, but in order to do that she would have to break the circle and reach below her skirts, all without anyone seeing. Her heart began to race. How could it be done?

'Spirit. Did someone try to kill you?' persisted Carter, fast losing patience.

Luna turned agonised eyes on Aidan and Konstantin. What could she do?

Aidan took the hint. 'Ah!' he cried, jumping up from his chair and breaking the circle. He ran to the flap of the tent, taking everyone's gaze with him. Quick as a flash, Luna reached beneath the table and secured Chronos back in position. It was not easy, what with the wire loops at her wrists, and she struggled with her skirts, but she did it. Chronos was securely fastened to her knee once again.

'What's the matter?' said Konstantin, playing along.

'Something touched me on the shoulder!' stuttered Aidan, twisting around to brush at his waistcoat, giving a very good impression of being completely terrified.

'That means the spirits are close,' said Conan Doyle, improvising too. 'Sit down, Mr O'Connell. We are getting to the meat of the matter.'

By the time Aidan returned to his seat, Luna's hands were back on the table, and she was back in her trance.

'King Tutankhamun,' said Carter, for the third time. 'Did someone kill you?'

YES.

'Who?'

AY.

'Why?'

FOR LOVE, intoned Chronos in his strange disembodied voice, just as rehearsed. *FOR ANKHESENAMUN.*

Carter gave a long sigh. 'Confirmed,' he said, and sat back in his chair. 'Confirmed!' He looked around the table. 'It's a pet theory of mine,' he said. 'That King Tut's death was the earliest political assassination of all time. I formed the notion from my own researches – when I discovered that Ay had married Tut's wife Ankhesenamun within a year of the young king's death, and then become pharaoh of all Egypt. It would explain why Tut died so young, if there was foul play. And it would change the game in terms of where he might be buried. But I only told His Lordship, and I don't suppose he told anyone else.' He looked at his sponsor questioningly.

'I didn't,' said Lord Carnarvon, holding up both hands. 'I didn't even tell Evelyn, did I, my dear?'

'That's true,' put in Lady Evelyn. 'I haven't the foggiest idea what you're all talking about.'

'There you are,' said Carter, utterly convinced. 'And I have never heard another living soul put forth that idea.'

'You said it,' said Conan Doyle. 'Another *living* soul. You have now spoken with Tutankhamun himself.' He sat back too. 'So there you are. And now' – he checked his pocket watch – 'I think we should turn in. It grows late, and you have a dig tomorrow.'

Carter grabbed his wrist. 'Wait, man, are you mad?'

Mr Conan Doyle feigned surprise. 'I thought you had heard all you needed to convince you.'

'To *convince* me, yes,' said Carter. 'But I have one further question. *The* question.'

'*The* question?' queried Conan Doyle.

'The *only* question,' said Carter. 'What's all this about? His whereabouts.' He placed his hands back on the table, and all the others followed suit.

Luna waited, her heart thumping. This was it. This was what the whole charade had been for. Would Howard Carter give his secret away?

Carter wetted his pale lips again then, quite clearly, he said, 'Are you buried beneath the storm drain by the tomb of Ramesses VI?'

YES YES YES.

And then,

VERILY I AM HERE WHEN THOU CALLEST.

This time when Carter pushed his chair back he almost upset the table. That final phrase, borrowed from Professor Petrie's golden shabti, and repeated by Chronos, had utterly convinced him.

Taking her cue, Luna gasped, blinked and shook her head. She looked about her as if dazed. 'Where am I?'

'Miss Conan Doyle,' exclaimed Howard Carter, fixing her with an intense gaze. He rose, rushed around the table and grabbed her hand. He raised it to his face and she knew then that it was all over.

He had seen the wire loop in her sleeve and would now expose her.

But he merely shook the hand he held warmly. He smiled for the first time in their acquaintance. 'After five long years you have given me the breakthrough I needed.' He dropped her hand and began to pace excitedly. 'My Lord, we must wake the labourers. We need to go *now*.'

'Don't be an ass, man,' said Lord Carnarvon. 'It's nearly midnight. They'll all be in their beds.'

'Goodness, yes,' said Mr Conan Doyle, stifling an enormous pretend yawn. 'It is late indeed.' This was the cue for all the time-thieves to start pretending they were tired.

Luna didn't even have to fake it. She was exhausted and her knees were raw. More than once she'd thought that Chronos would slide through the garter on to the floor. The boys though, taking their cue, began to yawn and stretch admirably, hoping their guests would take the hint. They did.

'King Tut's been at rest for three thousand years,' declared Lord Carnarvon. 'A few more hours won't make any difference. And we'll shift much better with a good night's sleep behind us.'

'I suppose you're right,' grumbled Carter, visibly trying to calm himself down. 'Waterboy,' he barked to Abdel. 'Wake me with the dawn.'

3 NOVEMBER 1922
11.45 p.m.

Night had transformed the Valley of the Kings.

Camels lay down in the sand, forming their own shadowy humpbacked dunes. Torches lit the tents from within, turning them into canvas lanterns, and burning brands thrust into the sand illuminated the way between the digs. Little fires further into the desert spoke of the workmen cooking meat or brewing coffee, and delicious smells wafted from their cauldrons. The men sang a strange and melodious song as they brewed, a sound that seemed to come from the back of the throat, mournful and thrilling at the same time. Those songs could have been as old as Tutankhamun himself.

The time-thieves and Abdel − who wouldn't have missed this for the world − followed Mr Conan Doyle past the fires into the secret dark beyond. There was to be no sleep for them that night. Now they knew where the tomb was, it was vital that they got there first.

They hadn't gone very far before their way was blocked by a crowd of burly men. Luna's heart pounded with fear, but she needn't have worried. The author had not been idle that afternoon. He'd hired his own team of diggers ready and waiting in the valley with picks and shovels, far enough away from the Carnarvons' tent to avoid suspicion.

As the time travellers approached, the leader of the gang said in broken English, 'Are you Lord Carnarvon and his daughter?'

Mr Conan Doyle took Luna's arm. 'Yes, that's us,' he answered confidently. Then he whispered to Luna out of the side of his mouth. 'Since Egyptian Independence you need a permit to dig in the Valley of the Kings, and we didn't have one.' He winked. 'But Lord Carnarvon does.'

'Where to, honoured sir?' said the musclebound foreman.

'Allow me,' said Abdel, beginning an animated conversation in his own language, with lots of pointing and gesturing and nodding. Then he mounted Cleopatra and set off to lead the way, and the whole gang followed with the time-thieves bringing up the rear. The men moved in silence through the warm night; there was no singing for them, only an unspoken agreement that they must be secret.

They all walked along unspeaking for a while, then when they were far enough from the camps, the workmen kindled the lamps, which weaved and bobbed ahead of them, lighting up glimpses of the eerie rocky valley. After a time, their feet struck a sort of channel in the sand – a natural pathway in the desert bordered by stones. Abdel held up his hand and the lamplit procession stopped. 'Storm drain,' he said.

Conan Doyle looked down the track. 'It's still a long stretch,' he said doubtfully. 'Where do we start?'

'The tomb of Ramesses VI is over there.' Abdel pointed to a dark mouth in the rock. 'So if we head towards that we must be going in the right direction.'

Just then, Cleopatra stumbled and Abdel fell to the sand with a thump.

Konstantin ran to help him up. 'Are you all right?'

'I'm fine, thank you, Konstantinkass,' Abdel replied, his teeth glinting in the moonlight as he winced. 'I just banged my elbow on this stone.' He thumped the offending slab with his hand. Then he looked at it hard. 'This is not a stone,' breathed Abdel, sinking to his knees so he could look more closely. 'It is a step.'

'A step?' asked Aidan, catching them up.

'Yes. Look at the size of the other stones.'

Luna had a look too. 'They're smaller,' she said. 'And less regular.'

'Yes,' said Abdel. 'This is longer and neater. It looks like the top of some stairs.'

Stairs.

The time-thieves looked at each other, eyes so wide that the whites could be seen in the darkness.

This was it.

Abdel called the team back with a single sharp cry that could have been a night bird, and they turned at once.

Everyone began to dig frantically. Luna, wishing very hard that she had her trousers back, rolled up her sleeves and hitched up her skirts and joined in too, and even Mr Conan Doyle stripped down to his shirtsleeves and bent to the task. The rubble around the long stone was very loose and soon the team had uncovered a second step, then a third. It was a long business, and the time-thieves began to talk as they dug.

'I don't understand the significance of the Tutankhamun murder story,' panted Luna. 'Carter said it changed the game. But how?'

'I don't know,' said Konstantin. 'Why does the fact he was murdered make any difference to where his tomb is?'

'I think I know this one,' said Aidan the engineer. 'When he showed me the map it was clear that up until now he was digging in all the quadrants that were *far away* from existing tombs, because he expected the tomb to be the size of the one we saw this afternoon belonging to Hatshepsut. That wasn't so much of a tomb as a mortuary temple – it was huge.' He wiped his brow. 'I think the murder changes things because it was an unexpected death of a very young man – he was buried in haste. They didn't have years and years to build a magnificent tomb far out in the desert for an ageing pharaoh. They had to build the tomb quickly and that's why Carter thought it would be worth looking close to an existing tomb after all – in this case of Ramesses VI – because Tut's tomb would be small and could fit somewhere unexpected. And it looks like he was right.'

In the space of an hour the team had revealed twelve steps in all. Conan Doyle, eyes as bright as the lamps, gazed down the stairway into the dark. 'You men may rest,' he said to the excavators. 'We'll call if you are needed. Take your ease. Children, take a light apiece.'

Abdel stood forward. 'May I come with you? Please?'

Arthur Conan Doyle tore his eyes away from the steps, looked at Abdel and smiled. 'My dear fellow. You *found* the bally thing. You may *lead* the way.'

Abdel, with a delighted smile, snatched up a lamp too and started to walk slowly down the stairs – aware of the honour of being the first soul to do so in three thousand years. The time-thieves, trembling with excitement, followed with Conan Doyle bringing up the rear.

They all gathered at the bottom of the steps. There was a door, ancient and entire, with the seals intact. 'Look,' said Luna. 'The cartouche of Tutankhamun, remember? The little basket, the sun, the scarab and the three lines.'

'Go on,' said Conan Doyle to Abdel. With shaking hands, Abdel broke the seals, the door opened with a centuries-old croak, and they were inside.

There was a short, narrow passageway, smelling of ancient stone, and for a moment they thought they were heading for disappointment. But in a very short time they found themselves in a chamber — small, crowded with things and quite untouched.

'Lift the lamps high,' said Conan Doyle in a voice choked with emotion.

They did.

They were standing in a treasure chest of gold, pure gold.

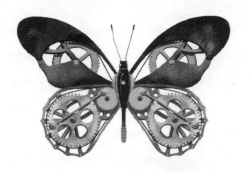

4 NOVEMBER 1922
1 a.m.

As their eyes adjusted to the brightness the travellers began to see shapes resolving from the treasure heap. Strange animals, statues, and everywhere the glint of gold. To the left, four dismantled gilded chariots, inlaid with jewel-bright glass, lay in disarray, as if they had crashed all together in a heap. The jumbled tomb did indeed look like a rushed job after the untimely death of a young man.

On the other wall, two golden couches, in creature form. One had the head of a hippopotamus, another a cow. 'The hippo is the goddess Taweret,' whispered Abdel. 'She protects the sleeper, and assists with the transit to the afterlife. If she is here, that's a good sign that *he* is too.' There was no need to explain who Abdel meant by 'he'.

The time-thieves and Mr Conan Doyle began their search. The golden couches were piled high with furniture – chairs, stools and garment boxes. There was even a gilded throne just the right size for a young man – it would have fitted Aidan or Konstantin perfectly.

Underneath the couches were piles upon piles of rounded wooden boxes. 'What are they?' asked Konstantin.

'Lunchboxes,' said Abdel.

Aidan looked sharply at the waterboy, suspecting a joke, but Abdel seemed perfectly serious. 'They are full of meat and fish, to sustain the dead to the afterlife. Another good sign. He is close.'

Overseeing everything were a couple of man-sized black statues wearing golden headdresses, so lifelike it was as if two sentinels from ancient Egypt were actually in the room. 'It's odd,' said Luna. 'What are they guarding? There's nothing there.'

'No,' said Abdel. It was almost a shout. 'He *has* to be here. I *have* to find him.'

Everyone looked at him in surprise.

'We,' he stammered. 'I mean we. *We* have to find him.'

'Why do you care so much?' said Aidan belligerently, swaggering over to the waterboy. 'What's in it for you?'

Abdel did not answer, but looked at his feet.

'*Everyone is a rival, no one is an ally,*' quoted Aidan. He grabbed a handful of the front of Abdel's robe. 'Is someone paying you? Is it that one-eyed fiend?'

'Shut up,' said Konstantin, a thought suddenly occurring to him. He shoved Aidan away. 'It's not that.' He put a hand on Abdel's shoulder and spoke gently. 'Did they ever find your brother's body? Did they ever bring Karim home from the Great War?'

'No.' Abdel shook his head and tears flew from his eyes. 'They never found him.'

Then Konstantin saw how it had been. 'I'm so sorry. I'm so, so sorry.' He felt, once again, as if he was apologising for Germany as well as himself, which was just ridiculous.

'Sorry for what?' said Aidan hotly. 'Look, just what is going on?'

Konstantin dragged Aidan into the passageway where they couldn't be overheard. 'Leave him alone,' he hissed. 'His brother, Karim, was killed in the Great War. I think he's been looking for him ever since.'

Aidan was appalled. 'But… but… I didn't know.'

'I know you didn't. But just be… *nice*, would you?'

'Of course.' Aidan thought for a moment. 'But he doesn't think… He doesn't believe that Tutankhamun *is* his brother, does he? Because that would be completely cuckoo.'

'No, of *course* not that,' whispered Konstantin. He tried to think of a way to explain. 'No one seems to like my country much at the moment but back there we have some very clever doctors whose field is the human mind. They would call what Abdel is feeling "transference". Abdel couldn't see his brother's body, couldn't give him any funeral rites and there's no grave to visit. So it has become very important to him to find Tut, who was the same age as Karim when he died. D'you see?'

Aidan frowned. Machines were so much more straightforward than people. 'I *think* so.'

'All right. Now – forward march?'

'Forward march,' said Aidan, grinning.

Back in the chamber, Luna and Mr Conan Doyle were still examining the two sentinel statues, which were standing a few feet apart, facing each other. Abdel stood a little aside, his mouth compressed into a line as if he was trying not to cry. He held his lamp high so that the others could see, but he was taking no further part in the proceedings. Abdel looked at Aidan doubtfully when he re-entered the chamber, and Aidan knew it was time to do the right thing.

'Look,' he said, going right up to the waterboy. 'I'm sorry I ever doubted you. I didn't know about your brother.

I've got six sisters, and if any of them… well, I don't know what I'd do. Pax?'

'Pax,' said Abdel, and he lowered the lantern slightly as he shook Aidan's hand.

The lowered light illuminated something in a flash.

'The writing's on the wall,' said Mr Conan Doyle suddenly, interrupting this touching scene.

'Yes.' Luna sighed. 'I'm afraid you might be right. It looks like we will have to admit defeat.'

'No,' said the author. 'The writing is *actually* on the wall. Abdel, have the goodness to lower the lamp again.'

Abdel's lamp illuminated a strange patch of wall between the two guards. A discoloured area, darker than the rest. 'Mud plaster,' said Abdel, the quarrel forgotten. 'Newer than the rest but not by much.'

'Yes, and look,' said Aidan, backing him up. 'Something's carved into the darker plaster.'

Luna went closer and ran her fingertips over the characters. It was hard to believe that they had been carved into the wall several millennia ago. 'What does it say?' she wondered aloud.

'It's a curse,' whispered Abdel, his voice cracking with fear. 'It says, "Death will come on swift wings for he who disturbs the tomb of the pharaoh."'

There was a horrible silence. 'Well, that's pretty clear,' said Aidan, trying to sound braver than he felt. 'It means keep away.'

'It means something else too,' said Mr Conan Doyle, straightening up. He looked at the time-thieves and Abdel. 'If there is a sign saying "Beware of the Bull" you can bet your last sixpence there is a bull in that field. If there is a sign saying "Danger, Deep Water" then you may be assured the water is deep. If there is a sign saying "Beware of the Dog" there is a dog waiting to take your hand off. People do not put up warning signs unless there is something to fear. If there is a curse on this wall, it is because there is something behind it.' Mr Conan Doyle laid his hand upon the plaster, as if he could feel the vibrations through the centuries. 'He's here,' he said in a hoarse whisper. 'I think there's another chamber. I think Tut's behind this wall.'

It was the work of a moment to break through the false wall with a couple of picks borrowed from the Egyptian excavators.

On Aidan's advice they made the hole high in the wall, up in the right-hand corner. 'That will keep the integrity of the structure,' he said, now in full engineering mode. 'You dig a hole at the bottom and the whole bally wall will come down.' Aidan and Abdel, working as a team, made a good-sized hole while the others moved the rubble. As the dust cleared, a dazzling screen of gold and blue emerged on the other side of the wall. They all clambered through, boosting each other up and through the hole, passing lamps from the outer chamber to the inner one. Once through the wall, they could tell at once that they were in an even more significant chamber. It was a small room, gloriously painted with white-clad gods and goddesses in profile, and in its centre stood an immense rectangular stone sarcophagus, crawling with hieroglyphics and carved with four winged beings. And, guarding it like a faithful hound, an ebony image of a dog.

'The black jackal,' hissed Luna. 'I saw him at the British Museum!'

'Anubis,' whispered Abdel. 'The jackal-headed deity who accompanies souls to the underworld. He's here. King Tutankhamun is here.'

'Well, Mr Conan Doyle,' said Luna in a voice strangled with emotion. 'You *did* detect something after all.'

4 NOVEMBER 1922
1.15 a.m.

As the time-thieves walked into Tutankhamun's burial chamber, their feet struck some objects which were standing upright on the floor, knocking them over like skittles.

'Lower the lamps a moment,' said Aidan suddenly.

They all did so and the light illuminated a sight to behold. A miniature golden army, ranks upon ranks of little identical figures, each no taller than a bottle of lemonade.

'Shabtis,' breathed Konstantin. '*Hundreds* of them.'

'Just like the one Flinders Petrie showed us in the British Museum,' exclaimed Luna.

Mr Conan Doyle stooped and picked one up. 'Not just *like*,' he said. 'Identical. And remember, Flinders said his was made of solid gold. This army alone is priceless.'

They cleared a way through the little golden figures and Konstantin laid his hand on the stone tomb. It was cold to the touch. 'Is his mummy in there?' he wondered.

'Has to be, doesn't he?' said Aidan confidently.

'We're going to need the team,' said Mr Conan Doyle. 'There might be some heavy lifting.'

Abdel ran for the men, and in an instant the burial chamber was full of people. Even so, it took every last ounce of strength of every one of those present to shift the stone lid of the sarcophagus. It gave way with a grudging, grating sound, and, too heavy to hold, fell to the floor with a boom. All those present jumped back to save their toes, and breathed in the choking, musty cloud of three-thousand-year-old dust. Then those lucky, chosen few craned forward to see what was inside the tomb.

It was almost a disappointment – something bulky and soiled, completely covered in linen shrouds. 'Abdel,' said Mr Conan Doyle softly. 'Could you thank the men and ask them to wait outside?'

When the team had left the burial chamber, he said, 'Time to meet the king. Ready?'

Luna didn't think she would ever be ready for such a moment, it seemed so significant. But Tutankhamun was why they were here. 'Yes,' she said.

As the first shroud was rolled back, all the travellers let out a gasp of wonderment at the gorgeous sight that met their eyes – a golden effigy of the young king, wearing a magnificent headdress, his hands crossed, holding the sceptres of kingship. He was clothed in feathers, and every little filament of each one was exquisitely carved.

'It's the lid of the coffin,' said Aidan. The coffin was over seven feet long, and the rest of it was painted gold and etched with hieroglyphics.

'And look,' said Luna. '*Flowers.*'

For the image of the young king had a small wreath of dried flowers resting on his brow, discoloured and desiccated by the passing centuries, but meant, once, as a tribute to one who was loved.

'Careful now,' said Abdel. He lifted the flowers as reverently as if they were made of gold, and laid them gently aside. Then everyone placed their hands on the coffin lid no one had touched for millennia and started to lift. But they were not destined to meet the king just yet. Inside the first coffin was another, even more glorious.

The second coffin, also made of wood and gold leaf, was decorated with iridescent blue and green glass inlay. And when they lifted the lid of the second coffin they found a third, nested inside the first two like the belly of a Russian doll.

The third coffin was solid gold.

This priceless coffin lid was almost too heavy for them to lift without the men – but after a superhuman effort they shifted it to the floor.

A peerless face stared back at them, a magnificent death mask perfectly crafted of gold and blue. 'Blue – it is the most precious of the colours,' murmured Abdel reverently. 'Blue lapis is the colour of the Nile, the seas, the sky. Everything Egyptians hold dear.'

Gently, Mr Conan Doyle lifted the wondrous mask to reveal, at last, the actual face of Tutankhamun.

After all those riches the reality was strangely sad. The skin was the brown of a Duke of Burgundy butterfly, and the texture of shoe leather. The eyes were closed and the mouth was open as if in sleep. It was the detail that was so heartbreaking. Tutankhamun had eyelashes, and pierced ears, and scraps of hair still clinging to the scalp. And below the face, a pitiful and shrivelled form, but still undoubtedly the body of a young man. He was armed – they found a wicked little dagger with an iron blade and a gold sheath by his side – but stripped of the wealth and glory he seemed almost vulnerable, and his hands were crossed protectively across his chest.

Mr Conan Doyle began to feel gently around the skull in a professional manner. Luna remembered then that the author had trained as a medical doctor. 'It looks like Mr Carter was right,' he said. 'Blunt force trauma to the skull and a four-inch-long fracture on the cranium.'

Konstantin's eyes grew wide. 'So he *was* murdered.'

'I'd say so,' said Mr Conan Doyle gravely. 'Yes.'

Three thousand years melted away. All the gold and the riches didn't matter. Here was a young man, taken before his time, to be respected and mourned. They all, without even discussing it, lowered their voices to a whisper.

'What do we do now?' hissed Luna.

'We winkle him out,' Mr Conan Doyle whispered back. 'And then we hot-foot it back to Flinders Petrie and the British Museum. This mummy's what we came for.'

'No,' said Abdel, more loudly than anyone had spoken for a while. 'He should stay here. This is his resting place and he shouldn't be moved.'

For a moment no one stirred. Then Konstantin came to stand next to his friend. He put a hand on Abdel's shoulder. 'I agree.'

Abdel put his own hand on Konstantin's. '*Thank you*, Konstantinkass.'

Luna looked at the shrivelled corpse, and then back at her friends. She went to stand with Abdel also. 'I agree too.'

All three looked at Aidan. He walked over to Abdel. 'I've been the worst,' he said. 'I doubted you. So I owe you this.' He put his hand on the waterboy's other shoulder. 'He stays.'

Mr Conan Doyle said nothing, but stood, chewing his lip, frozen in thought.

Then Abdel stepped forward. He pointed at the flowers, which he'd laid tenderly aside on the coffin lid. 'Look at that wreath. Someone laid it here.'

Mr Conan Doyle's eyes followed the pointing finger.

'Tutankhamun was loved once,' declared Abdel. 'In all this… splendour, have you seen anything so beautiful as those few withered flowers?'

'No,' said Mr Conan Doyle softly. 'No, I have not.'

'My mother would have laid such a wreath on Karim's breast if she'd had the chance. If you move him you'll have to do it without me, and probably without the men too. No Egyptian would stain his soul by moving a buried friend.' Abdel looked up, the flames of the lamps flickering in his dark eyes. 'He stays.'

Now the time-thieves looked at Mr Conan Doyle. It didn't really matter what they thought, a bunch of mere children. The author was leading this expedition. It was his opinion that mattered – he was the grown-up. He looked at them all in turn with a troubled expression on his face. 'The moral dimension is inarguable,' said he, 'but I am a member of the Butterfly Club, the very organisation that has sent us here on the specific mission of bringing back this mummy. An organisation founded by your aunt, Luna. And your father, Konstantin. Which employs your father, Aidan. I'm sorry. We must take him.'

He turned back to the sarcophagus, slipped his doctor's hands under the leathery body and began to lift.

As he did so there was a horrible noise – the unearthly howl of a dog.

The sound seemed to tear through the musty air of the tomb, and it echoed simultaneously like it was very far away in the desert, and there in the tomb with them. Of course, all the tomb raiders thought the same thing at the same time – that the god Anubis himself was howling at them for daring to disturb the tomb. They all jumped back from the coffin, and there was an abrupt silence, broken by – if possible – an even more terrifying sound. It was the whispering of a lone voice in a dead language. The voice chilled the flesh, and the time-thieves looked around in horror, but they were alone in the tomb. Alone, yet not alone. Something nameless was there with them.

'What's it saying?' Konstantin asked Abdel, his grey eyes wide with fear.

'I cannot fully make it out,' said Abdel. 'It's a very ancient dialect. But it's some sort of warning.'

Then the voice multiplied – there were two, then three, then ten, then a multitude. The whispering became louder and louder, then unbearable.

Luna opened her mouth to say something that she knew would sound completely mad, and yet she had to say it. 'Is it… is it the *shabtis* speaking?'

No one laughed, no one mocked her – because it really did sound like the golden shabtis, the hundreds upon hundreds of them standing sentinel on the stone floor, were whispering a terrible warning.

Konstantin began to back away towards the wall they had broken. 'We should go.'

'You think?' brayed Aidan. 'Let's get out of here.'

'Wait,' said Mr Conan Doyle. 'We need to take the mummy.'

It took all the courage they had to return to the sarcophagus. But when they got there, any courage that they'd gathered disappeared completely.

With a dreadful gurgling, rushing sound, the sarcophagus began to flood with liquid – a thick liquid with a funny metallic smell. Mr Conan Doyle, with a horrified fascination, dipped three fingertips into the fluid. He carried his fingers to his nose and sniffed. 'It's blood,' he said.

'Oh God,' said Aidan. 'It's just like the Puzzle Chamber of Thutmoses.' He turned to Mr Conan Doyle. 'Do you know your scripture, sir? Have you heard of Egypt's plague of blood?'

'Exodus 7:19,' replied the author in an awful whisper which echoed round the tomb. '*Blood will be everywhere in Egypt, even in vessels of wood and stone.*'

They stood, rooted to the spot, unable to look away. The leathery mummy remained completely dry, but the stone sarcophagus around him filled up with blood like a bathtub. All the horrified watchers could see what was about to happen, before it happened – the coffin filled right to the top, then spilled over, splashing on to the shabtis. In a moment, the golden figures disappeared under the flood. The tomb began to fill incredibly fast.

'Aidan,' said Mr Conan Doyle, never taking his eyes off the sarcophagus. '*Now* we can go.'

The time-thieves and Abdel ran – no easy task, because the blood was already up to their knees, snatching at Abdel's robes and Luna's skirts.

The horrible bit was getting back through the cursed wall. They'd made such a small hole, and quite high up, that there was a real chance that the tide of blood would drown them before they could escape.

'Luna, go first,' yelled Mr Conan Doyle above the roaring flood.

'Why should *I*…' she began.

'Niece,' he spluttered sternly, 'now is not the time for your suffragette nonsense. I will not save my skin ahead of a young lady. Just GO.'

'No, but listen,' she protested. 'You should go first. You are the tallest and strongest. We'll need you on the other side of the wall to help the rest of us through. I'd be no earthly use.'

It took him no more than a second to see the sense in this, for the blood was already at waist height. Together, they bundled the eminent author unceremoniously through the gap, followed by Aidan, who was deemed the next strongest. Next went Luna, weighed down by her skirts, which were saturated and slimy with blood.

It was worst for Konstantin. He insisted that Abdel should go before him, for a very particular reason. In that panicked moment, with the blood rising around them, he was unable to accept the thought that Abdel's mother would lose her only remaining son. His own father would mourn him, of course, but he was the youngest and sickest of four brothers, and his father would have many sons left to cheer his old age. That was not the case for Abdel's mother – she'd already lost her eldest – and Konstantin was determined that she should not lose her youngest too. He shoved Abdel upwards with an enormous effort, when gravity and his blood-soaked robes were determined to drag the boy down.

Once Abdel was clear and he was alone in the flooded burial chamber, Konstantin experienced the worst moment of his life. The blood had reached his throat and was flooding into his mouth. It was that horrible taste of metal that he remembered from nosebleeds or split lips, but multiplied ten thousand times. He honestly felt it would close over his head before the others could pull him up. His clothes were soaked, making him enormously heavy, and despite eight grabbing hands hauling him ever upwards, towards the hole in the wall, their grip kept slipping on his bloody garments, and he knew he would die there. With one desperate effort, he jumped toward the jagged gap and the torchlight and the grabbing hands, scrabbled at the blood-soaked plaster until he found a foothold and launched himself through the hole. He slithered on to the floor of the antechamber like a new-birthed foal.

The blood was already starting to pour through the jagged hole in the plaster, covering, character by character, the curse that they should have heeded. They slipped and stumbled along the stone passageway, pursued by a torrent of blood, and scrambled up into the starlight, to lie panting on the dunes.

After a moment of recovery they sat up slowly, looking at each other in horror. They were doused head to toe in blood – only eyes and teeth catching at the moonlight.

'Jesus, Mary and Joseph,' said Aidan, looking from one to the other of his almost unrecognisable companions. 'What in God's name have we done?'

4 NOVEMBER 1922

2 a.m.

'We have to fill in the steps,' said Mr Conan Doyle urgently, as soon as he could speak. 'We have to make sure no one finds the tomb again. And we just have to hope that no one else saw us digging tonight.' He seemed to have entirely changed his mind about Tut, having seen what power the long-dead king possessed.

He beckoned the team, and Abdel gave them instructions. Slightly bemused, the burly men filled in the twelve steps with the rubble they'd only just removed. Then the time-thieves smoothed a layer of sand over the top, so that no sign of excavation could be seen. Mr Conan Doyle thanked the team and paid them. Aidan watched them go into the night with a doubtful eye. 'Will they hold their tongues?'

'I purchased the kind of silence that only British gold can buy,' said Mr Conan Doyle. 'Let's just hope it's enough.'

When the time-thieves reached their tent, bloodstained and exhausted, all they could think of was going to sleep. But a commotion next door, at Lord Carnarvon's tent, brought them to the door of their dwelling. Hiding their filthy appearance behind the canvas, they peered out into the night. Howard Carter's digging gang were preparing for his own excavation at the storm drain, with Carter at the centre of them all, ready and immaculate in a cream suit.

'I've been thinking,' said Mr Conan Doyle. 'If we want Tut to stay where he is, we need to stop Mr Carter and Lord Carnarvon finding his tomb. And that means,' he said apologetically, 'no sleep just yet. We should contrive to go with them if we can, and divert them from the true site. We must tidy ourselves first, though. We look like the butchers of Smithfield market.'

They washed and changed but were still a bit of a mess as they walked to Lord Carnarvon's pitch. Luckily Carter's team were all too excited by the upcoming dig to notice smudged faces or damp hair.

Mr Conan Doyle approached Lord Carnarvon. 'Mind if we tag along? Just as casual observers, don't you know. Hate to miss the show.'

'My dear chap, not at all,' said the earl warmly. 'After all, I'm sure you'd like to know if your spiritual jiggery-pokery did confirm Tut's whereabouts.'

'As long as you stay out of the way,' added Carter ungraciously.

For the second time in the space of a few hours, the time-thieves made their way to the storm drain by Ramesses VI's tomb – this time following Howard Carter and his team of excavators.

'He's probably at the far end,' said Mr Conan Doyle, attempting to direct Mr Carter away from the location of the tomb. 'More space and all that.'

'I think you're right,' said Mr Carter, beckoning to his team of diggers. 'Down the far end.'

The team moved off – it was going to be all right.

Then, disaster.

Cleopatra the mule tripped at exactly the same place on the storm drain. Abdel rolled off Cleopatra with a cry, just as before. Quick as a cat, he was on his feet, but Mr Carter turned back.

'It's all right,' cried Abdel. 'My mule stumbled on a stone.'

There was a footstep behind them, and a familiar voice sounded from the night. 'That's not a stone. It's a step.'

The flash of watchglass glinted from the dark, and Arthur John Priest, disguised as Arthur Cruttenden Mace, stepped forth into the lamplight. He pointed at Abdel. 'This boy has stumbled upon the tomb of Tutankhamun.'

At that moment, the time-thieves knew he had seen everything. He had followed them, seen them digging earlier that night, seen them filling the steps in again.

'Why the devil should we listen to you?' snarled Carter. 'You're working for the enemy.'

Arthur Cruttenden Mace smiled. 'The war is over. There are no enemies now, only friends.'

'Why should we trust you, then?' persisted Mr Carter.

'There is no need to trust me,' said Arthur Cruttenden Mace. 'You may trust the evidence of your own eyes. You are an Egyptologist of many years' experience. Look at that stone and tell me it is not a step.'

Carter lowered his lamp and studied the long and strangely regular stone which had tripped Cleopatra. 'It *is* a step,' he said, his voice shaking with emotion. He looked up at the intruder. 'What do you want from me?'

'Nothing,' said Arthur Cruttenden Mace, holding up both hands, palms outwards. 'In the spirit of international relations, I will leave you to your find.' And, to everyone's surprise, he melted away into the night.

Carter barely noticed. Excitedly, he called his team at once to start digging.

The time-thieves, Abdel and Mr Conan Doyle watched, hearts sinking as the sun rose. There was nothing they could do as the loose rubble around the staircase was once again excavated and the twelve steps revealed.

Carter walked down the stone staircase in the new daylight. He stopped at the ancient portal, like a man in a dream, and touched the timbers of the door with quaking fingers. This was the moment he'd been waiting for for five long years, but his face screwed up into a scowl. 'Dammit!' he exclaimed.

'What's the matter?' called Lord Carnarvon from the top of the steps. 'You found the door, didn't you, man? I thought you'd be turning cartwheels.'

'This is Tutankhamun's cartouche, see?' Carter called back. 'The basket, the sun, the three lines and the scarab. So it's most definitely his tomb. But the seals are broken.'

'What does that mean?' asked the earl.

'Grave robbers,' said Carter curtly. 'Tomb raiders. This door has been opened.'

'When?'

'Probably three thousand years ago.'

The time-thieves exchanged glances. They knew very well that the seals had been broken hours before.

As Carter's team collected at the bottom of the steps to carefully open the doors, the time-thieves were not the only observers. Figures began to converge on the tomb from all over the valley, at first tiny blots on the landscape, then coming closer and closer and resolving into a crowd of hungry-looking young men.

'Word spreads fast,' said Mr Conan Doyle drily. 'This will be that fiend's doing too.'

'Who are they?' asked Luna nervously.

'It is a swarm worse than the ten plagues that smote ancient Egypt. A species more ravenous, more bothersome and more destructive than any locust.' He gave a sigh. 'That, my dear, is the world's press.'

The young men, all carrying notebooks and pencils, jostled for position at the top of the tomb for a glimpse of the English lord entering the ancient grave. His was to be the honour of going in first, as he had paid for the whole enterprise. As Carter stood back to let him by, Lord Carnarvon was smiling and laughing with excitement, as a lifetime's dream became reality.

'If 'e goes in like that I don't give him six weeks,' said a sardonic voice over Mr Conan Doyle's shoulder.

The author turned. 'What did you say?'

A pressman stood behind him, hat pushed back from a sweating forehead, face grinning ghoulishly. 'I said, if 'ee goes in like that I don't give him six weeks.'

'Why?' asked Konstantin.

'You mess with them mummies, they comes to get yer.'

Luna shivered, looking back to Lord Carnarvon, who was now raising both fists above his head like a boxer who had just won the final round. But then she saw something else. A jackal, just like the one Luna and Mr Conan Doyle had seen on the steps of the British Museum, trotted to the top of the stairway. He looked down at Lord Carnarvon in a most peculiar way.

'Look,' said Luna. For a moment nobody moved, then one of the burly guards stooped and chucked a piece of rubble at the jackal. It wheeled on its hind legs and slunk away.

'We're making history today,' said Lord Carnarvon, who hadn't noticed anything amiss.

He pushed open the door and entered the tomb, followed by Carter and Lady Evelyn, with Conan Doyle and the time-thieves bringing up the rear.

4 NOVEMBER 1922
9.15 a.m.

For Luna, the second time she entered the treasure chamber was even more frightening than the first.

They'd left the tomb filled with blood, and the gore had covered every piece of treasure. But spookily, there was no sign of the flood, and there was not even any residue of red. The floor was slightly damp, and a faint tide mark was visible around the walls if you knew what to look for. But the desert had thirstily drunk the liquid, and the tomb was dry again.

Carter and Carnarvon were almost tearful at the end of their five-year treasure hunt. Carter keenly set up his professional archaeology lamps and the earl began sorting through the funerary objects like a child on Christmas morning, not sure what to open first. It was Carter, though, who found the greatest prize in the antechamber. Opening a chest of ebony and ivory he found an exquisite jewelled pendant, a great heavy thing set with carnelians, gold solar discs and vivid blue scarabs as big as plums.

He held it up to the light.

'It's beautiful,' breathed Lady Evelyn.

'A pectoral pendant,' Carter said. 'Halfway between a piece of jewellery and a piece of armour.' Then, quite unexpectedly, he turned to Abdel. 'What's your name, boy?' he asked.

Konstantin felt rather angry on Abdel's behalf. The waterboy had been working for Carter for five years, and in all that time the Egyptologist had not bothered to learn his name.

Abdel, however, did not seem hurt. 'Abdel, sir.'

'*You* should wear this,' he said. 'For it was you who found this place.' And he hung the heavy pendant around the boy's neck, placing the breastplate over his chest, as if he was bestowing a medal. Abdel, who had been thoroughly miserable since he'd stumbled on the tomb for the second time, looked touched by the unexpected generosity of the gesture. He centred the scarab at his heart, suddenly transformed into a boy king.

Konstantin instantly forgave Mr Carter. He had never warmed to him, but he liked him very much at that moment. They hadn't wanted the tomb to be found at all, but if it was to be uncovered, Abdel certainly deserved the credit. He clapped Abdel on the shoulder. 'Just one of those scarabs will buy you that coffee shop you dream of,' he said.

Lord Carnarvon and Lady Evelyn joined in the joyous inventory of the treasure, exclaiming at the golden couches, the tumbled chariots, the gilded throne and the lunchboxes for the beyond. 'All this glitter and gold and youth!' exclaimed Lady Evelyn. 'He really is a jazz age pharaoh.'

'Haven't seen his mummy yet, have you?' said Lord Carnarvon.

'No, but…' began Carter. Then he stopped. He picked up a lamp and carried it to the dividing wall, illuminating the words of the curse. '*Death will come on swift wings for he who disturbs the tomb of the pharaoh,*' he read aloud, and for the time-thieves the words hit differently to how they'd heard them the previous night. For of course, *they* had been the ones to ignore the curse and wake the pharaoh. Carter held the lamp higher and saw at once the jagged hole in the plaster – the very hole the time-thieves had clambered through, blood-soaked and desperate, the night before. He pulled a little throne close and stood on it to peer through the void.

'What can you see?' asked Lady Evelyn breathlessly.

Carter's voice broke. '*Wonderful things*,' he said.

Utterly downcast, the time-thieves, Abdel and Mr Conan Doyle walked out of the tomb into the late morning light. The sun was already high in the sky and the heat was becoming fierce.

'Let's take a stroll down to the river to lift our spirits,' said Mr Conan Doyle. 'This heat is oppressive and it will be fresher there.'

'What do we do now?' asked Luna as they walked in the direction of the Nile.

'Not much we can do at the moment,' said the author. 'Carter and his team will begin the long process of extracting the treasure first and then the sarcophagus. Might as well let him get on with it while we think of a way to stop him taking the body itself.'

'Rather him than us,' said Aidan. 'If I never see that skellington again it will be too soon. I don't want him spitting blood at us again.'

'If it even happened,' said Konstantin, ever rational.

'What are you *talking* about?' brayed Aidan. 'You were there when the tomb flooded. You were the one who nearly drowned like a rat.'

'Oh, I'm not doubting that it flooded,' said Konstantin. 'But it was late, we were scared. Maybe we just disturbed some sort of well leading to an oasis. Perhaps it was just water.'

'But it even *smelled* like blood,' protested Luna. 'And our clothes were saturated with it. We can check the laundry back at the tent.'

Konstantin shrugged. 'Maybe it had dissolved some minerals from the sand to give it the red colour.'

'So you're saying we imagined it all?' said Abdel.

'*I* don't know,' said Konstantin uncomfortably. 'Maybe.'

'What do you think, Mr Conan Doyle?' asked Luna. The author had been silent throughout this argument.

'It is possible, I suppose,' he replied thoughtfully. 'The power of suggestion can be very strong. And I am partly responsible. I quoted Exodus at you – all that talk of blood.'

As they drew closer to the Nile they could barely see the river for the crowds – dense rows of people congregating on the banks, talking excitedly and pointing.

They found a gap in order to enjoy the river breeze – and what they saw made them stop and stare.

The river was red – entirely red.

Bison and camels stood, confused, at the water's edge, not sure whether to dip their heads to drink. Long-billed cranes rose from the scarlet water to wheel above and shriek their displeasure. Young boys were dipping their fingertips in the water and shouting one word over and over. It sounded like '*dam, dam!*'

'What are they saying?' asked Konstantin of Abdel, even though he already knew the answer.

'*Aldam*,' replied Abdel. 'Blood.' He clutching the pendant at his heart as if it was a talisman. 'They're saying it's blood.'

'Still think we imagined it, Konnie?' said Aidan shakily.

Sickened, her heart thudding with fear and foreboding, Luna looked across the red river. Something drew her eye in the midst of the crowd on the opposite bank. A flash of watchglass caught the sun.

From the other side of the Nile, Arthur John Priest, watching them intently from his single eye, lifted his panama hat in greeting.

4 NOVEMBER 1922
10.30 a.m.

Thoroughly frightened by what they might have unleashed, the time travellers and Abdel returned to their tent.

They could barely get near it, for at every step they were plagued by the gentlemen of the press, who were waiting for Lord Carnarvon's return. They swarmed around, firing questions and pressing their business cards into Mr Conan Doyle's hand.

'No point questioning me,' he barked irritably, shoving a path through them. 'I have nothing to do with the dig. I am a mere observer like yourselves. You must direct your enquiries to Lord Carnarvon or Mr Carter – they're the only ones who can give you the story.'

Back inside at last, the time travellers flopped into the wicker chairs, but there was no rest for poor Abdel, who had to return to work. No sooner had they rested their weary limbs than Sallah came into the tent. 'Letter for you, honoured sir. From journalist.'

Wearily, Conan Doyle looked up. 'I *told* those tiresome fellows. It won't be for me.'

'Fellow said the English sir who is travelling with a young lady,' persisted Sallah.

'It'll be for Lord Carnarvon,' said Conan Doyle tiredly, stretching his long legs out in front of him. 'He's travelling with his daughter.'

Sallah was adamant. He waved the letter in Mr Conan Doyle's face until the famous moustaches stirred. 'No, honoured sir. It's for *you*.'

'Very well.' Conan Doyle took the thing and sat up a little. 'It *is* for me. That's odd. Who could know I am here?'

He tore it open and read rapidly. Luna watched him, something niggling at the edges of her memory. She thought the writing looked vaguely familiar.

'Is it a good letter?'

'It *is* a good letter. A very good letter. Most newspaper journalists can't string a sentence together.'

'What does he want?' asked Aidan, almost too tired and dispirited to care.

'An exclusive,' replied the author. 'He wants an interview with me. Well, there's no doubt he can write.' He looked at the next page. 'Careless fellow though. Look. He's blotted the ink.' He showed Luna the second page – blank except for a curious black blot across the fold.

As if in a dream, Luna reached for the page. Her head spun, and with the heat and the tiredness she thought she might faint.

The Rorschach ink blot.

The sign of the butterfly.

That was why the writing looked familiar.

It was Papa's.

She said urgently. 'I know this reporter. He is a gentleman of good standing and well worth a hearing.'

As Sallah was still hovering she didn't want to tell Conan Doyle who the journalist *really* was, but she tried to signal to him with her eyes.

'Very well,' said Conan Doyle, catching her tone. He turned to Sallah. 'Where is this man?'

'Outside, sir. On the dunes.'

Luna ran outside as the others followed. In the morning sun, the man on the top of the dune was just a silhouette. Tall and rangy, wearing a panama hat. As she looked up at him, the figure raised one hand in greeting. Very faintly, she could hear him whistling a few bars of a familiar song.

Yesterday.

Luna's heart began to thump.

Sallah led them up the dune to where the man was standing. Konstantin had no idea who he was. Aidan vaguely recognised him as the man on the *Titanic* who had rescued him from the clutches of Arthur John Priest, and, as for Luna, well, it was all she could do not to throw herself into his arms.

The journalist took care not to look at her. 'Sir Arthur Conan Doyle, I presume,' he said putting out his hand. 'A pleasure.'

'Likewise.' Conan Doyle guardedly shook the hand. 'But you have the advantage of me.'

'How's that?' asked the journalist.

'You know my name, but I'm afraid I don't know yours. You did not sign your letter.'

'Ah yes, of course.' The journalist looked at Luna, very fleetingly. 'My name is William Boot of Fleet Street.'

Conan Doyle looked amused. 'A noble address,' he said sarcastically.

Mr Boot ignored the insult. 'Perhaps you'd be good enough to invite me to breakfast. To discuss my proposal… and other matters.'

'You take a good deal on yourself, I must say—' began Mr Conan Doyle, but he was quickly interrupted by Luna.

'*Please*, Uncle?

'I declare I indulge you more than any of my real nieces,' said Conan Doyle with a sigh. 'Very well.'

4 NOVEMBER 1922
11 a.m.

The first thing Luna did, once Papa was safely inside the tent, was to run into his arms.

'My Luna,' he said, squeezing her hard and giving her their special butterfly kiss with his lashes fluttering against her cheek, just like he always did.

'I spotted the Rorschach blot,' she said, 'so I knew it was you.'

'Good girl,' said Papa. 'I thought you might.'

Mr Conan Doyle looked from father to daughter, nonplussed. 'Look here. Just what exactly is going on?'

'I ought to introduce myself properly,' said Papa. 'I'm Daniel Goodhart.'

'Grace's brother?' Mr Conan Doyle registered surprise.

'That's it. And, more importantly, Luna's father.' He crushed Luna tight to his side. 'I'm not really a journalist.'

'Then what are you?'

'I suppose you would call me a time traveller.' Papa looked at Aidan, Konstantin and Mr Conan Doyle in turn. 'Like yourselves.'

'And why exactly are you here?' asked the author.

Papa looked troubled. 'I'm here for precisely the opposite reason you are. I'm here to *stop* Tutankhamun being taken out of Egypt.'

'So you are working *against* your sister?'

'On this occasion, yes.'

'Why?' asked Conan Doyle, interested.

'Because it is the right thing to do,' said Mr Goodhart. 'He belongs here. Egypt is now independent, she is no longer under British rule and her artefacts are her own.'

At that moment, Sallah brought breakfast, and they all settled around the table. Luna sat as close to her father as their chairs would allow, and picked up the thread of conversation. Once Sallah had safely gone, Luna said, 'But Papa, we *agree* with you that Tutankhamun should stay in Egypt. We had already come to that conclusion ourselves.'

He looked relieved. 'Well, that makes things considerably easier.'

'It does,' said Mr Conan Doyle. 'I won't enquire as to the particulars of your Goodhart sibling quarrel. Just to say that on an ordinary day, I would be a Butterfly Club man to my bootstraps. But this is no ordinary day. And since our aims chime so completely with each other I suggest we work together.'

'Gladly,' said Daniel Goodhart, smiling. But then the frown returned. 'The question is, how are those aims to be achieved? Carter is, even now, cataloguing and packing up Tutankhamun's artefacts from the treasure chamber to be shipped to the British Museum. It will be the burial chamber next, and the king's sarcophagus will be sent there too. And that's precisely why I gatecrashed your breakfast. There is not much time before they lift the body.'

At that, Aidan crossed himself, jumped up, turned around three times and spat over his shoulder.

Daniel Goodhart regarded him with astonishment. 'Good Lord, lad, whatever's the matter with you?'

'That bleedin' mummy, that's what,' said Aidan.

'*Literally* bleeding,' said Konstantin, the bookworm.

'Luna,' said Mr Goodhart, appealing to his daughter. 'Could you explain what on earth is going on?'

Quickly, in a low voice, Luna told her father about the bleeding tomb of the night before. She brought their clothes from the laundry basket and Daniel Goodhart looked seriously at the stained red garments.

'And that's not all,' said Mr Conan Doyle.

'It's not?' said Luna's father.

'I take it you have not been down to the Nile today?'

Daniel Goodhart shook his head.

'It is running red with blood,' said the author. 'I'd be surprised if that's not all over the papers by—'

He stopped suddenly.

'Sir?' said Daniel Goodhart. 'Are you quite well?'

'*All over the papers*,' said Mr Conan Doyle, holding up his hand as if to halt all interruptions. 'That… that newshound – one of the press pack that were crowding the mouth of the tomb – *he* said, when he saw Lord Carnarvon looking so jolly, "If he goes in like that I don't give him six weeks". He seemed to think that Tut would put some sort of… some sort of *curse* on Carnarvon.' He looked at the others. 'What if he's right?'

'You don't really believe in curses, surely?' asked Konstantin.

'It doesn't matter what *I* believe,' said Mr Conan Doyle. 'We just have to make Carter and the Carnarvons believe it. We have to make them believe that Tut doesn't want to leave Egypt, and will lay a curse on anyone who tries to take him away.'

'I think I'm beginning to see,' said Luna. 'We have to make them *fear* the mummy. But how? Would you write a story?'

'No, that would take too much time, and wouldn't have enough reach out here. But what's the modern equivalent of a short story? What arrives on the doormat every day, and is read at every breakfast table in England?'

It was Konstantin who answered. 'Newspapers.'

'*Precisely*,' said Mr Conan Doyle. 'You might not be a journalist, Mr Goodhart, but you are about to become one. And not a reputable one either, but the lowest of the low. A gutter reporter of the tabloid press.'

'Go on,' said Papa, his eyes kindling.

'Your stories will not be accurate or scholarly. They will be sensational, and lurid, and they will sell like hot cakes.' He looked around at all of his fellow conspirators in turn. 'Together,' said Arthur Conan Doyle, 'we are going to create *the Mummy's Curse*.'

4 NOVEMBER 1922
11.15 a.m.

The author began to pace up and down the tent. 'We're going to put such a hoodoo on King Tut that Carter won't want to touch him, much less take him back to his beloved Britain. Goodhart – you can use your alias and your press credentials to sell stories to the papers.'

'And you have something that all reporters need,' said Luna.

'And what's that?' asked her father.

'An inside source,' she said. 'Us.'

'But my darling Luna,' said Papa. 'I am no writer.'

'But I *am*,' said Mr Conan Doyle. 'You don't need to write a word. I will feed you, daily, with stories to build up the curse. And the first one shall be *The River Of Blood*.'

Just by the way he said it, the time-thieves could tell he was adding capital letters to the headline. 'Goodhart, I'll have something for you by this afternoon. In the meantime, get one of those picture people…'

'Photographers?' supplied Daniel Goodhart.

'… to take a photogram of the river. We need to break the story before anyone else does.'

'But won't it already have been reported?' asked Konstantin.

'Not like this,' said Mr Conan Doyle. 'We're going to link it to the opening of Tut's tomb. And if we do a similar story each day, the legend will soon grow.'

Daniel Goodhart looked to the tent flap, as if, even here, he was fearful of being overheard. 'I must go, without being seen. There should be nothing to connect Mr Conan Doyle to a member of the gutter press.'

'Sallah,' called Mr Conan Doyle. 'Could you bring a clean turban and robe for our friend?'

Sallah came in with a length of white cloth and a pale robe. Mr Goodhart began, in a practised way, to wind the turban round his head. Then he shrugged on the robe. Suddenly he was transformed from foreign journalist to Egyptian workman. 'That should do it,' he said with satisfaction. 'In fact, we should be careful not to meet when we transfer the stories, or our deception will be revealed.' He thought for a moment. 'Do you know the Ramesseum, the Temple of King Ramesses II?'

'We know someone who will know,' said Konstantin, thinking of Abdel.

'Good. One of the massive idols of Ramesses is broken – a huge head fallen into the dust. Under the head there is a natural cavity. Leave me messages there, in the hole. Then you may pretend you are merely tourists and I too. But always, *always* use the Rorschach blot when you write me letters.'

Mr Conan Doyle looked confused.

'Luna will explain,' said Papa, butterfly-kissing her goodbye. 'And now I must go.' But as he laid his hand on the tent flap he turned and said, 'There's one more thing to say, and I'm afraid it is a note of warning.'

The listeners all looked up.

'There is someone here in the Valley of the Kings, and you should fear him much more than any curse.'

'It's Arthur John Priest, isn't it?' said Luna. 'We met him at Hatshepsut's tomb.'

'Disguised as an Egyptologist,' said Konstantin with marked disapproval.

'And then he gave the game away at Tut's tomb last night,' added Aidan.

'Ah,' said Mr Goodhart with a twist of his lip. 'You've already seen the gentleman.'

'Yes, but I still don't understand,' said his daughter. 'If he wants the mummy himself, why would he give the find to Carter, and the British dig?'

'My guess is that he will let Carter do all the heavy lifting, extract the sarcophagus, and then when it is ready to transport, Arthur John Priest will steal it for the Germans,' said Mr Goodhart. 'And if we don't want the British to have Tut, we don't want the Germans to have him either.'

'Why not?' asked Konstantin, bristling slightly.

'Nothing against your great nation,' said Mr Goodhart. 'But there are dark forces within it who were not best pleased with the treaty that ended the Great War.'

'That Treaty of Versailles thingy?' said Aidan, recalling the conversation at dinner.

'Yes. These dark forces think that Germany was crushed and humiliated by the terms of the treaty, and needs to be made great again. A find like Tut could restore their reputation on the world stage.'

'Well, what's wrong with that?' said Konstantin in a prickly voice.

'Nothing in itself. But the gathering of great artefacts might lend their power to a man who already has too much of it. A man,' he said, 'by the name of Adolf Hitler.'

Then Daniel Goodhart vanished into the light.

4 NOVEMBER 1922
6.45 p.m.

The time-thieves slept the afternoon away, and when Luna woke, the ghost of the sun, a pale disc shining through the canvas, was already low in the sky. She pushed aside the mosquito net that surrounded her divan, stood and stretched. She didn't need to dress, for she'd never *un*dressed, and she went through to the main atrium of the tent, feeling rather wobbly from sleeping at the wrong time of the day.

In the living area, Mr Conan Doyle was awake, ink pen in hand, scribbling away at the table. He'd covered half of the page.

'Here we are,' he said, dotting the last 'i' and crossing the last 't'. He waved the page so the ink would dry. 'The lurid story of a river of blood, visited on Egypt's people by a vengeful Tutankhamun who was disturbed from a three-thousand-year sleep. Would you like to take it to the Ramesseum for your father?'

'*Would* I?' said Luna, eyes shining.

She woke the boys and together they went to find Abdel filling his water jars by the well, the priceless pectoral pendant clanking against the terracotta as he bent. They told him about their meeting with Luna's father, and the plan to create the mummy's curse to keep Tut in Egypt. The only thing they left out was the time travel aspect – there seemed no good way to raise such a thing in a normal conversation. 'So can you show us the way to the Ramesseum?' begged Konstantin.

'Yes, of course, Konstantinkass,' said Abdel, who would do anything for his new friend. 'But there is something else we can do.' He turned to Luna. 'If your father is telephoning, get him to call a man called Monsieur Pierre Lacau. He is the Head of Egyptian Antiquities at the Egyptian Museum in Cairo. He is a Frenchman but he lives as an Egyptian and he is on our side. I've often heard Mr Carter complain of his interference. If we tell him about Carter's discovery, he will not let Tutankhamun be taken out of Egypt.'

The time-thieves looked at each other. 'It can't hurt,' said Luna. 'Anyone got a pencil?'

Konstantin, who was the very useful sort of boy who had lots of things in his pockets, produced one. At the end of Mr Conan Doyle's sensational article, Luna wrote:

Also Papa, please telephone to M. Pierre Lacau at the Cairo Museum. Tell him that Tut has been found and to come at once.

Then, just so he would know it was her, she added,

Yours until the end of time, Luna x

The Ramesseum at sunset was a sight to behold. It was a massive mortuary temple built of golden pillars of stone, with vast statues of Ramesses II standing sentinel like an army of giants. Sunset had brought out the mosquitoes, but the cooler evening had encouraged droves of tourists too, buzzing about in twos and threes. Many of them had easels; amateur painters hoping to capture the majesty of the red sun setting behind the temple. There were photographers also, sticking the legs of mahogany box cameras firmly into the sand, hoping, in their more modern way, to capture the moment too. Boys dressed like Abdel sold iced sherbet and postcards from the backs of willing mules, who plodded patiently, tails swishing away the flies and hooves kicking up clouds of sand. Much-less-willing camels, dressed in bright tasselled saddles, strode around the stones, their disdain showing on their long furry faces as they gave rides to customers.

But despite the crowds, the place had a strange power to it, and was somehow more than just a tourist attraction. The wind through the massive idols sounded an eerie, mournful note as the time-thieves and Abdel walked the ancient pavings, seeking the broken statue Mr Goodhart had told them of. At every turn they thought they would be observed by an eye and a watch, but they saw no sign of Arthur John Priest, or Arthur Cruttenden Mace, or whatever other persona their old enemy had adopted that day.

At last, they saw a quartet of statues of Ramesses, the last one in the line was broken and tumbled. The legs still stood, but the torso and head had fallen into the dust.

'This is it,' said Luna. 'You boys keep watch, I'll leave the note.'

'Wait,' said Konstantin. 'Did Mr Conan Doyle use the Rorschach blot method?'

Luna unfolded the paper to check. 'Yes.' She crouched in the sand and slid her hand under the massive fallen head.

'What is this Raw Shack method?' asked Abdel.

Luna showed him the system they'd pioneered on the *Titanic*. 'Look. When I write to my father, he always makes me put an ink blot across the fold. It looks like a butterfly and there's one "wing" on each piece. I tear it along the fold and leave his message here for him to collect.' She suited the action to the words. 'If he writes back, we already have the other half, so if any enemy tries to leave a message in his name, we will know it is false, because the two wings of the butterfly blot won't match. The Rorschach blot is impossible to replicate, because however many times you make it, it is never the same twice. See?'

Abdel smiled and nodded. 'Yes, I see. Clever.'

'Well, we shouldn't stand around jawing,' said Konstantin. 'Or someone will know we're up to something. Come on.'

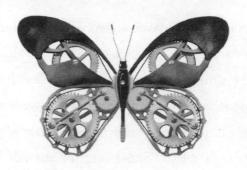

9 NOVEMBER 1922
8.45 a.m.

Howard Carter completed the painstaking process of meticulously moving and cataloguing the artefacts in the outer chamber of Tutankhamun's tomb, and the time-thieves viewed the process with disquiet.

'Don't worry.' Mr Conan Doyle laid a comforting hand on Abdel's shoulder as the waterboy nervously watched the procession of priceless gold objects being carried to the Carnarvons' tent. 'They won't be moving the mummy itself for a good while yet.'

'He's right,' said Aidan the engineer. 'Getting the sarcophagus out of that burial chamber will be like getting a ship out of a bottle. They'll have to dismantle the gilded screen, then carefully remove the roof of the shrine. It could take months.' He pushed back his cap and scratched his head thoughtfully. 'We might be here for longer than we think.'

And the time spent waiting had not been dull thus far. The time-thieves had spent much of their days with Lady Evelyn, not just so they could keep track of what was happening with Tutankhamun, but because they enjoyed her company. They took to breakfasting with her every morning, sitting outside in the shade of the Carnarvons' tent. The earl liked to have an English breakfast, so Sallah had done his best to find English tea and English marmalade; of course the bread was different and the milk was different and nothing quite tasted the same as it did at home, but somehow infinitely better.

Five days after the tomb had been found, and the Nile had run red, the time-thieves were at just such a breakfast when Sallah walked in.

'The Englishes' newspapers, milady,' he said, laying them down on the table in front of Lady Evelyn.

Idly, she sorted through them. 'They've all gone Egypt-mad. Papa and Tut are plastered over every front page. *The Times*, *The Telegraph*, *The Daily Mail*.'

Lady Evelyn picked up *The Times* first, reading the headline with wide eyes. 'Oh, gosh, look!'

The time-thieves looked at one another. Luna's father had worked fast.

NILE RUNS RED WITH BLOOD AS TUT'S TOMB OPENED!

shouted the headline in inky black.

There was a picture of Lord Carnarvon entering the tomb, a picture of the river and the crowd, and another photograph of an Egyptian boy, his fingertips dark with blood.

The sub-heading read:

Could King Tut be laying a curse on those who dare to wake him from his centuries-long sleep? For the full story on THE MUMMY'S CURSE turn to page 4.

'Dear God,' said Lady Evelyn, turning to the story and reading with growing concern. 'It says here that Tutankhamun was angered when he was disturbed, and is unleashing his wrath on the people of Egypt. This is jolly worrying. I think we ought to tell Papa.'

Lady Evelyn was obviously upset, and the time-thieves exchanged guilty glances. Aidan, who'd always felt a particular bond with Lady Evelyn, felt terrible. She was due to visit Tutankhamun's tomb that morning and they agreed to accompany her. As they made their way across the valley to the tomb, Abdel kindly let a distressed Lady Evelyn ride on Cleopatra the mule, and the time travellers hung back so they could talk.

'That worked a bit *too* well,' said Aidan. 'I didn't mean for us to upset Evelyn.'

Luna noticed, once again, how concerned Aidan seemed for their new friend. The noticing made her a bit sharp. 'Let's worry about saving Tut for Egypt, shall we?' she said tartly. 'That's what we're here for.'

'*I* think we should worry about what our next sensational story is going to be,' said Konstantin. 'Whatever it is that dyed the river red – algae, or perhaps mineral deposits, we can't expect nature to oblige us a second time.'

Just as he said this, something hopped heavily over Luna's foot. She screamed and jumped back, then looked down at the sand. There, glistening wetly in the sun, was a fat green frog. 'Ugh!' she shrieked.

Lady Evelyn looked round at the commotion. 'What is it?' She slid off the mule and she and Abdel turned back towards the others.

'Just a frog,' called Luna, hand over her hammering heart.

'Not just one,' said Konstantin. 'Look!'

Coming towards them over the rocky terrain of the Valley of the Kings were tens, then hundreds, then thousands of frogs, in all shades of green and yellow and brown. There were big ones the size of your shoe and small ones the size of a halfpenny. They passed the travellers without fear, hopping and flopping over their boots as they went, like an army of amphibians.

Aidan crossed himself. 'It's the curse,' he said, white-faced. 'I *told* you.'

'Calm down,' Konstantin said, hopping over the creatures as if he was a frog himself. 'There will be a perfectly rational explanation for this too.'

'Go on then,' challenged Aidan.

'Well.' Konstantin considered. 'Perhaps the frogs don't like what happened to the river. Perhaps whatever's in the water to make it red makes it an inhospitable habitat for them, and they're on the move to find somewhere else.'

This *did* sound rational, even to Aidan. But all of them hastened their footsteps to Tut's tomb, where, in the cool and dark of the chamber, they could leave the hopping invaders behind.

9 NOVEMBER 1922
10.30 a.m.

As the time-thieves and Lady Evelyn approached King Tut's tomb, it became clear that they weren't the only visitors to the site.

A group of official-looking men were approaching the excavated stone stairway. They all wore dark suits, and red fez hats on their heads. A man in the middle, leading the pack, had a distinctive white beard.

'Hallo,' said Lady Evelyn. 'Who's this lot?'

'The man with the white beard is Monsieur Pierre Lacau,' said Abdel excitedly, 'the Head of Antiquities from the Museum of Cairo.'

Lady Evelyn narrowed her eyes. 'What's he doing here?'

'I think,' said Abdel, careful to conceal his joy, 'that he has come to stop Tutankhamun being taken to the British Museum.'

Monsieur Lacau and his team walked down the steps and had a prolonged conversation in Arabic with the burly guards on the door of the tomb before the sentinels reluctantly let the officials pass. Lady Evelyn, who descended the stone stairs behind them with the time-thieves, was, of course, well known to those same guards, and was immediately nodded through.

The time-thieves found the burial chamber hot and crowded with people. Howard Carter was engaged in brushing aside the dust within the sarcophagus, and Lord Carnarvon stood watching him, clearly fascinated by the process. As the party from Cairo entered, Carter looked up with annoyance at the interruption to his work.

'Oh, God,' said Lord Carnarvon, rolling his eyes. 'Pierre Lacau. No need to ask what *you're* doing here.'

'Yes,' said Monsieur Lacau, his voice as dry as sand. 'It has come to my attention – not, it has to be said, from your own lips, which might have been the courteous thing to do – that you have made this rather important discovery of tomb KV62. And I must tell you that if your intention is to take Tutankhamun out of this country, I will fight you with every bone in my body.'

'What do you care?' growled Carnarvon.

'I care very much,' said the newcomer. 'The fact is, this' – he pointed to the sarcophagus – 'is not a box of bones, but the body of a young man. Even that is enough to deserve our respect. But, added to that, he is an Egyptian pharaoh, one of this country's monarchs. Should your own king, George V, die…'

Konstantin had to remind himself that England's monarch was now, as he had learned on the *Titanic*, Queen Victoria's grandson.

'… which God forbid, would you expect him to be brought here to Egypt for me to show in a glass case in my museum in Cairo?'

'No: But you are forgetting that Egypt was a British protectorate for many years. When I began this dig, in fact,' Lord Carnarvon shot back.

'*Was* being the important word in that sentence,' Lacau countered. 'Egypt is newly independent. You are now a guest in this country, my lord, and as such, the Egyptian Antiquities Service has every right to inspect your progress.'

'Inspect away,' said Howard Carter, waving the hand that held the brush. 'But you know as well as I do that British excavators have the right to keep their finds.'

'They did once,' said Lacau sternly, 'but you are living under Egyptian laws now.'

The tomb seemed to be getting hotter; it was fraught with tension and felt like a cauldron about to boil over. Then Lady Evelyn piped up, all charm and good humour. 'Forgive me for butting in and all that. But as far as I know, Egypt is *still* a British protectorate until a parliament and prime minister are elected. So I suppose the jolly old point is – are any of these laws of which you speak yet passed?'

There was a silence, during which Lacau squirmed a little. 'Well,' he said eventually. 'Not strictly speaking, no.'

'Well then.' Lady Evelyn smiled pleasantly. 'Seems to me like you've got yourself into a bit of a tight spot, old bean. Not to put too fine a point on it, if I were you I'd make a noise like a hoop and roll away.'

Monsieur Lacau straightened up and stuck his chin in the air. 'Very well. But I'll be back.'

'I'm sure you will, Pierre. And it's always a pleasure to see you,' said Lord Carnarvon in a voice that meant quite the opposite. 'But when you do, try to come back with some paperwork that is actually — what's the word I'm looking for? Oh, yes! — *legal*.'

There was nothing for it but for Monsieur Lacau to turn and leave the tomb. But at the doorway he turned back. 'King Tut is Egypt's ancestor and he has come back to see his nation reborn. He will not be taken away.' His words had a strange power to them, almost like an incantation, and as he uttered them the desert air seemed to shift and swirl within the tomb. Somewhere in the distance the howl of a dog could be heard once again, a cry that chilled the blood. Luna thought of the red river, and the army of hopping frogs, and shivered. Whatever Konstantin said, perhaps Tut did have some strange, elemental power.

When Monsieur Lacau and his team had left the tomb Lord Carnarvon stepped across all the rubble and hugged his daughter warmly. 'Well done, my dear,' he said. 'I knew I was right to educate you out here in Egypt, no matter what your mother said. Now you've seen off that appalling Frenchman, let's go and have a drink.'

At the top of the stairs Luna could see the party from Cairo disappearing over the horizon. Lord Carnarvon watched them, shaking his head. 'Fancy trying to take our mummy! What with a Frenchman trying to keep him in Egypt and the Germans trying to take him to Berlin, anyone would think he didn't belong in Britain!'

The time-thieves and Abdel all looked at each other. This wasn't going at all as planned. Monsieur Lacau had been defeated, and Lady Evelyn seemed to have forgotten all about the warning she had for her father. Then Luna felt another pair of eyes on her.

The lone black jackal sat on the top of a nearby dune, and kept on watching them until they left. Once again, Luna had the uncomfortable feeling that they had set something in train that would not easily be stopped.

9 NOVEMBER 1922
11.45 a.m.

As the party walked back to their camp, the sun climbed higher in a sky that was a scorching blue. There was not a cloud in it – except one. A black mass rose over the desert horizon and moved towards their party, undulating and changing shape like a dark phantom.

'What on earth is that?' asked Aidan, pointing. 'Is it a sandstorm?'

'Not sand,' said Abdel. 'Gnats.'

Suddenly the cloud was upon them and the insects were everywhere; buzzing, bothering gnats that settled on their lips and eyelashes to be batted away. Only the placid Cleopatra plodded on, swishing the gnats with her long white tail. 'Ugh, I can't bear this,' said Lady Evelyn from the back of the mule. She dug her heels into Cleopatra to get back to camp as soon as possible, and her father hurried after her on foot. The time-thieves and Abdel followed but the gnats stayed close, like their own personal raincloud.

The white tents, when they reached them, were black with gnats. They all piled through the flap, but the interior was not much better. Mr Conan Doyle, with a pained look on his face, was swishing a horsehair fly-swatter from side to side, to little effect. 'Is this normal?' he was asking Sallah.

'I've never seen them this bad, sir,' said Sallah, waving the fringed end of his turban at the pests.

'Is there anything you can do?' pleaded Mr Conan Doyle.

'Keep the tent flaps shut,' said Sallah briefly. 'I'll burn some reeds; they don't like that. And set some honey traps. Make sure you sleep in your nets, honoured Englishes. Most of these are gnats, but there are mosquitoes mixed in. Same family,' he declared, pointing helpfully at Mr Conan Doyle and his 'niece', Luna.

Sallah bustled about efficiently, and as the young people seated themselves and Abdel brought iced lemonade, he lit long black Nile reeds in earthenware vases, which gave off white smoke and a cloying scent. The gnats thinned out to a bearable number, and those who didn't flee the smoke were drowned in the flat dishes of honey Sallah left about the place – the golden liquid soon turning black with little corpses.

Once Sallah had gone Aidan turned to the others. 'Well,' he said. 'We've no shortage of things to tell the papers *today*.'

'You're right,' said Konstantin. 'Makes you wonder what on earth will be next.'

Aidan looked at him, a faintly astonished look in his blue eyes. 'You're joking, aren't you?'

Konstantin looked back at him, his eyes steady and grey. 'What do you mean?'

'I mean,' said Aidan, 'we know exactly what's next. Flies. Flies are next. *Bright Friendly Girls Frown Less By Having Laughing Dimply Faces.*'

Mr Conan Doyle blinked. 'I'm not following you.'

'Don't you see?' said Aidan, a little wildly. 'I don't know how or why, but it seems as if our friend Tut is unleashing the Ten Plagues of Egypt, one by one. No one knows the order better than we do – we had to get them in the right places to escape the Puzzle Chamber of Thutmoses. We've had the river of blood. We had the frogs on the way to the tomb this morning. And now we have gnats.'

'Hold on,' said Mr Conan Doyle. 'Lord Carnarvon was kind enough to give me access to his books. Quite a library he has with him, and I saw a family Bible among them.' He went next door and was back in a moment, holding a small but ancient volume. 'Here we are,' he said. 'The Book of Exodus. "Seven days passed after the Lord struck the Nile",' quoted Mr Conan Doyle, as if in a dream, '"the Lord said I will send a plague of frogs on your whole country. Then the Lord said, throughout the land of Egypt the dust will become gnats, and gnats came on people and animals."'

The time-thieves looked at one another, round-eyed and terrified. 'This is on us,' said Luna. 'We disturbed Tutankhamun. What do we do now?'

'Well, we can't stop what has been set in train,' said Mr Conan Doyle, closing the good book with a snap. 'We can only hope to make amends by preventing Carnarvon from taking Tut from his grave and his homeland. And we do that by ramping up the stories of the Mummy's Curse. To that end, this long-dead pharaoh is actually *helping* us.'

He took up his pen and ink, and interrogated the time-thieves about the army of frogs. He wrote the story that afternoon, fattening it up with legend and hearsay until it was as lurid as could be. The next day he wrote about the gnats, and the following day the flies which had almost seamlessly replaced their winged cousins overnight. '"I will send swarms of flies on you and your officials, on your people and into your houses,"' copied Mr Conan Doyle from the Carnarvon family Bible. '"The houses of the Egyptians will be full of flies; even the ground will be covered with them."'

The time-thieves duly dropped his scribblings off at the Ramesseum, under the great fallen stone head, marked by a Rorschach blot butterfly. A few days later the stories miraculously appeared in newspapers.

The sensational headlines were working. Already some of the foreign excavators, beaten to the golden prize by Carter and frightened by the curse, were packing up and going home. The only one who didn't seem at all frightened was Lord Carnarvon. Despite the mounting evidence of something sinister in the Valley of the Kings, and his daughter's fond warnings, he pronounced all talk of the curse to be 'piffle and poppycock'. He seemed blissfully unaffected by the insects that plagued his camp, apart from a rather nasty mosquito bite on one cheek. He seemed more determined than ever to bring Tut back to the British Museum. Work on Tutankhamun's tomb was progressing slowly and surely. And, taking his lead from his boss, Mr Carter, who was a practical sort of fellow not given to flights of fancy, just concentrated on his work.

Day by day, Mr Carter meticulously cleaned, extracted and catalogued every single one of the grave goods that he found in Tutankhamun's tomb.

'They have to lift everything out extremely carefully,' explained Aidan at afternoon tea. 'Say what you like about Carter, he's a cold fish but he is a good archaeologist. He's a stickler for procedure. They'll be weeks in that burial chamber before they get to the actual mummy.'

'We've got plenty of time until they think about moving him,' said Konstantin comfortingly.

'And the longer it takes, the better it is for us,' said Mr Conan Doyle. 'I'm sure Abdel's Monsieur Lacau is working on a legal means to keep Tutankhamun in Egypt, but the wheels of the law grind slowly, and he will need time. And *we* need time for this curse idea to take hold. We need some more supernatural happenings.'

But the vengeful pharaoh, having sent four plagues, seemed to be taking a break. There was no sign of the fifth plague, the death of livestock. Mr Conan Doyle was frustrated, but the time-thieves were relieved. If nothing else happened, then maybe – just maybe – those terrible occurrences could be written off as coincidences.

Konstantin argued that one event logically led to the others. 'Something went funny with the river,' he argued. 'So the frogs all left. And who usually eats all the gnats and flies? Frogs do. So in the absence of the frogs, the gnats and flies could thrive.'

Mr Conan Doyle grumbled, his fingers twitching for his pen – but he need not have worried.

Very soon, the time travellers would have more proof of the curse than they could ever have desired.

14 NOVEMBER 1922
9.15 a.m.

A few days later, when the time-thieves were arriving for their customary breakfast at the Carnarvons', Lady Evelyn flew out of the tent to greet them. Her normal composure had gone, her severe hairstyle was all awry and her face was streaked with tears.

'Look at what happened,' she cried. 'The beast! Oh, the beast!'

She held out her hand to show a sad little bundle of vivid yellow feathers. Her pet canary was curled up in her palm, seemingly asleep.

'She's dead!' Lady Evelyn cried. 'Alexandria's dead!'

Aidan threw an arm round her. 'Calm down. What happened? Who is the beast?'

'Tutankhamun, of course. He cursed my canary!'

At this point Lord Carnarvon hurried over, his face all concern. As his daughter repeated the story he said calmly, 'Nonsense, darling. It would have been the heat. It was just too much for her.'

Even though it was indeed hot, Luna had a cold sense of foreboding in her chest. The very first time she'd been at the Butterfly Club she'd told Aunt Grace she wouldn't be a canary in the coal mine. What if Lady Evelyn's canary dying was some sort of omen? But she said nothing and just helped Lady Evelyn to bury her beloved pet in the sand.

'That'll confuse future archaeologists,' said Konstantin flippantly.

'Shh,' said Aidan. 'She's really upset.'

'Chin up, Evie,' said Lord Carnarvon. 'We'll get you another one in Luxor.'

'It's not the same,' sobbed his daughter, inconsolable. 'Alexandria used to sit on my shoulder and eat crumbs. She's irreplaceable.'

'Don't be silly, darling,' said Lord Carnarvon, not unkindly, but with his mind obviously elsewhere.

'Well, how would you feel if it was Susie? Is Susie replaceable?'

Lord Carnarvon's face took on an oddly shuttered look. 'Susie is different.'

'Who in the wild world is Susie?' asked Aidan.

'Papa's little three-legged dog, back at Highclere Castle,' sniffed Lady Evelyn. 'He dotes on her. Well, you *do*, darling. You love her quite as much as you love Mother.'

'Much more,' said the earl, rather shockingly. 'At least she's loyal.'

'You'd never pet another dog the way you pet her.'

'Susie and your canary are hardly comparable,' said Evelyn's father stiffly. 'Susie's more like a person than a pet. And she has a personality.' He smiled fondly, as if he was somewhere else entirely. 'She's so determined. Remember her when she gets hold of a bone? She won't let go of it.'

'You're Susie, aren't you?' said his daughter, looking at him through her tears. 'You won't let go of Tut – Tut is your bone.'

'You're right,' said Lord Carnarvon. 'I cannot deny it. Speaking of Tut, why don't you come with me to the tomb today? Take your mind off your feathered friend. Waterboy!' he called.

Abdel appeared, looking most peculiar. In his own way he looked as miserable as Lady Evelyn.

'Pack up that mule of yours – Lady Evelyn wishes to visit the tomb.'

Lady Evelyn, who didn't much want to do anything, kept a miserable silence. But Abdel shook his head. 'I can't.'

'*What?*' Lord Carnarvon, so used to being obeyed, looked as if his daughter's dead canary had talked back to him.

'I can't,' repeated Abdel in a very wobbly voice, and it was then that Luna noticed that Abdel too had tear tracks on his face, making a lighter path through the grime on his cheeks. 'She's dead. Cleopatra's dead.'

The time-thieves all gasped in unison. They knew how much Abdel had loved his placid white mule. But Lord Carnarvon simply shrugged in exasperation. 'Then get another one.'

'Don't be so insensitive,' said Konstantin, his clockwork heart racing. 'You just told us your own dog would be irreplaceable. Well, Cleopatra was so much more than some pampered pet of a rich person. She was a companion, a helpmate and a *working* animal. Cleopatra was Abdel's livelihood. She wasn't a luxury. She even found Tut's tomb for you, when she stumbled on the storm drain.'

Lord Carnarvon drew himself up to his full height. 'Are you addressing *me*, you insolent young Hun?'

Luna and Aidan gasped at the slur. They weren't sure what it meant, but it sounded bad.

'How dare you talk to a British peer of the realm in that manner?' continued Lord Carnarvon, icy with rage. 'Especially after the shameful conduct of your nation during the war. I do not wish to see you around my camp, or my daughter, ever again.' He held out his hand to Lady Evelyn. 'Come, my dear'. His voice changed entirely. 'We found a treasure chest of ceremonial jewellery yesterday. That will cheer your spirits.'

As father and daughter left for the tomb, Lady Evelyn turned back to send an apologetic glance in Konstantin's direction.

'You should not have done that, Konstantinkass,' said Abdel, once the young people were alone. 'I am only a servant. And now he has banished you from his sight.'

'I'll live,' said Konstantin, who was still angry. 'Now, let's see about giving Cleopatra a decent burial.' He knew Abdel's feelings on the need for a grave. The waterboy had been so sorry that his brother Karim had never had one, and so insistent that his king, Tutankhamun, should keep his.

It was hot work digging a grave in the searing sand that was big enough for a mule, but Konstantin, Aidan and Abdel swiftly completed their grim task. While they dug, Luna made a wreath of flowers to be buried alongside Cleopatra, just like the one they'd found in Tut's tomb. This kindly gesture made Abdel her friend for ever. They covered the body and flattened the sand, and Abdel said a prayer in Arabic.

'Right,' said Aidan, almost before Abdel had finished. 'Now we have to find you another mule.'

'Aidan,' Konstantin scolded. 'Cleopatra's barely cold. Have some respect.'

'Respect is for the rich,' said Aidan. 'Lady Evelyn can afford time to grieve, then she can wait a few months, then she can choose a new bird. But Cleopatra was not just a friend but a work animal. You said it yourself. Abdel needs to work to support his mother and save up for that coffee shop.' He grinned at the waterboy.

Abdel nodded. 'He's right. But I can't afford to buy another mule.'

'Well, I know someone who can,' said Konstantin. 'Wait here.' He led Aidan and Luna inside their own tent. Mr Conan Doyle was busy writing something in his chamber so Konstantin brazenly went to the bureau and found the purse of sovereigns. He took two. 'That should do it.'

Aidan's eyes grew as round as the coins. 'Isn't that stealing?'

'How is it stealing?' countered Konstantin. 'We are the ones who earned that money. It came with the Gabriel Prize for Communication, which we won with the Marconi radio. There are loads left – I think we can take a couple.'

As it turned out, money was not the problem. As Abdel led them up and down the Valley of the Kings, from one mule dealer to another, they slowly realised the horrible truth.

There were no mules to be bought, even if they'd had a hundred sovereigns.

They were all dead.

14 NOVEMBER 1922
Noon

It was a tragic morning, filled with sad sights.

The time-thieves and Abdel walked from dig to dig, mule dealer to mule dealer, only to hear the same story. The unfortunate animals had just died, that very morning. Some had expired where they stood, for as mules could sleep standing up, they could apparently die that way too. Some had keeled over on the sand, their burdens lying with them. Some entire teams had died at once, still tethered together. The bodies were covered with canvas, or unfurled turbans, and their miserable owners dug makeshift graves in the sand before the flies could feast.

'All right, Konnie, now explain *this*,' said Aidan grimly as they turned back to camp.

The strange occurrences in the Valley of the Kings were getting harder and harder to account for, but still Konstantin had a try. 'Perhaps Alexandria and Cleopatra, and all those poor mules, died of insect bites. You saw all the flies and gnats the other day. The frogs that would have eaten them fled from the red river.'

Aidan scoffed at this. 'People don't die of insect bites. No – it's the curse, sure as eggs is eggs.'

'What will you do now?' said Luna to Abdel.

'I will carry the water on foot, until I can find another animal,' he replied. 'It is not such a hardship. But Lord Carnarvon and Mr Carter have a bigger problem.'

'What's that?' asked Konstantin.

'They used an army of mules to take the hardcore out of the tomb – that's the rubble that they dig away.'

'So what will they do now?' wondered Aidan.

'I imagine they will rush to complete the underground railroad,' said Abdel. 'They'd already begun building it. There are miles of track that wind under the rocks between the tombs.'

'With actual trains on them?' Aidan perked up.

'No, not trains. Those, what do you call them...' Abdel mimed pumping a handle up and down. 'Trolleys, that are operated by two people working a handle.'

'Oh yes. Handcarts.' Aidan had used these himself, on the Trans-Siberian railway.

'I'll show you if you like.'

'Yes *please*,' said Aidan, who was always fascinated by engineering projects. Even Luna and Konstantin, who were less interested, thought it sounded fun, and they certainly needed fun after the mournful morning they'd had.

Abdel led them in the direction of Tut's tomb, where the sand was rising from the diggings and the picks sounded on the rock. Konstantin hung back a little, having no wish to run into Lord Carnarvon again, but he needn't have worried. Abdel led them into a deep, rocky channel with a little iron train track at the bottom, leading into the dark mouth of a cave. Little pig-iron trolleys, about the size of half a Time Train, were ranged along the track. Ranks of local workmen in robes and turbans were passing baskets of rubble to each other, to be dumped into the trolleys with a clatter. The trolleys were then rolled down the line, operated by two workmen pumping the handles up and down in turn.

'Looks like fun,' said Aidan. 'Can we have a go?'

'Let's not,' said Konstantin. 'I don't want to get into more trouble with His Lordship.'

Aidan was peering down the track into the dark. 'How far does it go?'

'Miles,' said Abdel. 'All the way to the Nile Delta. Most of the rubble gets dumped in the river.'

'That's a helluva project,' said Aidan admiringly. 'Digging out of flat rock is no mean feat.'

'Well, but the diggings were mostly already there,' said Abdel. 'The engineers used the tunnels made by the ancient Egyptians, when they were creating the tombs in the first place. There's a whole network down there. But the railway is incomplete. Right fork finished and ends in buffers on the bank of the Nile. So the rubble can be transported by river, you know. Left fork' – he drew a finger across his throat – 'sheer drop. I imagine they'll finish it in double time now the mules are gone.'

He drooped sadly and Konstantin put a hand on his shoulder. 'Come on. Let's go back. I've an idea that Cleopatra can do one last labour for you.'

Back at their tent, Konstantin led the others into Mr Conan Doyle's chamber and explained his idea to the author. 'So I thought,' he concluded, 'if we can use Cleopatra's death, and that of all the other mules, to create another sensational article, then her death won't have been in vain. It's the fifth plague, you see – the death of livestock.'

Mr Conan Doyle reached for the Carnarvon family Bible and turned once again to the book of Exodus. '"The hand of the Lord will bring a terrible plague on your livestock in the field,"' he quoted.

'That's the one,' said Konstantin. 'We can make a big splash out of it.'

Mr Conan Doyle waved the paper he'd been writing. 'I'm one step ahead of you, my boy. Sallah told me about this morning's occurrences. My condolences to you, my friend,' he said to Abdel, who bowed with his hand on his heart. 'But I've taken a slightly different tack. We need to concentrate not on the mules, but the canary. You see' – the author stood, as if he could better make his point standing up – 'we have to make it *sell*. Nobility sells. Celebrity sells. Besides, we're really trying to change the mind of one person – Lord Carnarvon. If the story is about his daughter, and his daughter's precious bird, that's very close to home. It might finally persuade him that Tut is dangerous.'

Aidan looked doubtful. 'I dunno. It seems a bit cruel. Lady E was awfully cut up about her pet.'

Luna shot him a sharp glance. Once again she noticed how defensive Aidan was of Lady Evelyn. But Mr Conan Doyle waved away his objections.

'The ends justify the means, dear boy,' he said. 'If we want Tut to stay in Egypt, this is how we do it.'

So the time-thieves duly took the article, complete with Rorschach blot, to the Ramesseum and hid it under the fallen stone head of Ramesses for Luna's father to collect.

A few days later, Aidan, Luna and Mr Conan Doyle were at breakfast with the Carnarvons (the banished Konstantin tactfully stayed away) when Sallah brought the English papers. The *Daily Mail* stood out, with its eye-catching red banner, and Lady Evelyn picked it up first, reading the headline with wide eyes. 'Oh, gosh, look!'

PEER'S DAUGHTER'S PAMPERED PET SLAIN BY DEADLY CURSE!

There was a picture of Lady Evelyn, a library picture of a canary, and another library picture of an Egyptian pharaoh. The sub-heading read:

Could King Tut be widening his revenge to Lord Carnarvon's family? For the full story on Lady Evelyn's Agony turn to page 3.

'The *beasts*!' said Lady Evelyn, turning to the story. 'How could they know about Alexandria? Who told them?'

'What the devil is going on?' asked her father. 'Who the hell is Alexandria?'

'Papa,' said Lady Evelyn reproachfully. 'My canary. She died suddenly the other day, remember? On the day all the livestock died.'

Lady Evelyn looked very upset, and the time-thieves squirmed uncomfortably.

'Speaking of livestock,' said Lord Carnarvon with distaste, 'the bally press are no better than jackals and vultures. Look, chin up, old thing,' he said, throwing a careless arm round his daughter and jiggling her until she smiled through her tears, obviously a trick he'd been using since childhood. 'I know we're in a desert, but we don't need a rain shower.'

Lady Evelyn looked at her father through her tears. 'Papa. Don't you think we ought to listen to King Tutankhamun's warnings, before something even more terrible happens?'

'Warnings?' said Lord Carnarvon. 'Eh? What's that? What warnings?'

'Five plagues to date, darling,' said Lady Evelyn. 'And they're growing increasingly closer to home.'

'Nonsense,' said her father. 'You forget. Savage happenings are commonplace in a savage country. We are far from civilization. It's to be expected.'

Luna felt that squirmy feeling again beneath her bodice. It seemed from all she'd learned of ancient Egypt that it was one of the most advanced civilizations in the world, and predated the British Empire by thousands of years. But she didn't want to butt in to what seemed to be a very family quarrel.

'Besides,' said Lord Carnarvon, 'what do you suggest we do? Cover him back up, after I've spent half my life searching for him?'

'No,' said Lady Evelyn. 'Not that. But the treasures could be in a museum here, and his body – well, it could be left where it lies.'

'Tut, stay in Egypt?' Lord Carnarvon scoffed. 'Over *my* dead body.' He wiped his mouth on his napkin. 'Now, if you'll excuse me, I must away to the tomb. Come along, Evelyn. We must finish what we started.'

'In the name of God,' exclaimed Mr Conan Doyle once the Carnarvons had safely gone. 'What will it take to convince this stubborn nobleman to leave Tutankhamun alone?'

Those were words Arthur Conan Doyle was soon to wish he had never uttered. Because in the coming months, the Mummy's Curse would reach its deadly climax.

4 APRIL 1923
6.30 p.m.

By the spring the first painstaking phase of the excavation of King Tutankhamun's tomb was complete. Every priceless item from the outer treasure chamber had been lifted out, photographed, packed in cotton wadding and wooden crates, and stacked in a warehouse ready to take to the British Museum. Every golden shabti from the burial chamber was swaddled like a baby, and prepared to travel with its master. With every week that passed, the time-thieves expected more strange and horrible happenings, but for the moment the pharaoh lay quiet in his grave.

Then came the tricky part, the bit Aidan had once described as 'getting a ship out of a bottle' – the process of removing the sarcophagus itself from the burial chamber.

Work began to dismantle the gilded screen, then carefully remove the roof of the shrine. The Mummy's Curse was never very far from the time travellers' thoughts, and, sure enough, as soon as work began to remove Tut's body from his tomb, it reared its deadly head again like a cobra ready to strike.

It began with something so simple. In late March the time-thieves were breakfasting outside their tent in the spring sunshine, when Abdel walked out of the Carnarvons' tent with a basin of water. He greeted the others and tipped the water into the sand. The sand turned red.

'Gosh,' exclaimed Luna, shocked. 'What happened?'

'It's nothing,' shrugged Abdel. 'Lord Carnarvon cut himself shaving. You recall the mosquito bite he got during the plague of gnats? Well, he sliced it off with the razor. He's bandaged it up now.'

Lord Carnarvon took to going about with a sort of small flesh-coloured bandage on his face, which was apparently called a sticking plaster. After a few days he got rid of the plaster and went about with the wound on full show. The time-thieves had expected a small cut, but what they saw was a large, round, angry-looking bump.

Konstantin, son of a doctor, did not like the look of it. 'That's not healing as it should,' he pronounced to Luna and Aidan. 'It should be a clean little cut. But that looks more like…'

'… a boil,' said Aidan. 'I've been thinking the same thing.'

As usual, Mr Conan Doyle was ready with the Carnarvons' Bible. He turned to Exodus and found the right verse. '"Festering boils will break out on people and animals throughout the land,"' he read.

'The sixth plague!' hissed Luna. 'D'you think we should say something?'

'Not if there's just *one* boil,' said Mr Conan Doyle. 'One is hardly a plague.'

'And this boil came from the gnat infestation, which came from the frogs leaving, and they left because of the dirty river,' said Konstantin. 'This could still all be the same logical sequence of events. Can I borrow this Bible?'

'Becoming a believer, are we?' twinkled Mr Conan Doyle. 'Of course you can. But don't lose it. It's not mine.'

Konstantin tucked the good book in his coat and no one thought any more about the boil until the next day. Lord Carnarvon didn't turn up at the tomb to oversee the removal and cataloguing of the artefacts as he always did.

'Oh, he's feeling a bit under the weather,' said Lady Evelyn airily. 'It'll pass.'

But it didn't.

Lord Carnarvon missed a second day. And a third. A local doctor was called from Luxor. Then a more important doctor was called from Cairo. It was pronounced that Lord Carnarvon had developed pneumonia. Lady Evelyn lost her happy-go-lucky manner and became visibly worried. Her lips seemed a little less red, her bobbed hair less blunt and neat, and her eyes lost their sparkle. She talked of nothing but the curse, convinced that the evil eye of Tutankhamun had fallen on her father, and of course the time-thieves all felt terrible about that.

On the fifth day after the bowl of blood, Lady Evelyn was breakfasting with them outside their tent when Sallah handed her a letter. Her face fell as she read. 'Oh, God…'

'What is it?' asked Luna breathlessly. 'Is it the curse?'

'Worse.' Lady Evelyn grimaced. 'It's Mother.'

'Has something happened to her?' asked Aidan with concern.

'Worse again,' said Lady Evelyn. 'She's coming here.'

Luna had never known a mother but she was fairly sure this wasn't the usual way to talk about one. 'Don't you like her?'

'Other way round,' said Lady Evelyn. 'She doesn't like *me*.'

'At least your father likes you,' said Luna, thinking of her own papa.

'Yes, he does,' said Lady Evelyn, 'but I'm just not quite as important as my brother Porchey. Papa was so relieved when he came back from the war, because there'd be someone to inherit Highclere Castle.'

'Wouldn't the castle have come to you?' asked Aidan.

'No, darling,' said Lady Evelyn drily. 'It would have gone to some male cousin. That's what comes of being a woman, I'm afraid.'

'That's hardly fair,' said Aidan decidedly. 'What about that pharaoh queen? What about… Hap… Hap…'

'Hatshepsut? Yes,' she said ruefully. 'Sometimes I think that for women, things have gone backwards.'

Lady Carnarvon arrived on the evening of the 4th April, just as the sun was leaving.

The Valley of the Kings was bathed in a beautiful rosy gold light as the sun sank behind the rocky cliffs. The countess cut an elegant figure, picking her way down the dunes leaning on the arm of a tall man.

As if she had dressed for the sunset, she was wearing an exquisite flowing gown of peach satin with a billowing shawl hung with little amber crystals. There was an elegant rose-pink close-fitting hat on her neat head. She was not carrying her own suitcases but was followed by a procession of Egyptian servants in white robes and white turbans, carrying a seemingly endless collection of cases, bags and hatboxes.

As she came closer the time-thieves could see that she was basically an older version of Lady Evelyn with one crucial difference.

She didn't smile.

Lady Evelyn stood as her mother approached, as if she was in school and a particularly strict teacher had just walked into the classroom.

'Evelyn.' Lady Carnarvon nodded her elegant head, but made no effort to kiss her daughter. Luna thought about the way her father always greeted her, with a bone-crushing hug and a butterfly kiss on the cheek – this was very different.

'This is my... *friend*... Colonel Dennistoun.' The countess indicated the tall man hovering behind her. Colonel Dennistoun was tall and handsome, and his black hair, slicked back from his forehead, was as glossy as his patent leather shoes. He smiled weakly, looking wholly uncomfortable.

Lady Evelyn raised her pencil-thin eyebrows. 'And these are our *friends*,' she said, giving the word the same emphasis. 'Mr O'Connell, Mr Kass and Mr Conan Doyle, and his niece Luna. Chaps, this is my mother, Lady Almina Herbert, Countess of Carnarvon.'

The countess's gaze swept over the time-thieves and Mr Conan Doyle with absolutely no interest. Lady Evelyn, in contrast, stared beadily at the colonel. 'You have some business in Egypt, Colonel?'

'Darling, don't *pry*.' The countess raised her pointed chin. 'The fact is that Colonel Dennistoun is here to accompany *me*. You wouldn't want your beloved mother to make such a perilous journey alone – among all these filthy savages?' She looked down her nose at Abdel. 'I'm very grateful to Ian, and so should you be.'

'Oh, it's *Ian*, is it?' muttered Lady Evelyn, but all she said out loud was, 'Can I offer you some refreshment, Mother?'

'*God*, no.' Lady Almina sniffed. 'I'm not staying. We just came to pick up your father. I'll nurse him now. Can't trust the local quack doctors and their snake-oil cures.'

'Take him where?' asked Lady Evelyn.

'To the Winter Palace Hotel in Luxor. It's not exactly the Ritz, but it'll have to do. You, boy, don't just stand there.' She snapped her be-ringed fingers at Abdel. 'Come and help. I wired Carter to arrange a motor – it will be here soon.'

'But... but...' stuttered Lady Evelyn. 'Doesn't Papa want to stay here in the Valley of the Kings?'

'Haven't the faintest, darling,' said her mother airily. 'But *I* don't. I'm not staying in a fleapit like this. I'll be at the Winter Palace too. Ian,' she barked.

The colonel sprang to attention. 'Right you are, old thing.'

As Lady Carnarvon disappeared into their tent, with 'Ian' at her heels, Konstantin spoke out of the side of his mouth. 'Do we stay or make ourselves scarce?'

'I don't know,' said Luna out of the side of hers. 'It feels like a very family thing.'

'Well, but,' said Aidan, 'they might need a hand with the old man.'

So they stayed, and soon wished they hadn't.

Lord Carnarvon came out of the tent, leaning heavily on Colonel Dennistoun on one side and Sallah on the other. He was very thin, and his breath came in painful gasps. The boil on his cheek had become an angry red lesion, but the rest of his flesh was the greeny-yellow of a Clouded Yellow butterfly and his lips had a blue tinge to them. His eyes were red and seemed not to know what they looked upon. This noble man had become a horrible spectre. It was hard to believe that this change had been brought about by something so small, so inconsequential as a mosquito bite.

At the sight of him Mr Conan Doyle sprang to his feet. He went over to the invalid and laid a hand on Lord Carnarvon's forehead, but the earl took no more notice of it than he would a fly. He didn't seem to recognise the author at all. 'See that he has a physician as soon as he reaches the hotel,' said Conan Doyle urgently. 'I would diagnose blood poisoning, and possible septicaemia. He *must* see a doctor with all haste.'

Abdel, looking grave, followed the family to the waiting motor car, carrying Lord Carnarvon's cane and hat. Once the motor had pulled away with Lord Carnarvon in it, the time-thieves were at a loose end, feeling troubled and restless. Luna suddenly wanted her own father very badly. 'We can't just sit about worrying,' she said. 'Let's go to the Ramesseum to see if there are any messages from Papa. That'll blow the cobwebs away.'

On the way across the valley Luna was silent and troubled. One by one, the Ten Plagues of Egypt seemed to be coming true and that only led in one direction. As Luna was normally so chatty it didn't take the boys long to realise something was wrong.

Aidan nudged her with his shoulder. 'What's the matter?'

'It's nothing,' said Luna unhappily. 'It's just… just something you said in the Puzzle Chamber of Thutmoses.'

'What?'

'The plague you couldn't remember. The last and the deadliest. It was the Death of the Firstborn.'

'What about it?' said Aidan uneasily.

'Well, we are slowly making our way through the ten plagues. And that means that, eventually, we get to the death of the firstborn. And I'm afraid…' Luna took a deep and shaky breath. 'I'm very afraid that might be *me*.'

'You?' said Konstantin, who'd been listening to the exchange. 'Why you?'

'Because Tut seems to be taking his revenge on all those who interfered with his tomb. The Carnarvons. The mules that were working on the dig. So far, we've been getting away with it. But we are the ones who woke him. We're the worst – we are the ones who are responsible for disturbing him in the first place; we were the first eyes to see him for three thousand years.'

'So?'

'So what if, when it comes to the death of the firstborn, he claims one of *us*? It won't be you, Aidan, with your six older sisters. Nor you, Konstantin, with all those soldier brothers. But me, well, I'm an only child. A firstborn, and a last.'

The boys looked at each other, considering this dreadful thought. Konstantin attempted to be comforting. 'Well, if you're lucky, he might come for someone else.'

'Who? Abdel had an older brother. Lady Evelyn has an older brother too, remember, Porchey – he's the one who inherits the castle. And besides, they are my friends. I don't want the curse to get *anyone*.'

'All right,' said Aidan. 'Supposing that there *is* a curse. Which there definitely is. I don't think Tut would come for us anyway.'

'How d'you work that out?' said Luna.

'Because we are trying to do the right thing,' said Aidan. 'We are trying to keep him in Egypt. Surely that will avert his evil eye?'

'We'd better hope so,' said Luna, a little comforted. 'For my sake.'

The sun was well and truly setting by the time they reached the vast statues. They went to the fallen stone head of Ramesses II and Luna put her hand beneath it as the boys kept watch – feeling, as she always did, a slightly tingly feeling in her arm as if a crouching scorpion was waiting in the dark recess to sting her. Her searching hand found a folded paper with a message written on it and half a Rorschach butterfly along the edge. She drew out their previous letter and compared the two wings. They matched, and she read the message aloud.

Dearest Luna,

Pierre Lacau is staying at the Winter Palace Hotel. He has vowed not to leave Luxor until he has ensured that Tutankhamun will remain in Egypt.

Yours until the end of time,
Papa x

'What does that mean?' wondered Luna.

'Well, it's obvious, isn't it?' said Aidan. 'Pierre Lacau, the fellow from the Museum of Cairo who we met in Tut's tomb, has stayed in the area to make sure his wishes are carried out, rather than going back to Cairo. He is determined that Tutankhamun stays in Egypt, and so are we. We should go and see him.' He looked at Konstantin, blue eyes narrowed against the lowering sun.

Konstantin nodded once. 'To use a military expression,' he said, 'it's time to join forces.'

5 APRIL 1923
7 p.m.

A bdel was at a bit of a loose end since his master was laid up with his illness, so he agreed to guide the time-thieves to Luxor. He led them across the valley, the last light of day kindling the scarabs of Tutankhamun's pectoral pendant, making them glow through his thin robe. The low sun beat down upon them as they crossed the Valley of the Kings, which made what happened next all the more extraordinary.

To begin with, Luna thought someone was throwing stones at them as they walked. But no – something round and hard was raining down from the sky. She put out a hand and something landed in it. A tiny ball of ice, perfectly round, like a minute snowball. Then the deluge gathered pace and soon the ice was pounding down on them with almost the power to pierce the flesh.

'It's the hail,' yelled Luna. 'The seventh plague.'

'You think?' Aidan shouted back.

There was nowhere to hide, nowhere to shelter. They held hands, jackets, caps, turbans, anything they could above their heads to stem the flow. They began to run but this almost made it worse, as if the hail came faster the quicker they moved.

Abdel, who was in the lead, shouted something that sounded like 'Leaves!' and pointed. There on the horizon was a ruined city of sand and stone, and they pelted towards it as fast as they could. Soaked and shivering, they sheltered with their backs to enormous columns, and the rooves of an ancient temple kept the hail off their heads. Panting, they looked out on the absolutely extraordinary scene.

They'd gone from being roasted in an oven to being deluged with ice in an instant. The hail showed no signs of abating, and was so heavy it was actually settling on the sand before it melted. From the shelter of the ancient city they surveyed the scene. The sky was the purple-black of a bruise and the sun was no more than an eerie yellow light behind livid clouds. Then, almost as soon as the hail had come, it stopped; the clouds cleared, the sky brightened again, and the white covering of hail melted away in the fierce gaze of the sun.

Aidan stood with his hands on his hips. 'Well. I've been all the way to Siberia and back and I've never seen anything like that before. Good job you spotted this place, Abdel, else we'd have been as full of holes as a cheesecloth.'

'This is the ancient city of Thebes,' said Abdel. 'So it *has* seen something like that before. Thebes was here the last time the plagues came to Egypt.'

'So strange,' said Luna.

'And inexplicable,' said Konstantin.

'*Finally*,' said Aidan. 'You actually admit something funny's going on now?'

'Yes,' said Konstantin. 'A weather event like this is hard to link to back to the river of blood, unlike all the other plagues. And it does seem as if we're going to get all ten, so let's get to Luxor before anything else happens.'

They were completely dry by the time they entered the city, and although everyone looked a bit dishevelled it was as if the hailstorm had never been.

Luxor was such a contrast to the canvas and sand of the Valley of the Kings that the time-thieves and Abdel were struck dumb with shock. Camels jostled for space on the road with shining motor cars, and the pavements were one long market lined with baskets. Instead of cold drumming hail, there were lots and lots of pale green leaves blowing around on a warm breeze. A babble of sellers waved their merchandise in the time-thieves' faces – there were colourful fruits both familiar and unfamiliar to the time-thieves, bright vegetables and bitter-smelling spices.

Luna stopped before one of the baskets. It was full to the brim with strange long pale leaves, dry and desiccated. They seemed to be seething and moving.

'Oh!' she said to Abdel. 'What are these?' She'd never seen a spice or vegetable like it before. She put out a hand, a second before Abdel caught at her wrist.

'Locusts,' he said.

And as Luna reached out her fingers, the pale leaves rose as in a cloud, startled by her touch, to fly at her face. She cried out and began to bat at them, and the locusts shimmered and shifted on the air, flying high over their heads. There they joined the other things blowing about on the warm air, and the time-thieves realised these were not leaves but more locusts.

'The eighth plague,' gasped Aidan, as the market traders began to shout and beat at the insects with brooms, for fear they would lose all their produce. For the second time that day the travellers were obliged to run, just to get away from the flapping plague that threatened to blind and choke them. And very unpleasant it was too – there were so many locusts on the ground that the pavement couldn't be seen. The creatures were impossible to avoid and they made a horrible crunching underfoot.

The time-thieves and Abdel pelted down the main street until they came to the Winter Palace Hotel – a wonderful ornate frontage with creamy pillars and balconies and big glazed windows. A double staircase carpeted in red and gold swept up to the entrance, but at that moment it had the very odd addition of hundreds and thousands of locusts, clinging to the gilding like unwanted decorations.

The time-thieves fled through the grand doors into an even grander marble reception. Because the doors were the revolving kind, they immediately left the plague of locusts behind, except for a few hardy souls who came in clinging to their clothes. There were wicker chairs, green palms in big brass pots, silver tea pots carried by staff wearing red fez hats, and revolving ceiling fans kept the air cool and fresh. 'Gentlemen of the press' stood around in little huddles, clearly also hiding from the locusts. They flipped through their notebooks while their photographers smoked patiently, their modern box cameras slung around their shoulders. Egyptian messenger boys dodged around these islands of people like bright fishes, carrying trays and glasses and sandwiches to feed the hungry press pack.

'What are they all doing here?' wondered Luna aloud. 'They're as plentiful as the locusts.'

'Two words,' said Abdel. 'Lord Carnarvon.'

In the mosaic atrium they found a table and no sooner had they sat down than Konstantin took the Carnarvon family Bible out of his coat. He turned to Exodus, his hands shaking a little. They were all thoroughly frightened by that morning's happenings. 'Right,' he said. 'We've just had hail and locusts. Here we are: "I will send the worst hailstorm that has ever fallen on Egypt, from the day it was founded till now. Give an order now to bring your livestock and everything you have in the field to a place of shelter, because the hail will fall on every person and animal that has not been brought in and is still out in the field."'

'What about locusts?' asked Aidan, flicking one of the offending creatures off his sleeve.

'"I will bring locusts into your country,"' said Konstantin in reply. '"They will cover the face of the ground so that it cannot be seen. They will devour what little you have left after the hail, including every tree that is growing in your fields." Sound familiar?'

'Very,' said Aidan grimly, as Konstantin closed the pages.

Just as he did so, Luna said suddenly, 'What's that?'

Konstantin turned the Bible over. 'Not another damned locust, is it?'

'No,' said Luna, taking the book from his hands. 'I saw a sort of a drawing, just as you were closing the pages. Here.'

She turned to the front of the Bible, where there was a sort of diagram. It was drawn in many different inks, obviously over many different years, and it had little lines branching off with names below.

Abdel leant over her shoulder, his pendant falling forward from the neck of his robe. 'What is it?'

'A family tree,' said Luna. 'Often people draw them in the front of their family Bible. Look, here are all the Carnarvons. Here's the current earl, the first branch on his line. Then this double line means he married Lady Almina. And below him, Lord Porchester, another firstborn, and then Lady Evelyn.'

'That's all very interesting,' said Konstantin, taking the book back, 'but shall we return to the matter at hand? I feel like we're getting to the endgame.'

'What's that mean?' asked Aidan.

'It's a chess term,' said Konstantin. 'I played a lot on my sickbed – not much else to do really. The endgame is the very last stage, when the game is won or lost. There are only two plagues left, the darkness and the death of the firstborn. Maybe, just maybe, if we can make it so that Tutankhamun definitely stays in Egypt, he'll be at rest again, and we can stop the Mummy's Curse before he does something *really* terrible.'

Abdel said, 'In order for that to happen we have to find Monsieur Lacau as soon as possible. He's our best chance at getting Tut to stay. You all wait here. I'll try to sneak behind the desk and take a look at the register. That will have everybody's names and which rooms they are staying in. They'll just think I'm one of those messenger boys.'

The time-thieves waited, trying to blend in, which wasn't very easy, seeing as their clothes were thirty years old. Luckily, there was a raucous party drinking and laughing in the bar at the front of the hotel, and they captured most people's attention.

'Who are all those drinkers?' asked Aidan. 'More gentlemen of the press?'

'No,' said Konstantin. 'They're wearing those uniforms we saw in Hatshepsut's tomb. With the swastika on the sleeve. And they're speaking German. I'll go closer and see if I can hear anything.'

He picked up one of the English newspapers on the reception desk and went to loiter by the table of uniformed men, leaning against a pillar, half-hidden by a pot plant, pretending to read but actually listening carefully.

While Aidan and Luna were waiting for Agent Abdel and Agent Konstantin to return with information, they made a discovery of their own. At a corner table, tucked away from prying eyes, was Lady Almina Carnarvon, snuggled up with her 'friend' Colonel Dennistoun. Her scarlet nails caressed his cheek, while the other hand held a cocktail to lips as red as Lady Evelyn's.

'Hmm,' said Aidan. 'So much for friendship.'

'What do you mean?' asked Luna innocently.

'Well, I don't treat my friends like that, do you? Imagine if you and I were sitting here together, having a drink, and a bit of a *craic*...'

'A what?'

'A *craic*. A chat and a laugh. Would you be pawing at me like that?'

The idea of stroking Aidan's face made Luna feel most peculiar. 'Of *course* not,' she said hurriedly, her cheeks feeling suddenly hot.

'Well, there you go. Friend, my foot. They're billing and cooing like a pair of lovebirds.'

'But... but she's *married*,' said Luna, shocked to the core. 'And her husband is lying ill somewhere upstairs.'

'Takes all sorts, Duch,' said Aidan. 'Maybe Lady Evelyn was right about her. Maybe old Ma Carnarvon ain't exactly a plaster saint.'

Suddenly Konstantin was with them, sliding into the velvet booth beside Aidan.

'Did you find anything out from the Germans?' Luna asked him.

'Not much,' he replied. 'There was rather a lot of jaw about the locusts. The only interesting thing I did find out is that they're here to pick something up and take it back to Berlin.'

Aidan surveyed the uniformed Germans with his blue eyes. 'There's rather a lot of them just for a parcel.'

'Well, but they're not postal workers. They're soldiers,' said Konstantin.

'Soldiers?' Luna was surprised.

'Yes,' said Konstantin. 'They are storm troopers from a political organisation.'

'Which political organisation?' asked Luna.

'The National Socialist Party, apparently. But I've got no idea what they stand for. How did you get on, Abdel?'

'It was easy, Konstantinkass.' Abdel had a twinkle in his eye. 'Monsieur Lacau is in Room 17 on the first floor.'

The time-thieves walked up the mahogany staircase and along a carpeted corridor until they came to a door with the number 17 stamped into a brass roundel.

'Here goes nothing,' said Aidan, and knocked.

5 APRIL 1923
9.30 p.m.

A faint voice came from within. *'Entrez!'*

Pierre Lacau was sitting in a chair by the window, reading a newspaper in the last of the evening light. He looked up in mild surprise when the time-thieves and Abdel walked in, and folded the newspaper. When he saw Luna he got to his feet politely. 'Can I help you?'

Encouraged by his manners, Luna stepped forward. 'We'd like to talk to you about Tutankhamun, and what's going to happen to his mummy.'

The Egyptologist's face shuttered at the sound of her accent. 'I'm sorry, but if this is another appeal to take him to the British Museum I will not be moved. Tutankhamun belongs here. He will *not* be going to London, or Berlin, or anywhere else.'

Luna said, 'We absolutely agree with you.'

Now Monsieur Lacau looked even more surprised. 'You do? But you're English, surely?'

'Yes,' said Konstantin. 'Abdel is Egyptian, Aidan here is Irish, I'm German.' He supposed he would have to get used to saying that instead of 'Prussian'. 'And we all agree.'

Monsieur Lacau started to smile. 'Well, I'm very glad to hear it,' he said, much more warmly. 'Although I confess I wish that all your fellow countrymen shared your view. Here, sit down, won't you?' He studied them all in turn. 'I've seen you before. In tomb KV62.'

'Yes,' said Aidan. 'We are... friends... with the Carnarvon family.'

Monsieur Lacau sat forward. 'Are you here on their behalf?'

'No, not that,' said Luna. 'We don't speak for them – in fact, they don't even know we're here. We were just wondering if you could think of some way to persuade them to let Tut stay.'

Pierre Lacau stroked his white beard. 'Well, as you heard that day in the tomb, the new parliament and the laws of the independent Egypt are not yet in place. At the moment, under the old British law, the excavators do

have the right to take the artefacts, including the body.'
He sighed. 'I was hoping,' he said, 'that these mysterious
happenings and the stories of King Tut's curse would
deter them, but now I think we need another inducement.'

'What kind of inducement?' asked Konstantin.

Abdel spoke for the first time. 'Money,' he said.

Everyone looked at him.

'Monsieur Lacau,' said the waterboy. 'What is
Tutankhamun worth?'

'He is priceless,' said the Egyptologist gravely. 'He
would be invaluable to our country. To tourism, yes – but
more than that. To Egypt's national identity.' He stood and
looked out of the window. Darkness had fallen, pinpricks
of electric light warmed each window, but he spoke as if
he was seeing way beyond the bustle and the chaos of the
city, out into the lone and level sands of the desert. 'Egypt
is in the odd position of being one of the newest countries
with one of the oldest civilizations. King Tut could define
its rebirth. And there's something else.' He turned to face
them. 'So many sons of Egypt never came home from
the Great War. Boys Tutankhamun's age. Mothers, fathers,
brothers and sisters had no body to visit, no one to mourn.'

'Then that's something, isn't it?' said Abdel, his eyes
suddenly mirrored with tears.

'Yes, young man,' said Lacau looking at him piercingly. 'It is everything.'

He strode to the door with sudden decision and threw it open. 'Leave it with me. I will talk to the museum and we will come up with a financial offer to take to Lord Carnarvon.'

The time-thieves and Abdel shut the door behind them, allowing themselves to share a hopeful smile as they walked back to the stairs. Despite what Mr Conan Doyle said, they felt they had found not just an ally, but a friend.

But soon the smile was wiped from their faces, as two things happened almost simultaneously.

From inside one of the rooms there came a horrid, anguished cry: the torment of a soul in hell.

And, at that very moment, all the lights went out.

5 APRIL 1923
9.45 p.m.

They clung together in the dark, terrified by that awful scream and the sudden blackness.

'What happened?' asked Luna. Used to the warm reliability of candles and oil lamps, the travellers from 1894 had never known such a sudden blackout.

'Power cut,' said Abdel briefly. 'The electric light has gone out. Look.' He felt his way along the wall and the others followed him. Through the window at the end of the corridor they could see the city in total darkness – there were no lights at the windows now. The only illumination came from the silvery moon sailing above. Everything was unnaturally quiet and truly eerie.

'The Darkness,' whispered Luna. 'The ninth plague.'

Then a figure burst out of a nearby room and cannoned into them, giving them an enormous shock. 'Gosh, I'm so sorry,' said Lady Evelyn's voice. 'Can't stop. My papa's calling for my mother. I have to find her.'

At the sound of her voice, which seemed like it was at breaking point, the time-thieves forgot Tutankhamun.

'It's us,' said Konstantin. 'Your mother's downstairs in the bar. I'll show you.'

That was easier said than done, as the passageways of the grand old hotel were in total darkness. Fortunately at that point, members of staff were coming up the stairs with oil lamps. Konstantin grabbed one of the lights, and Aidan grabbed another.

'We'll tell him she's coming,' assured Luna. '*Go.*'

Konstantin and Lady Evelyn ran downstairs to the bar, and Luna, Aidan and Abdel entered the open door of Room 13.

What they saw there none of them would ever forget.

By the dim light of the oil lamp they could see a figure lying on the bed, a figure that they knew must be Lord Carnarvon, but he was almost unrecognisable.

'He looks *terrible*,' whispered Luna, appalled.

But it was Aidan who got it exactly right. 'He looks like Tutankhamun.'

It was true. Lord Carnarvon looked like a desiccated corpse – his yellow flesh drawn tight over his cheekbones; his eye sockets hollow like a skull; his dry, cracked lips drawn back in pain. He was so thin his arms were like sticks and his fingers twigs. His hair had almost all fallen out and his breath came in short, laboured gasps. He resembled, almost completely, the three-thousand-year-old body the time-thieves had found in the sarcophagus: a vital being, shrunken to nothingness.

It was a shocking change from the man they had seen being helped to the motor car, and an even more shocking change from the man they had met on their first day in Egypt, whacking golf balls into the dunes.

'He has an infection of the blood,' Abdel stated, too low for the invalid to hear. 'I have seen it before.'

Sensing there was not much time, Aidan walked forward and laid a gentle hand on the twiglike arm. It was clear that it was only when he touched Lord Carnarvon that the earl noticed them for the first time. 'Don't worry,' said Aidan. 'Your wife is coming.'

As if she'd heard her cue, Lady Carnarvon entered in a flurry of chiffon and diamonds, a cloud of gin fumes and cigarette smoke following her. Behind her came the ever-present Colonel Dennistoun, sheepishly wiping lipstick off his cheek.

'I just don't see why *he* has to come,' Lady Evelyn was saying, not troubling to lower her voice.

'Darling, don't be rude,' said Lady Almina. 'Ian is here for *me* – such a *difficult* time for your dear mama.' She touched her handkerchief to a totally dry eye, taking care not to dislodge her make-up.

'Shhh – Daddy's trying to say something.' Lady Evelyn leant over her father again and all those gathered, even the countess, fell silent.

The time-thieves glanced at each other. Would he say something damning about the mummy who cursed him?

The syllables escaped from the dry lips. 'Sooooo-eeeeeeee. Sooooooo-eeeeeeee.'

'Papa, I can't hear you,' said Lady Evelyn. 'Try again, darling.'

'Soooooozzzzzzz. Sooooo-zeeeeeee.'

Lady Evelyn turned to her mother, almost smiling through her tears. 'Susie! He's asking for Susie.'

'That damned dog!' cried the countess wildly. 'Can't he shut up about her, even now?' She turned to Ian. 'I told you that he thought more of her than me.'

She pushed Lady Evelyn out of the way and leant over her husband. 'Susie's not *here*,' she shouted, as if to an imbecile. 'She's *dead*.'

Lady Evelyn gasped in shock and shook her head, her bobbed hair swinging like a shiny bell. 'Mother! What a thing to say!'

'What?' said Lady Almina, all innocence. 'It's true. She died a few months ago, back at Highclere.'

'Yes, but even *so*,' protested Lady Evelyn. 'Could such a piece of news not wait until Father is better?'

'I don't think he understands much at the—' began Luna.

'When did Susie die?' Konstantin said, cutting across her. 'It's important.'

Lady Almina looked vaguely startled. '*I* don't know. I think it was… yes, it was November 10th. I remember it being an awful nuisance because I had to get my hair done for the ball at Badminton. I had all the bother of getting the gamekeeper to throw the body away.'

Luna hated Lady Almina very much at that moment. Imagine being so callous about a beloved pet! But Konstantin's mind was on something else. 'November the 10th,' he said, almost to himself. 'That was the day of the death of the livestock.'

'It was rather eerie,' said Lady Almina, shivering prettily. 'She just let out a great howl and died. So if my husband thinks there's a dog in this room, he's losing his mind.'

Just then there was a sound from the passageway, the sound of claws skittering on marble. Luna turned her head and saw a familiar figure. A jackal, whippet-thin and black as night, stood in the doorway, large ears pricked up attentively, almond eyes watching them all.

The others looked round, and the countess was the first to react. 'Ugh, how dreadful! It must be a stray. Filthy thing – shoo! Shoo!'

Abdel stepped forward, waving his hands. 'No, madam. No shoo. It is unlucky. The jackal is the messenger of the pharaohs. You must let him pass in peace.'

'Yes, do dry up, Mother,' said Lady Evelyn impatiently. 'He's not going to bother Papa now.' She nodded at the bed, where Lord Carnarvon lay quite, quite still. The haunted eyes were closed, and his shallow breathing could barely be heard.

The jackal, untroubled by the countess's reaction to his presence, trotted forward. He nudged his sleek head under the bony yellow hand that hung down outside of the covers.

The countess stepped forward to chase the jackal away but her daughter caught her wrist in a vice-like grip. 'No,' she said.

Everyone watched in frozen fascination. The earl's lifeless fingers animated and stroked the dog's silky black head, playing with the pointy ears. The eyes flickered once more and the arid lips moved, stretching into what would once have been a smile. 'Susie,' whispered Lord Carnarvon, much more clearly now. 'You're here. Stay now, there's a good girl. Stay.'

And then he died.

Numbly, the time-thieves and Abdel fumbled their way downstairs to the hotel bar. It seemed such a family moment that they knew they should leave the Carnarvons alone to grieve. They sat down at a table once more, now lit by oil lamps of jewel-coloured glass, a little island of stillness in all the hubbub of guests and waiters that flowed around them.

Konstantin said it first. 'It's over.'

'Of course,' said Luna. 'The death of the firstborn. The tenth plague.'

'How d'you figure that out?' said Aidan.

'Remember the family Bible?' said Luna, tapping Konstantin's pocket. 'Lord Carnarvon was the firstborn of his family. Must have been, because he was the earl.'

Konstantin pulled the Bible out of his pocket. Now it opened at Exodus almost by itself, so often had they looked up the plagues. He read: *'Now the Lord said, I will bring one more plague on Pharaoh and on Egypt. The firstborn son in Egypt will die, and there will be loud wailing throughout Egypt – worse than there has ever been or ever will be again.'*

Luna looked at the three boys in turn. 'It wasn't any of us. It was *him*. We found Tut but Lord Carnarvon made the mistake of wanting to move his body – not just out of his grave but out of the country.'

'And Anubis the jackal came to collect him for the underworld,' said Abdel. 'The Mummy's Curse has completed its terrible work.'

Aidan, who was thinking of how sad Lady Evelyn must be, said, 'Can't we flip back and stop this happening to him? We have the Time Train, after all.'

Konstantin shook his head. 'And do what? Stop one in a million mosquitoes from biting Lord Carnarvon? I know Professor Lorenz said change one small thing, but I think that might be a bit too small, even for him.'

'I suppose,' said Aidan soberly. 'So, what now?'

'We stop the articles,' said Luna. 'This is too serious to be part of some silly story. We can't write up this one.'

'I don't think we'll need to,' said Konstantin.

'What do you mean?' asked Abdel.

'Look.' Konstantin pointed to the men who crowded the lobby, all those eager young men with notebooks and cameras and trilby hats. 'The "gentlemen" of the press are all over this place like ants on an anthill. This story will get out without any of our help, believe me.' He shook his blonde head. 'Lord Carnarvon will be considered Tut's biggest scalp.'

6 APRIL 1923
9.30 a.m.

The following day the Carnarvon family returned to their tent, and Mr Conan Doyle, having heard the dreadful news, suggested that they all visit to offer their sympathies.

Mr Carter was at the tomb, but they found mother and daughter seated at the table. They were reading through the newspapers as Abdel served them coffee. The ever-present 'Ian' hung about in the tent folds, looking desperately uncomfortable.

In reply to their sympathies Lady Evelyn brought her fist down on the table so firmly that the coffee cups jumped. 'It was that confounded Mummy's Curse!' she exploded. 'Just like all the newspaper johnnies are saying.'

She pointed to the jumble of newsprint almost covering the table. Every newspaper carried the news of the earl's death, and every one had been published that day with a black border, as a mark of respect. But the respect did not extend to the headlines. Even the more respectable papers had followed the lead of the tabloids, and the stories were as lurid and sensational as they could be.

According to the British press, there was no doubt that Tut's curse had killed the Earl of Carnarvon. 'That blasted bag of bones got him in the end,' raged Lady Evelyn. 'Well, that's it. Porchey and all those brave young men fought for England and we are not taking that… that *thing* back to curse the country thousands died for. King Tut obviously doesn't want to leave. He can stay here and rot in the sand of his own country.'

'Nonsense, darling,' said her mother, who seemed to be handling the loss of her husband remarkably well. 'I was thinking we would give the mummy to the British Museum and take some of the treasure back to Highclere. You know, have a sort of little museum in the cellars.'

But Lady Evelyn wasn't having that. 'Nothing that belongs to that mummy – nothing he ever touched, sat on or drank from – should come over the threshold of Highclere Castle. Remember Papa did no more than lay eyes on him. Never even touched the body, to my knowledge. But if we dig that mummy out of his grave it will never rest until we're all in ours.'

The countess lit a cigarette and blew out a plume of smoke before she answered. 'Rubbish, Evelyn,' she said. 'You're just overwrought. Give it a couple of days and you'll see that I'm right. Tut goes back to England and that's that.'

The time-thieves looked from mother to daughter, silently cheering Lady Evelyn on to win this battle of wills.

Then Mr Conan Doyle, who had been watching this exchange with keen eyes, said something quite unexpected. 'Quite right, Lady Almina,' he said. 'I'm sure it would be quite safe to take Tut home.'

The time-thieves goggled at him – whatever was he doing?

Lady Almina inclined her glamorous head. 'Thank you, Sir Arthur,' she said absently.

'After all, it's not as if you were considering getting married,' he said casually. 'Or, rather, I should say, *re*-married.'

Now he had Lady Almina's full attention. Her head snapped round and she fixed her eyes on the author. 'Whatever do you mean?'

'Ah, perhaps you don't know, as you have just lately arrived. It is said,' Conan Doyle confided in his soft Scottish voice, 'that Tutankhamun reserves a particularly grisly end for women who remarry shortly after the death of their husbands. The reason being, of course, that the boy king's beloved wife Ankhesenamun remarried within a year of his death. She wed his vizier, Ay, the very man who murdered Tutankhamun. So the story goes that Tut's spirit stalks this earth, smiting hastily married widows, righting the wrong that was done to him.'

Lady Almina's face, despite the make-up, went as white as paper. She shot a look to the colonel, who was fidgeting shiftily in the shadows.

'But in your case,' said Mr Conan Doyle happily, 'I'm sure it is well worth taking the risk, as no such union is likely.'

Lady Almina glanced at 'Ian' while she finished her cigarette. 'Still.' She stubbed the thing out and sat up very straight. 'One wouldn't want any… repercussions if… one day… *far* in the future of course… one wanted to marry again.' She looked at her daughter. 'That ghastly little Frenchman – the one that's gone completely native – did offer me thirty-five thousand pounds if the mummy stays in Egypt. He approached me at the hotel in Luxor, just after your father died.'

Lady Evelyn clapped her hands together. 'There you go. *Much* better to take the money and leave Tut here. Because I have to tell you, Mother, that I think the only body that should come back to Highclere is Papa's.'

Lady Almina lit another cigarette and blew out a plume of smoke before she answered. 'Very well, darling. Have it your way. Boy!' She beckoned to Abdel. 'Go back to the Winter Palace Hotel in Luxor and tell that appalling Frenchman – what's his name? Latrine?'

'Monsieur Lacau, madam.'

'Tell Lacau to come and see me after my siesta, and bring the papers he wants signing. He can have his blasted mummy.'

Abdel couldn't prevent a sunburst of a smile. 'Yes, madam. At once, madam.'

'There, darling,' said the countess to her daughter. 'You've got your way. Just remember that in the near future, when your dear mama might have a request of you.'

Lady Evelyn pushed back her chair and stood up. 'I'm going to be sick,' she declared, and ran out of the tent.

Aidan followed her, and had to run up the dunes to catch up. 'Are you all right?'

'Yes,' said Lady Evelyn, sinking down on the sand. 'I'm not really ill. I just couldn't stand all that "dear mama" stuff. She's clearly going to marry Ian before Papa's cold, and gave me what I wanted so I wouldn't stand in her way. That's what made me want to be sick.'

Aidan sat down beside her on the warm sand and they looked out over the extraordinary landscape of the Valley of the Kings. 'What will happen to you now?'

'I'll go home, I suppose,' she said. 'They'll find someone for me to marry too.'

'Is that it?' Suddenly, to Aidan, Lady Evelyn's future seemed as bleak as the landscape. All her strength and eccentricity, her trousers, her bobbed hair, her outspoken confidence – what was it for? She'd been so outgoing, so original, but now, on the death of her father all the rules came into play. Highclere Castle would pass to the son – from the fifth earl to the sixth. And the daughter? This extraordinary girl who had come all the way out to Egypt to follow her father in his passion? She was now nothing more than a marriage prize.

At that moment, Aidan, a lowly navigational engineer, felt sorry for a lofty young lady of the English nobility. He could see how much more freedom he had than her, in this life that he had made for himself, and could see too that it would be many years before a woman would be able to live the life that he did.

He could think of nothing comforting to say, so he leant in and kissed Lady Evelyn Herbert on her wet cheek.

6 APRIL 1923
10.30 a.m.

When Aidan got back to Mr Conan Doyle's tent, he found his fellow time-thieves sitting with the author. Mr Conan Doyle was deep in thought, his fingers steepled together.

Aidan joined the circle and turned to Mr Conan Doyle. Always a planner and a doer, he asked his usual question. 'Now what?'

'Now nothing,' said Mr Conan Doyle, echoing the words Konstantin had spoken in the reception of the Winter Palace Hotel. 'It's over. The curse is up and running on its own at this point, and the Carnarvons have agreed that King Tut should stay in Egypt.' He looked at Luna. 'Take a final note to your father at the Ramesseum. Tell him we're finished.'

'And then?' asked Luna.

'Then we go home. To 1894.'

Abdel returned from Luxor with Monsieur Lacau, and the Egyptologist spent the afternoon in the Carnarvons' tent, drawing up the paperwork which meant that Tutankhamun would stay in his own country.

'It's terrible that Lord Carnarvon had to die to convince them to leave Tut where he is,' said Luna as they walked through the valley to the Ramesseum for the last time.

'It is terrible,' said Abdel. 'But at least they have a body. He will have a magnificent tomb of his own. They can visit it, and mourn.'

Konstantin knew he was talking about his brother Karim, and laid a hand on Abdel's shoulder sympathetically.

'Come *on*,' said Aidan impatiently. 'Never mind all this weeping and wailing. Let's take the letter to the Ramesseum and finish this thing.'

Abdel looked, briefly, furious. But he led them to the Ramesseum without a word, walking ahead with Konstantin, who made valiant efforts to cheer him up.

As they entered the temple complex Luna hung back and turned on Aidan. 'That was jolly rude. Why don't you like him?'

'Why don't I like who?' asked Aidan.

'Abdel, of course.'

'I like him fine.'

'Well, you don't seem to have much sympathy for him. And never have, right from the start.'

'Look,' said Aidan testily. 'I'm sorry he lost his brother. I am. But some of us have got family back home – *living* family – who we wouldn't mind seeing again.'

Luna squinted at him in the bright sun. 'Where were you just now?' she said suspiciously. 'Before you joined us, I mean.'

'Comforting…' began Aidan before he saw the trap. He sighed. 'Comforting Lady Evelyn.'

'Interesting,' said Luna. 'You seem to have all the time in the world for *her* grief. But not for Abdel's. You're mean to him, but you're making sheep's eyes at her.'

'I am *not*,' said Aidan, 'making sheep's eyes at Lady Evelyn.'

'You most *certainly* are,' said Luna, her Goodhart temper rising. Really, she didn't know why she was quite so angry, but now her fury was like a runaway train that she couldn't stop. And it drove her to say something quite unforgivable, something she would have taken back at once if she could. 'Have you even told her who you really are?'

Aidan stopped walking. He turned to face her. 'And who am I "really", Duch?' he demanded, blue eyes blazing.

Luna said nothing.

He threw out his arms. 'This is it, Duch. This is me. *I'm* not the one living a lie.'

Luna's mouth fell open. 'How exactly am *I* living a lie?'

'You worship that dad of yours but you haven't got the cogs to ask him what he's doing, dotted about all over time.'

Luna suddenly felt like she couldn't trust her voice not to wobble. 'He came back from the dead. That's all I care about. Can't you see that?'

Aidan heard the wobble. He spoke with a little less heat. 'People don't come back from the dead, Duch. All I'm saying is, if it was *me*, I'd want to know what he's playing at.'

'Shut up, you two,' said Konstantin, turning back. 'You're drawing attention to what was supposed to be a *secret* message drop.'

Luna and Aidan fell quiet, each one simmering silently. Casually, they all pretended to be gazing in awe at the giant statues, and Luna, stooping as if to button her boot, slipped her half-letter under the massive, fallen stone head of Ramesses. She knew what it said. Mr Conan Doyle had written:

All over. Stand down. Going home.

With those three short sentences their adventure in Egypt was over, and Luna couldn't help feeling a little flat. So before she left the massive head for the last time, she slipped her hand across the cool sand under the stone, searching in the dusty shadow out of habit.

There was something there.

She drew out a paper. It had on it a Rorschach blot – just a half across the fold, one wing of a butterfly – and a couple of scribbled lines.

Dear Luna,

Tell me when the mummy will be unguarded. I have orders to move him.

Your loving Papa

A number of factors had Luna prickling with suspicion at once. The handwriting, so similar to Papa's, but not quite the same. The fact that Papa had not used his usual sign-off, always so appropriate to their adventures: *yours until the end of time*. And, most damning of all, the fact that there was no kiss after the name Papa. But she had to check to be sure. She retrieved the letter she had left and held the two halves together, so the two wings of the butterfly blot touched.

They did not match.

Aidan approached, the quarrel forgotten, followed by Konstantin. 'What's up?'

'Look,' said Luna, showing them the two letters. 'Someone wants to steal King Tut. It's definitely not my father. So who?'

'I think we all know,' said Abdel.

'Arthur John Priest,' agreed Aidan grimly.

'Otherwise known as Arthur Cruttenden Mace,' said Konstantin. 'I hate to say it, but this looks like a German plot to take Tut. Don't you remember, the soldiers I overheard at the Winter Palace Hotel were talking about something they were planning to bring back to Berlin?'

'And Papa even said that Arthur John Priest told Howard Carter about the burial chamber, so he would do the hard work of excavating the tomb, and *then* Arthur John Priest would steal the sarcophagus.' Luna started walking. 'Come on,' she called over her shoulder. 'We have to get back and warn Monsieur Lacau. His hard-won prize is about to be stolen right from under his nose.'

6 APRIL 1923
Noon

Fortunately, the time-thieves arrived back just as
Pierre Lacau was leaving the Carnarvons. The
Egyptologist found himself the victim of a friendly ambush
as he was almost dragged into Mr Conan Doyle's tent.

Slightly dazed, the Frenchman allowed himself to be
steered into a chair. He was given coffee and sweetmeats,
and an introduction to the greatest detective novelist of
the age.

'Monsieur Lacau,' said Mr Conan Doyle, 'would you
allow me to ask you if you have, just now, secured the
remains and treasures of Tutankhamun to stay in Egypt?'

'I am happy to report that I have,' came the reply.
'She drives a hard bargain, the countess, but eventually I
named a sum that would satisfy her of thirty-six thousand

pounds. As for the Lady Evelyn, she is convinced that the Mummy's Curse carried off her father and will not let a fingerbone of King Tut's past the white cliffs of Dover.'

'Well,' said Mr Conan Doyle, 'that is a relief. But we do have one more potential problem.' He set down his cup. 'The Germans. Specifically a man working for them. A fellow styling himself as Arthur Cruttenden Mace.'

Monsieur Lacau was no fool. '*Styling* himself?' he repeated, one white eyebrow raised.

'Yes. His real name is Arthur John Priest, and we have reason to believe he is trying to steal Tut's mummy and take it to Berlin.'

Luna explained about the letter from the Ramesseum, the instruction it contained, the incorrect Rorschach blot and the counterfeit signature.

'Arthur John Priest is working for the Germans,' said Aidan.

Monsieur Lacau sat up at this. 'Yes, I saw a whole platoon of German soldiers in the hotel bar earlier.'

'They are not the German army,' said Konstantin grimly. 'They are storm troopers from a political organisation.'

'Which political organisation?' asked Lacau.

'The National Socialist Party.'

'How do you know this?'

'I am German myself,' said Konstantin, a little nervously. He was not at all sure how Monsieur Lacau, who had lived through the Great War, would take this. 'I heard them talking. We think they want to take Tutankhamun to their leader. And we want you to help us stop them.'

Monsieur Lacau looked troubled. 'I am entirely on your side,' he said, much to Konstantin's relief, 'but I am not sure what I can do. We could guard the tomb, and will. But my team and I are academics, not fighters. If a whole troop of crack German soldiers decide they want to take him, there is not much I can do to stop them.'

'But that cannot be true!' cried Abdel, the pendant round his neck clanking in sympathy. 'We cannot let him go. There *must* be a way.'

Monsieur Lacau frowned for a moment. Then the light of inspiration brightened his eyes. '*Mon frère*,' he said to Konstantin, 'how do you like the idea of being a double agent? It will involve you going over, temporarily, to the other side.'

Konstantin's eyes began to shine too. 'I like the idea very much,' he said.

'First and foremost,' said Monsieur Lacau, 'you will have to find a way to have a conversation with your enemy Mr Priest.'

'Not a problem,' said Konstantin. 'I don't think he's ever very far away from the Carter camp.'

'Just a warning,' said Aidan. 'I know this man better than any of you. I spent many moments – far too many – in his company. He's relentless. He won't rest – and he won't let King Tut rest – until he gets what he wants.'

Pierre Lacau took a drink, and when he lowered his cup he revealed a conspiratorial smile. 'Young Konstantin,' he said. 'I've the beginnings of an idea. You come along with me now and I'll explain all. And if you others don't know, you can't be forced to tell.'

'Couldn't you just give us a hint?' wheedled Luna.

'Well,' Pierre Lacau said, 'let's just say we will be giving your Monsieur Arthur John Priest something to steal.'

6 APRIL 1923
8 p.m.

That night, when the others were at dinner, Konstantin sat on the low and ancient wall between the tents. The last time he had sat here as the others dined inside, it had been because he had been forced out. This time, it was entirely by choice.

A figure moved in the darkness like a walking shadow. Was it Arthur John Priest?

'Konstantinkass?'

Abdel's voice sounded from the night. The waterboy came to sit with his friend on the wall, just as they'd sat together that first day of their acquaintance.

Konstantin turned to him. 'Is it done?'

Abdel had been dispatched to the Ramesseum that afternoon with a note in Mr Conan Doyle's hand, saying that the British were handing over ownership of the tomb to the Egyptians, and that because of the changeover, for that night only, KV62 would be unguarded by either nation. 'Yes,' said Abdel. 'I waited and went back, and the note was gone. The trap is set.'

'Well done.' Konstantin smiled at him. 'Now, you'd better scram.'

'I do not know this scram.'

'Go. Vanish. Make yourself scarce. Our old friend might be here any minute.'

'Yes.' Abdel looked suddenly serious. 'There's something I want you to do for me. Will you?'

'If I can,' said Konstantin.

Abdel took the pectoral pendant from his neck. 'Could you give this back to Tutankhamun? It belongs to him.'

Konstantin looked at the priceless thing in his hands. The scarabs shone in the moonlight like stars. 'Are you sure? What about your coffee shop? Remember – just one of these scarabs would pay for the whole thing.'

Abdel shook his head. 'The pendant is his. And it's more than just a pendant – it's a breastplate. It offers protection, and I feel that he needs protection more than me tonight.'

'All right,' promised Konstantin. 'I'll return it. Now, you'd better…'

'I know.' Abdel's smile flashed in the moonlight. 'Scram.' And he was gone, reclaimed by the shadows.

Konstantin sat chewing his flatbread and drinking his can of coffee, waiting. He thought it would not be long. And he was right.

After only a few moments of solitude he saw the glint of a watchface in the dark. Arthur John Priest loomed out of the night. He was dressed in his immaculate three-piece cream suit and his panama hat shaded his missing eye. Only the watchglass betrayed him. He looked down at Konstantin for a moment and Konstantin looked up at him, his face showing surprise he did not feel. Arthur John Priest indicated the wall with one hand. 'May I?'

Konstantin shrugged. 'If you want.'

His old enemy sat where his new friend had been. There was a tense silence while Konstantin chewed and waited.

Then Arthur John Priest spoke. 'I am sorry that you and I have never become acquainted. I think if we knew each other better we might find common cause.'

'I doubt it,' said Konstantin shortly. 'What common cause could we possibly have?' It had been agreed that if he was too friendly too fast, Arthur John Priest would become suspicious.

'You could go into business for yourself,' said Arthur John Priest. 'Take the shilling of the piper who's willing to pay you. Be an agent of chaos. Like I am. Then we'd both be in the same boat.' He chuckled to himself. 'No *Titanic* pun intended.'

Konstantin did not deny this. 'What are you suggesting I do?'

'Do what I did,' said Arthur John Priest. 'If one side doesn't like you, you join the other.' He studied Konstantin with his single eye. 'You're a Prussian, aren't you? Well, now you're a German. You're the enemy. Embrace it. Germany is at an exciting moment of her history. She is experiencing a new dawn, under a new leader. You could be a part of that.'

Konstantin forced himself to look interested. 'Go on.'

'I am not, as you know, a German. I have been dealing with the Egyptians in English. But, for the transport of Tutankhamun's sarcophagus, the National Socialists have arrived from Berlin. Also known as the Nazis for short.'

Konstantin had never heard that word before, but it sounded, quite literally, nasty – like a buzzing hornet.

'I could do with a German speaker to communicate my orders to them. I could do with *you*.'

Konstantin let his eyes wander doubtfully towards the tent. Arthur John Priest saw it. 'What loyalty do you owe to them? They sent you out to chew your crusts in the night, like a dog.'

Konstantin threw the grounds of his coffee on to the sand and stood up with decision. 'You're right. I owe them nothing. I'll do it.'

Arthur John Priest stood up too. 'Good boy. Now, we must hurry. The British are due to surrender Tut to the Egyptians tomorrow, but I have it on good authority that tonight, when responsibility for the mummy transfers from Britain to Egypt, the tomb will be unguarded. Our task must be completed before dawn.'

6 APRIL 1923
9.15 p.m.

When the pair of unlikely allies approached the mouth of Tutankhamun's tomb, Arthur John Priest gave a low whistle and shadowy figures appeared out of the night.

The National Socialist troops lined up at the top of the stone stairs, as if they were well used to gathering in formation. In their khaki uniforms they were almost invisible, but for the fact that the funny black crosses on their arms were on white circles, and so, that odd twisted symbol shone out in the night. Konstantin felt his clockwork heart racing, hammering, at a pace that told him he was afraid. He would have run right then, but he knew he couldn't. He had a very important role to play.

He led Arthur John Priest down the twelve steps Abdel had found, to the temporary gate Carter's excavators had constructed over the tomb's mouth. As arranged with Monsieur Lacau, KV62 was completely unguarded, and the only security for the priceless treasures was provided by a flimsy-looking padlock. Arthur John Priest pulled at the padlock, but it held fast.

One of the troops, presumably their captain, growled, 'Pity we have no guns. We could have shot the lock off.'

'Are you crazy?' said Konstantin, also in German, his outrage giving him courage. 'The doors behind that lock are three thousand years old.' Then he realised what the captain had said. 'You're not armed?'

The captain jerked his head at Arthur John Priest. 'He said no guns. Secret operation, he said. No noise.'

'What are you saying?' said Arthur John Priest. 'What's going on?'

'Just passing the time of day,' lied Konstantin. 'Or rather, night.'

'Have you got a key to this lock?' asked Arthur John Priest.

'No,' said Konstantin. 'We'll have to pick it. Do you want to do it, or shall I?'

For once, Arthur John Priest looked slightly uncomfortable.

'Oh, come now,' said Konstantin, starting to enjoy himself. 'We both know you picked the lock in the crow's nest on the *Titanic*, and stole the only binoculars. So, would you like to do this one?'

Arthur John Priest sniffed. 'You do it,' he said.

It was not the easiest task in the world to pick a lock in a desert by night. But to Konstantin, who had picked a lock at the top of a mast in the freezing North Atlantic, it was child's play. He applied the picklock he'd brought expressly for the purpose, fashioned from a fork that Abdel had helpfully provided, and the padlock popped open.

The troops stepped forward and tore through the temporary gate, leaving the precious doors alone. Konstantin looked at the ancient portals, with King Tut's hieroglyphs carved into the wood. A little musty breath of stone and sand whispered out of the tomb, and through the gap between the doors. The soldiers stepped back, and even Arthur John Priest said, 'You first.'

Konstantin realised that these men – these rough, tough soldiering men and this time anarchist – were afraid, and this realisation made him fearful too. But he had to lead them to the sarcophagus – that was part of the plan. He put his hand to the ancient doors and pushed.

It was a very different proposition going into the tomb at the dead of night, compared to when Konstantin had last entered in the company of Lady Evelyn and the other time-thieves. Then, there had been noise and excitement and the entire Carter excavation team. Now he was trespassing in the dark, surrounded by the spirits, the ancient gods and the long-dead king himself.

At least the soldiers, following heavy-booted in his wake and exclaiming in his mother language, were a comfort. Once inside, with the ancient doors closed behind them, they lit lanterns with tiny little tinderboxes they seemed to carry in their pockets, and the candles cast crazy shadows, animating the hieroglyphics on the walls into celluloid strips of moving pictures.

The mouth of the inner tomb yawned blackly out of the dark and Konstantin's mechanical heart began to speed again. Would Monsieur Lacau's clever plan work? It was time to find out. 'This way,' he said in German.

In the burial chamber, the gold of the walls reflected the light of the lanterns a thousand-fold. It was almost as bright as day as the National Socialist troops encircled the tomb. Standing at the head end of the sarcophagus, Arthur John Priest's eyes kindled greedily. 'Tell them we must work fast,' he ordered Konstantin. 'King Tut must be on a truck to Berlin by dawn.'

'Take care,' said Konstantin to the men. 'The grave is as yet untouched.' And indeed, it looked almost brand-new − a beautiful varnished sarcophagus of enamelled wood, burnished with gold. The soldiers put their hands on the thing and started to lift.

'Stop,' called Arthur John Priest, his voice echoing around the tomb and his breath wavering the flames of the lamps. Although he was speaking English he held up one stern hand; the soldiers understood the action, not the word, and pulled back at once. 'Translate please,' said Arthur John Priest to Konstantin. 'We must check that the mummy is truly inside.'

Konstantin relayed this instruction and all of the soldiers looked at their boots. Clearly no one wanted to touch the cursed mummy − not with all the dreadful stories swarming around it like flies around a corpse.

'Let me put it this way,' said Arthur John Priest pointedly. 'What do you most fear? Touching this coffin here and now, or opening the tomb in Berlin in front of Herr Hitler to find it empty?'

On hearing the translation the soldiers stepped forward reluctantly and put their shoulders to the task. The lid of the sarcophagus came away surprisingly easily and was placed gently on the floor. Inside was a figure wrapped in white bandages.

'Who will lift the wrappings?' asked Arthur John Priest, clearly none too keen to do it himself.

'I will.' Konstantin swallowed. He must keep his nerve – Monsieur Lacau had planned for this eventuality. He started at the head, and unwound the bandages layer by layer. Something fell out, and Arthur John Priest caught it in his hands. It was the dagger with the iron blade and the gold sheath that they'd found on the first day.

Arthur John Priest held it high, and the wicked blade gleamed in the lamplight. 'His dagger,' he breathed. 'It's him all right.'

One of the soldiers, suddenly finding courage, pulled back the remaining bandages to reveal a skull, discoloured and dirtied up with sand.

'That's enough,' snapped Arthur John Priest tensely. 'We don't need to count the teeth. Get the lid back on and get him out of here.'

Konstantin translated this message to the soldiers and they did as they were commanded. Once the lid was back in place, the six soldiers hoisted the sarcophagus on to their shoulders as if they were pall bearers carrying a coffin at a funeral.

Konstantin glanced below the place where the coffin had lain, at the bed of palm leaves and twigs and sand inside the immovable stone surround. It looked entirely uninteresting, but even so, he made sure no one saw him looking. Quietly and covertly, he dropped the pectoral pendant from his sleeve. It slithered out, silently as a snake, to fall in a metal coil into the tomb. A promise was a promise.

As the soldiers left the tomb with the sarcophagus, every lamp was extinguished except one. At the top of the steps the king was laid on the sand, and the soldier with the one lone light waved it high above his head three times before blowing out the flame.

There was an answering growl from the blackness and Konstantin had a sudden dark notion that Anubis's jackal had grown to a giant hound of hell, with eyes of fire.

But as the thing approached, the eyes of fire and the roar switched off with the engine. It was a truck, painted and canvassed in camouflage to conceal it against the desert backdrop. The only bright spot was a white circle on the side featuring, once again, that jagged black cross.

The canvas at the rear was lifted and the troops slid the sarcophagus on to the flat bed of the truck. The soldiers clambered in alongside it, and helped Arthur John Priest up too.

The one-eyed traveller touched the brim of his panama hat to Konstantin. 'You did good service to your country tonight, son,' he said. 'And a good turn for me. And as one good turn deserves another, let me give you a piece of advice.' He leant forward and the moonlight caught at the glass casement of the watch in his eye. 'There will come a time, someday soon, when you will have to pick a side. Another war is coming, one that is even worse than the first. And once again, Germany will begin it. And with the help of the mummy's dark magic, this time they will win.' He tapped the glass of his eye. 'Make sure you know where your allegiance lies.'

Konstantin, who was much more afraid, now, of the future than of any hound of hell or Mummy's Curse, knew he had to keep up the pretence. 'I know already,' he said. 'It's Germany all the way.'

Arthur John Priest looked at him keenly with his single eye. 'Then here,' he said, and held out his hand.

This was it, thought Konstantin. One more handshake, and he would be free.

Reluctantly, he took the offered hand.

To his horror, Arthur John Priest hauled him upwards, and he found himself seated on a wooden bench. The tailgate was slammed shut.

Konstantin was in the back of the German truck.

6 APRIL 1923
10 p.m.

'What's happening?' Konstantin looked around him in a panic.

Arthur John Priest sat back and nodded at the unit commander, who banged his hand on the side of the truck as a signal to the driver. He looked at Konstantin in surprise. 'I'm doing you a favour, boy. I told you one good turn deserves another. I'm taking you home.'

'*What?*'

'You're welcome,' said Arthur John Priest. 'I'm taking you away from those who despise you, and giving you a free ride back to Germany. We'll be in Berlin within the week.'

Konstantin was horrified. If he was taken to Berlin, away from the time-thieves and the Time Train, he would be stuck in the future forever. And it didn't sound like a future he wanted to be a part of *at all* – another terrible war, with these… these Nazis as the aggressors. But if he tried to escape, Arthur John Priest would realise he was a double agent and know that something was amiss. In a cold sweat, Konstantin waited for the roar of the engine, waited for the truck to pull away into the warm night, bumping over the dunes and rocky outcrops of the Valley of the Kings.

But something was wrong.

The unit commander was barking at the driver, and the driver was arguing back, looking all around his seat and shrugging.

'What are they saying?' asked Arthur John Priest, impatiently.

Konstantin hardly knew what to reply, because the truth was they seemed to be arguing about keys, which didn't make any sense.

Just then there was a jingling sound from outside of the truck.

In the red tail light he could see Abdel, triumphantly waving something above his head. The something was jingling. 'Looking for these?' he crowed.

The keys to the truck.

Abdel smiled at him. 'Konstantinkass,' he said through his smiling teeth. 'Get out of there.'

Konstantin didn't need telling twice. He vaulted over the tailgate before grabbing hands could stop him and ran towards Abdel. 'Towards the storm drain,' hissed the waterboy. 'Quick.'

Konstantin veered left, into the dark natural channel they'd entered months before. A hand shot out of the dark and grabbed him, and he nearly jumped out of his skin.

'This way,' said Luna's voice.

They hurried down a torchlit tunnel and Konstantin tripped over a sleeper. He could see the gleam of an iron track snaking into the dark – they were in the underground railway.

There was a row of handcarts lined up on the rails; Aidan was sitting in the first one, hands already on the pump. He beckoned rapidly. 'Get in,' he said. 'Abdel's on his way.'

'We didn't trust Arthur John Priest,' explained Luna breathlessly as she clambered into the front of the cart. 'Abdel insisted we came after you. And when the Nazis tried to kidnap you, he stole the keys.'

'We couldn't outrun them over the sand,' said Aidan, 'as they have the truck. But we thought this way would be ideal. Here he is.'

Abdel came pelting down the rail and they hauled him into the back of the handcart. 'Go go go!' he hissed. 'They're after me.'

Konstantin and Aidan pumped the handle up and down, sending the cart speeding down the track into the rocky tunnels in the bowels of the earth below the Valley of the Kings. For a moment it was exhilarating, rocketing along the track, round bends and down slopes. The way was lit with sodium mining lamps giving an eerie orange light, and they were alone on the track, as of course no one was transporting rubble in the dead of night. The air rushing past their faces was hot and bitter as hell. The excitement lasted exactly until it became clear that they were being pursued. Arthur John Priest and three of the soldiers had piled into the handcart behind them, and with their adult strength at the pump, were gaining on them rapidly.

'Let's just hope they don't start shooting at us,' shouted Aidan.

'They can't,' replied Konstantin. 'They're not armed. Their captain told me. This was supposed to be a secret operation, and guns are loud.'

'Well, that's a relief,' said Aidan. 'I guess we just have to stay ahead of them.'

'We have another problem,' yelled Abdel from the back of the cart. 'Remember one of the tracks is incomplete. We have to take the right fork to the Nile. The left fork is unfinished.'

'How do we take the right fork?' Luna yelled back from the front of the cart.

'Points,' bellowed Aidan, as he desperately pumped the handle. 'Railways have things called points, which switch the train from one track to the other. There will be a handle to switch tracks. Luna, take over from me. Just go up when Konstantin goes down.'

Luna swapped places with Aidan at the handle, and Aidan hung perilously out of the front of the cart. He peered into the half-dark ahead, narrowing his eyes. He knew what he was looking for – a fork in the track, and a long lever that would switch the points from left (certain doom) to right (the Nile and safety). They were rocketing down an incline now, and Aidan could see the fork where the track divided into two and disappeared down two different tunnels. And sure enough, there was the lever that switched the points. He could see that it was in the left position, which would send them to the incomplete track and the sheer drop. It needed to be knocked over to the right, and he only had one chance to do it. As the cart approached, he punched out as hard as he could and knocked the lever to the right. The points switched, the cart swerved sickeningly to the right, so rapidly that he thought the thing would derail. But the cart righted itself again, and they were speeding along the right-hand tunnel.

Abdel, in the back of the cart, jumped up and down cheering. 'Hooray! Hooray for the Englishes! Hooray for the Irishes! Hooray for the Prussians!'

Aidan turned around. 'Calm down,' he yelled, 'we're still being followed.'

Something flew at them from behind, something dark and swift, like a bird that had been trapped in the tunnel. Suddenly he couldn't hear Abdel cheering any more, and he hoped he hadn't hurt the waterboy's feelings. They'd been getting on so well recently. He could see Abdel had sat back down, but he couldn't think about their new friend just now. Soon they would be reaching the end of the track and they'd have to slow the cart before they hit the buffers, the kind of metal barrier at the end of a railway line. It was a pity, he thought, that he couldn't have switched the points back in time for Arthur John Priest and his German friends to go over the sheer drop. Unfortunately their pursuers would get to the buffers just behind them, but that couldn't be helped – they'd just have to escape as fast as they could. He took the handle back from Luna and began slowing down the cart. 'As soon as we stop,' he shouted, 'everybody out.'

The cart hit the buffers. Aidan, Luna and Konstantin jumped out.

Abdel didn't move.

Konstantin ran back. 'Something's wrong.' He cradled his friend, who seemed to be sleeping. A handle was protruding from his stomach.

It was Tutankhamun's dagger.

The dagger taken from the bandages of the pharaoh, and claimed by Arthur John Priest. The dark bird that had flown from the other cart had found its target, and claimed Abdel's life.

Konstantin's face crumpled. 'No!' he yelled.

Appalled, Luna and Aidan pulled him away from the crumpled body. 'Come on. We have to go.'

Konstantin looked up at them as if they were enemies – the cold stare of a stranger. 'I won't leave him. He needs a grave, a grave his brother never had. A grave like Tut's.'

'That won't happen if we're captured,' gasped Aidan. 'Come *on*. We can't help him now.'

Konstantin looked up, with sudden clarity in his grey eyes. 'You're right,' he said. 'We can't help him *now*. We can only help him *then*.'

There was no time to ask him what on earth he meant. The three of them ran out of the tunnel on to the sandy banks of the moonlit Nile, just as they heard the second cart hit the buffers. Suddenly Konstantin was ahead and he ran back over the Valley of the Kings like a man on a mission. Luna and Aidan stumbled after him, no idea where he was going. They were no longer being pursued – presumably Arthur John Priest had prised the keys from Abdel's dead fingers and was heading back to the truck as fast as he could. After what seemed like miles through the starlit valley, Konstantin fell to his knees and began to dig, like someone possessed. The other two realised where they were, just before they realised what he was doing. Here was the cairn that marked the spot where they'd buried the Time Train.

'Konstantin,' panted Luna, her voice thick with tears. 'What are you doing?'

'I'm going back,' he said. 'We have to save Abdel.'

'But we talked about this before, when Lord Carnarvon died,' she said gently, taking his arm. 'It's impossible.'

'No!' shouted Konstantin, shrugging her off. 'We change something. We change one small thing, just like the professor said. We use the Butterfly Effect.' He looked at them in turn. 'For the earl it was a mosquito. This was a dagger. Please. Abdel's our *friend*.'

His fellow time-thieves looked at one another. 'Very well.' Luna and Aidan knelt with him and they all dug together, as a team, until the Time Train was completely uncovered. It stood, shining and powerful, in the moonlight.

Aidan sat at the console. 'What time?'

'Earlier tonight,' said Konstantin, sliding into the back seat next to Luna. 'When I was talking to Abdel. Just before I met Arthur John Priest. Eight p.m.'

Aidan nodded and set the dials. 'Hold on, then.' He threw the ivory lever, and the night-time desert disappeared.

THE VALLEY OF THE KINGS EGYPT

6 APRIL 1923

6 APRIL 1923
8 p.m.

Once again, while the others were at dinner,
Konstantin sat on the low and ancient wall between
wall the tents.

A figure moved in the darkness like a walking shadow.
'Konstantinkass?'

It was enormously moving seeing Abdel again,
living and breathing and walking and talking. It was all
Konstantin could do not to hug him, but of course that
would seem utterly bizarre to Abdel. Abdel came to sit on
the wall, just as they'd sat together that first day of their
acquaintance, and Konstantin knew that the waterboy was
about to have the most important conversation of his life.

Konstantin listened impatiently while Abdel told him
about leaving the note at the Ramesseum, the note that

told their enemies Tut would be unguarded that night. 'The trap is set,' finished Abdel.

'Well done.' Konstantin smiled at him, and waited for what he knew was coming next.

'There's something I want you to do for me. Will you?'

'If I can,' said Konstantin.

Abdel took the pectoral pendant from his neck. 'Could you give this back to Tutankhamun? It belongs to him.'

Konstantin looked at the priceless thing in his hands. Then he said, quite loudly and clearly, 'No,' and replaced the breastplate around Abdel's neck. 'In fact, you have to do *me* a favour. No, more than a favour. Make me a promise. That you will not take this pendant from your neck until dawn, *whatever happens*.'

Abdel looked up, surprised. 'The pendant is his. And it's more than just a pendant – it's a breastplate. It offers protection, and I feel that he needs protection more than me tonight.'

'No one needs protection more than you tonight,' said Konstantin solemnly.

Abdel looked troubled, but agreed. 'Very well,' he said.

'And another thing,' said Konstantin. 'Don't come after me, whatever happens. I'll be fine. Promise you'll stay away.'

Abdel pressed his lips together, and Konstantin could see he wasn't going to get the answer he wanted. 'All right. You better scram. Go, I mean.'

And Abdel was gone, reclaimed by the shadows.

After only a few moments of solitude Konstantin saw the glint of a watchface in the dark. Arthur John Priest loomed out of the night, and Konstantin listened while his enemy appealed to him. Anxious to get to the tomb, he agreed to join the Germans' side.

Deep in the Valley of the Kings, the National Socialist troops lined up at the top of the stone stairs to the tomb. Konstantin felt his clockwork heart racing as it had before, hammering, at a pace that told him he was afraid. But this time he was not afraid for Tut. He was afraid for Abdel.

Konstantin led Arthur John Priest down the twelve steps. As before, he picked the lock, and soon they were unwrapping the bandages of the pharaoh's body.

The iron knife with the golden sheath fell into Arthur John Priest's greedy hands, and Konstantin thought there was no harm in trying to change another small thing – if he got hold of the knife, it couldn't be used against Abdel. 'I'll take that, if you like,' he offered. 'I could give it to Monsieur Lacau for his museum.'

But appealing to Arthur John Priest's good side was a waste of time. He didn't have one. 'You must be joking,' he replied. 'This blade is worth a fortune. It stays with me.'

Once the lid was back in place, the six soldiers hoisted the sarcophagus on to their shoulders. At the top of the steps the king was laid on the sand, as he was the first time around, and the soldier with the one lone light waved it high above his head three times before blowing out the flame.

There was an answering growl from the dark and the truck backed up to the tomb.

The troops slid the sarcophagus inside and clambered in beside it, helping Arthur John Priest up. This time, Konstantin had no intention of giving his hand to Arthur John Priest, no intention of getting into the truck. He walked to the front of the vehicle and peered into the driver's side.

The keys were already gone.

'*Verdammt!*' he exclaimed to himself. Abdel had defied him, and had come to his aid. He heard a jingling sound from outside of the truck.

In the red tail light he could see Abdel, triumphantly waving something above his head. The something was jingling. 'Looking for these?' he crowed. Abdel smiled at him. 'Konstantinkass,' he said through his smiling teeth. '*Run.*'

Konstantin's heart sank. Clearly there was no way of altering time too much – things were destined to play out just as they had before. He ran left, into the storm drain. Luna's hand shot out of the dark and her voice said, 'This way.'

Aidan was sitting in the handcart, hands already on the pump. As expected, Abdel came pelting down the rail and they hauled him into the back of the handcart. 'Go go go!' he hissed. 'They're after me.'

It was in Konstantin's mind to swap places with Abdel – but then of course he would be in danger from the knife himself. He would just have to trust the Butterfly Effect, trust Professor Lorenz, and trust that the one small thing he'd changed would be enough. Konstantin and Aidan pumped the handle up and down, sending the cart speeding down the track into the rocky tunnels below the Valley of the Kings. Just as before, they were being pursued; Arthur John Priest and the soldiers were gaining on them rapidly.

As the cart approached the points, Aidan punched out as hard as he could and knocked the lever to the right. The points switched, the cart swerved sickeningly to the right, and Abdel, just as he'd done before, jumped up and down cheering. 'Hooray! Hooray for the Englishes! Hooray for the Irishes! Hooray for the Prussians!'

This was it, thought Konstantin, heart racing. This was the moment.

The dagger flew through the air and Abdel stopped cheering, but this time the waterboy gave a gasp, as if winded. Konstantin was at his side in an instant. 'Are you all right?'

Abdel was clutching his stomach, and Konstantin's own stomach turned over. Had his clever plan failed?

But then Abdel gasped, 'Something hit the pendant.'

He held the breastplate out to the light with shaking hands, as the cart sped along, and in the sodium light Konstantin looked at the pectoral pendant with disbelief. The central scarab, worn just over the heart, had a star-shaped crack like the centre of a flower. Abdel scrabbled around on the floor of the cart. 'It was this,' he said, holding the iron dagger in his hand. 'They threw this at me. The pendant saved my life.'

Konstantin enfolded him in a big bear hug, and sent up a silent prayer of thanks to Professor Edward Norton Lorenz, wherever he was.

'No time for all that,' said Aidan. 'We're about to hit the buffers.'

The cart slowed and stopped, and they all jumped out. 'We can't let them catch us,' said Konstantin. 'Throw them the keys to the truck. That's what they want. Then they'll go.'

Abdel goggled at his friend in disbelief. 'We can't just let them *have* King Tutankhamun,' he said. 'What has this all been for?' They could hear the cart of their pursuers approaching.

Konstantin took his friend by the shoulders and shook him a little. 'Trust me,' he said. 'We're friends, aren't we?'

This convinced Abdel. As Arthur John Priest and his soldiers emerged from the tunnel on to the banks of the Nile, Abdel threw the keys on to the beach. It bought them crucial seconds, and as the soldiers scrabbled around in the sand, the time-thieves were able to make their escape.

6 APRIL 1923
10 p.m.

The time-thieves scarcely stopped running until they had reached their tent. They burst inside, closely followed by Abdel, to find Monsieur Lacau having coffee with Mr Conan Doyle.

They all flopped into chairs, grabbing handfuls of sweet pastries, suddenly ravenous. The food cheered Konstantin up enormously, but nothing would put a smile on the faces of Luna, Aidan and Abdel. The waterboy, in particular, looked near to tears.

Mr Conan Doyle looked at them all with amusement. 'Goodness, you look like someone died!' he said. Of course, no one found this funny because of what had so nearly happened to Abdel. 'Whatever's the matter?' asked the author more gently.

'Just that it was all for nothing,' said Luna gloomily. 'The puzzle chamber, the plagues. All the headlines. We failed. Tut's been wrenched from his resting place and he's halfway to Berlin by now. Arthur John Priest must be laughing all over his stupid face.'

'Oh, I don't know about that,' said Monsieur Lacau. 'I get the feeling that once Herr Hitler discovers what "Arthur Cruttenden Mace" has brought to Germany, your acquaintance will have bigger problems to occupy him than our conspiracy.'

Konstantin laughed and his fellow time-thieves and Abdel looked at him with surprise.

'How can you laugh at a time like this?' asked Aidan, aghast.

'Because I know something you don't,' said Konstantin smugly. 'I know that the sarcophagus Arthur John Priest and his Nazi goons have taken to Berlin is not the *real* Tutankhamun.'

Mr Conan Doyle chuckled in a delighted way, and began to clap his hands. 'Bravo,' he said. 'Bravo. Perhaps, Monsieur Lacau, you would explain how you and your team achieved the deception? How did you swap the sarcophagus that the Germans stole for the *real* King Tut? I'm assuming that's what you did?'

'As your Mr Watson would say, it was elementary,' said the Frenchman, dabbing at his white beard with a napkin. 'The sarcophagus they took was part of a window display from a cigar store in Luxor.'

Mr Conan Doyle beamed appreciatively. 'And the skeleton?'

'Donated by our friends at the Cairo Medical School. He isn't even real. He is made of Bakelite plastic. I believe his name,' said Monsieur Lacau delicately, 'is Sphinxy.'

'Monsieur Lacau wrapped Sphinxy in ancient bandages from his museum,' Konstantin took up the tale. 'Then he tucked Tutankhamun's dagger inside the wrappings, just where we found it on the real skeleton, to make the whole deception more convincing. It was the dagger which convinced Arthur John Priest that he had the real Tut.'

'Neither the skeleton or the sarcophagus would fool a real Egyptologist. But as we know, Arthur Cruttenden Mace, or Mr Priest, or whatever his name is…'

'… isn't a real Egyptologist!' chorused the time-thieves delightedly.

'And the real Tutankhamun?' asked Abdel, with a catch in his breath.

'Safely in his stone tomb, in the real sarcophagus below the false one,' said Konstantin.

'My team protected him with cotton wadding,' said Monsieur Lacau, 'covered that with sand and palm leaves, and put the false sarcophagus on top. Now the *real* Tutankhamun will be treated with the reverence he deserves.' Monsieur Lacau checked his pocket watch and gulped his coffee. 'I must go.' The Egyptologist stood, bowed so low that his red fez nearly touched the floor, put his hand on his heart and said, '*Merci, mes amis.* You have done Egypt a great service.'

Once he'd gone Aidan looked around at the others. 'We've done all we can,' he said. 'Time for us to go back to where we came from too.'

'London, that is,' put in Luna hurriedly, before Aidan could say *1894* and give them away to Abdel as time travellers.

Mr Conan Doyle finished his coffee. 'I expect you're right.' He smiled at Abdel as the waterboy took his cup. Abdel looked sadder now than when he'd thought Tut was lost. 'But I think we can stay for a little longer.'

Abdel's face brightened.

'Young man, ask Sallah to light the lamps and bring some food. We'll have a proper farewell party before we go.'

6 APRIL 1923
10.45 p.m.

It was the time-thieves' last night in Egypt and it was a good one.

They'd agreed between themselves to leave, Cinderella-like, at midnight. Lady Almina and 'Ian' had not deigned to come, so it was just Lady Evelyn, and the party was all the better for it. They all sat outside under the rising stars, white dappling the black night like the wing of a Grizzled Skipper butterfly. Sallah and his team brought cushions and rugs to sit on, and fabulous things to eat and drink, and lit a fire pit in the centre of the group of friends.

For once, Abdel could take his ease, and he ate and drank with the rest of them. Konstantin and the waterboy sat together, chatting companionably until, at a nod from

Sallah, Konstantin disappeared. He returned leading a white mule on a rope. The mule looked vaguely familiar. Abdel jumped to his feet and began to caress the animal's ears, just as he used to do with Cleopatra.

'Meet Ptolemy,' said Konstantin. 'He's Cleopatra's son.'

Abdel could hardly speak. 'How did you…?'

Konstantin smiled. 'I gave Sallah a sovereign and asked him to see if he could find Cleopatra's foal. He went to Luxor to find the breeder.'

Abdel enfolded Konstantin in a crushing hug. 'Thank you, my friend. I won't forget you.'

'Nor I you. Take care of yourself.' He looked across the dark desert, as if he could see all the way to Berlin. 'Evil is not a long-dead pharaoh. It's what's happening now. It's what is coming in the future.' He shook his head, as if to shake the thought away, and smiled at Abdel. 'I hope you open your coffee shop one day. You could always sell your pendant.'

Abdel shook his head, vaulting up on to Ptolemy's back. 'I took a different form of payment from my pharaoh.' He took Tutankhamun's dagger from his robe and the blade flashed in the moonlight. 'Knives represent great evil. This one nearly killed me, so I'm going to use it for good. I think the price of this will be enough to start my coffee shop, don't you?' And he nudged Ptolemy's sides and rode off into the moonlight.

Aidan and Lady Evelyn had their heads together too, sitting a little apart from the others. Lady Evelyn was unusually thoughtful that evening, not at all the bright young thing the time-thieves had first met. Aidan thought he knew why. As she'd told him, things had changed for her now, with the death of her father. She would go back to England and be married off to some useless young nobleman.

They watched the flames in silence until Lady Evelyn sighed.

Aidan said, 'What's that sigh for?'

'It's a man's world,' she said. 'Always was, and always will be. You'd think things would get better not worse. Progress. But they don't. A pair of trousers, a haircut, a vote. It's meaningless. Women are still nowhere. We're still in the desert.'

Aidan said, 'Like your female pharaoh Hatshepsut?'

'You got her name right!' Her red mouth smiled sadly. 'That frieze I showed you in her tomb is one of the only surviving images of her. Her statues were broken, her portraits erased. When her jealous stepson, Thutmoses III, succeeded her, he literally had her chipped off the walls of

355

history. And once people are gone, they can't come back. Except for…' She stopped.

'Except for who?'

Lady Evelyn shook her head. 'It doesn't matter.'

'It might.'

She sat up, as if making up her mind. 'I was going to say apart from your employer.'

'*What?*' Aidan sat up.

'The reason we were all so surprised to see Sir Arthur Conan Doyle, especially Papa, was that he'd heard he died. Way back in the nineties. In some sort of anarchist explosion.'

'Oh.' Aidan thought about this, strangely unsettled. 'Well, he didn't.'

'Obviously. But Papa could have sworn that his knighthood was awarded posthumously.'

Aidan didn't really want to admit he didn't know what that word meant, but he was too interested for pride. 'Post… what?'

'It means after you're dead.' She looked at him. 'But of course, now we know it was our mistake – he's very much alive.'

She gazed moodily at the flames again. 'But, you know, even if he *had* died, at least he left a legacy. Men like him can write things; men like you can build things. He'll be known for his books, you for your railways and machines. I suppose the *real* curse is being forgotten. But what can women do? Get married.' She sighed. 'I suppose I just have to hope that whoever they hitch me to will be a good sport about all *this*.' She moved her hand in a sweeping gesture, taking in the beautiful moonlit valley. 'But I'll tell you what. Even if darling hubby never lets me come back to the Valley of the Kings, I'll always be interested in Egyptology, right to my dying day. At least there are no borders in a woman's *mind*.'

Aidan looked at her from under his dark lashes. He remembered what Luna had said to him – that he should be honest with Lady Evelyn about how he came to be who he was. Then, he'd been angry. Now, he knew he might never get another chance. He took a deep breath. 'I was born a girl,' he said. 'But now I live the life I was meant to live.'

Lady Evelyn turned to look at him – really look at him, like she never had before.

'Well, darling,' she said, 'if that's the case, I don't bloody blame you.'

They sat in companionable silence for a moment watching the fire, then Aidan heard Konstantin calling his name. It must be midnight. He held out his hand. 'Goodbye, Lady Evelyn. Good luck.'

She smiled. 'Goodbye, Mr O'Connell.' She ignored the hand, leant in and this time, she kissed *him* on the cheek.

As everybody else seemed to be in pairs, Luna wandered off on her own. She didn't feel at all left out but oddly content, just enjoying the evening and the desert. It must be approaching midnight, and then their adventure in Egypt would be over. She sat down on the sand, then lay back and looked up at the stars and her namesake the moon, riding high in the sky. Papa had chosen her name; they would always have that connection, whatever time period she was in, and she knew she would see him again. And sure enough, as if she had dreamed him, his face appeared above her.

She sat up and shook herself a little, the locks of her sandy hair slithering against each other like snakes.

Papa sat in the sand beside her and folded her hand in his. She looked at the joined hands. 'I won't ask if you will come with us,' she said, 'for I think I know the answer.'

He shook his head. 'Not this time. But one day.' He squeezed the hand he held. 'You all did a good thing here. It's very important that the real Tut stays in Egypt and the false one is on its way to Berlin with our mutual friend. I think that the more trouble Arthur John Priest is in, the safer we *all* are.'

'And exactly how much trouble is he in?' asked Luna.

'Herr Hitler is not known for being a very forgiving man.'

Luna looked at the figures around the fire. The evening had turned into the music hall – Sallah's crew had produced some traditional instruments and everyone was now clapping along as Sallah attempted to teach Mr Conan Doyle an Egyptian dance.

'I still don't fully understand what a platoon of German soldiers was doing in Egypt,' she said. 'Lady Evelyn told us that their symbol, the swastika, is a symbol of peace.'

'And indeed it was, once,' said Papa. 'But Luna, what you have to understand is that in the not-too-distant future that symbol will come to embody the greatest evil to walk the earth.' Papa gave a sad smile and said, 'But that is a long way away. The only future I want you to worry about is in the past.'

It was then that Luna remembered what Aidan had said to her. That she didn't have the cogs to ask her father why he was running all over time. There had been enough dark hints and warnings. It was time for some straight talking. 'Papa. What *are* you doing, running all over time?'

He sighed. 'I knew you would ask that question eventually,' he said, half-regretful, half-proud. 'You remember on the *Titanic* I told you there were time travellers and time anarchists?'

'Like Arthur John Priest?'

'Yes,' he said, not quite meeting her eyes. 'Well, I'm trying to prevent you being caught up in an act of time anarchy that is due to take place on the 15th of February, 1894.'

Luna remembered what the Carnarvons had said when they'd first laid eyes on Mr Conan Doyle. 'Is it an explosion?'

'Yes.'

'Will it kill Mr Conan Doyle?'

'Not if I can help it.'

He looked up to the desert moon hanging over their heads. 'You should go,' he said. 'And I should too.' He cupped her cheek in his warm hand. 'But if you heed what I said, you will be all right. Don't be *anywhere* near the Greenwich Observatory at 4.45 p.m. on the 15th of February, 1894.'

'When will I see you again?' she said, knowing what he would say.

He held her very close and murmured the answer into her hair.

'Yesterday.'

And he vanished into the desert night.

While everyone was busy watching Sallah performing a particularly hilarious comic song, the time travellers from 1894 tiptoed away over the dunes in the direction of the Time Train. Konstantin walked ahead with Mr Conan Doyle, but Luna hung back to talk to Aidan. She knew there was something she had to say.

'I'm sorry,' she said, 'for what I said to you at the Ramesseum.'

He grinned at her, and she knew that it was all right. He took her hand and gave it a little waggle, before letting it go.

'I did ask my father what he was doing, just like you said.'

He shot her an approving look under long dark lashes. 'Good for you, Duch. What did he say?'

Luna explained about Papa's warning of an explosion due to take place at the Greenwich Observatory. Aidan listened and said, 'Lady Evelyn was speaking of that very thing just now. Remember what the Carnarvons said when they first saw Mr Conan Doyle? They thought he'd died in some explosion, and been knighted after his death.' Aidan looked at the author's figure ahead of them, standing tall and straight like a bookmark, keeping his place in the world. It seemed inconceivable that he would ever die. 'But of course he *can't* have been killed. If he had been, he couldn't be here. It's the same as us, isn't it? If we were dead we couldn't be here either.'

Luna's brow cleared. 'Of course,' she said. 'Lord Carnarvon must have been thinking of someone else.'

A short silence fell and then Aidan said, 'You should know – I did what you suggested too. I told Lady Evelyn how I started life.'

'Oh,' said Luna. 'And what did she say?'

'She told me she didn't blame me.'

There was another pause, and this time it was Luna who broke the silence. 'If the future got really good for women, and they could really do what men do, would you change back?'

Aidan shook his dark head. 'No. It's not like that. I think when it began I did change because I wanted to do what boys did. I felt different to my sisters, and didn't want to play their games. And yes, I wouldn't have been able to become an engineer and work with my father if I'd been a… girl. But no, I wouldn't go back. Nadia is dead. Aidan is who I am.'

Now it was Luna's turn to squeeze his hand.

'And besides, I think the equality you're talking about is a long way off. Look at Lady Evelyn.' He shook his dark head. 'Jesus, Mary and Joseph, what a topsy-turvy expedition this turned out to be. We didn't come to make friends, but we did come to take Tutankhamun home. We left Tut here, and we made a whole bunch of friends.'

They'd caught the others up and had arrived at the cairn that indicated where the Time Train was buried. They all dug together, Mr Conan Doyle too, until the tarpaulin covering the Time Train was in sight; none too deep this time as they'd buried it in haste, only expecting to stay a few more hours.

'Pity we have nothing for the Butterfly Club,' Konstantin said, digging out the sand like a dog seeking a bone. 'And poor Flinders Petrie of the British Museum.'

'I suppose,' panted Luna. 'Oh!' She stopped digging abruptly, and the others straightened up and looked at her.

'What's up?' asked Konstantin.

'Hear me out,' said Luna. 'Shouldn't we just check Tutankhamun never actually *went* to the British Museum? Back in Greenwich, Professor Lorenz said he did.

Do we need to make sure that what we did here actually worked?'

'Do you mean travel forward?' Aidan groaned. The biggest homebody of them all, he just wanted to get back to his own time. 'We've been back and forth in time like a fiddler's elbow.'

'No,' said Luna. 'We don't have to *travel* again to know what we need to know.' She pulled the tarpaulin off the cab part of the Time Train, ducked her head in and turned the hands of the console's clock to 4.45. The little doors in the clock face flicked open and Chronos sprang forth. She turned the bird on his spring so he poked out of the window, as if perching on the sill. 'Chronos,' she said, turning his brass key clockwise, 'show us the professor.'

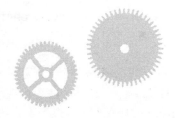

7 APRIL 1923
12.15 a.m.

It was perhaps the strangest visitation the time-thieves had ever had from the hologram of Professor Edward Norton Lorenz. Stranger than his appearance in the Butterfly Room of the Greenwich Observatory, or even in the waterlogged hold of the doomed *Titanic*. Here his hologram, luminous as the moon, appeared suspended in the infinite black nightscape of the Egyptian desert, like a silver-blue ghost.

'Are you in the library, Professor?' asked Luna.

'Honey,' smiled the professor. 'I'm an academic. The answer to that will almost always be yes.'

'Could you check something for us on your magic lantern?'

'On the microfilm reader? Nothing simpler.'

Mr Conan Doyle said, 'Professor. When we last spoke in the Butterfly Room at the Greenwich Observatory, you told us that King Tutankhamun was found in 1922 and taken to the British Museum. We think we have been able to change that. Would you be able to ascertain for us that he never in fact ended up at the museum, but remained in Egypt?'

'That Sir Arthur Conan Doyle?' exclaimed the professor, his smile widening. 'Say, I don't know if I ever mentioned but I sure loved those Sherlock Holmes stories of yours.'

'You did,' said Mr Conan Doyle drily. 'I thanked you then, and I thank you again.'

'Not at all, not at all. Goddamn shame you had to kill him off though.'

'Well,' said Mr Conan Doyle patiently. 'Each man has his own time on this earth, and when he's gone, you can't bring him back.'

Konstantin thought about Abdel, and was about to open his mouth to say that this wasn't *strictly* true. But the professor was speaking again. 'I think you left the door open, though, if you ask my opinion.'

'We are asking your opinion now.'

'Well, what if he *didn't* die when he fell off that old waterfall, and…'

'Professor Lorenz?' prompted Mr Conan Doyle gently.

'Yes, sir?'

'We're asking your opinion about *King Tut*. And the British Museum.'

'Oh, sure, sure.' The professor laughed good-naturedly. 'Let me just have a look-see here. Should be easy enough.' The professor seated himself and scrolled through his magic machine – and very strange it was to see in the night-black desert the backlit newsprint passing across his face. 'Well, it sure looks like the Brits went King Tut-crazy in 1922, from what I'm reading here.'

'In what way?' asked Konstantin curiously.

'Well, according to these reports in the *New York Times*: "There is only one topic of conversation… one cannot escape the name of Tut-Ankh-Amun anywhere. It is shouted in the streets, whispered in the hotels." Apparently the discovery sparked a Tutankhamun craze,' the professor went on. 'Images of the king or objects from the tomb appeared on jewellery, furnishing fabric, cigarette cards, penknives, biscuit tins and evening gowns. There was a King Tut dance, a stage magic act starring Carter the

Great, even a gramophone record called *Old King Tut*.'
Then he frowned. 'Huh.'

'What?' said Aidan.

'It all changed. Wow.' His hologram face fell.

'You mean, the public fell out of love with Egypt?'
asked Mr Conan Doyle.

'Did they ever. Looks like by 1923, folks were *terrified*.'

'Of what?' said Konstantin.

'Of the so-called Mummy's Curse.'

The time-thieves and Mr Conan Doyle exchanged
meaningful glances.

'You mean the Ten Plagues?' said Aidan.

'And the canary and mule?' put in Konstantin.

'And the Susie the dog?' supplied Luna.

'And Lord Carnarvon?' added Mr Conan Doyle quietly.

'Well, yes, all that,' said the professor gravely.
'But there was more. Much, much more. There's
a whole article here. Listen: American railroad
magnate Jay Gould died of pneumonia after visiting
Tutankhamun's tomb. French Egyptologist Georges
Bénédite had a bad fall on the steps of the tomb and
died. Sir Archibald Reid, a radiologist who X-rayed
some of Tut's artefacts, also died. Richard Bethell,

Lord Carnarvon's secretary, committed suicide. His father, Lord Westbury, on hearing the news, cried 'It's the curse of the Mummy!' and threw himself out of a window. In 1924, British Army major Sir Lee Stack was murdered in Cairo, after he'd been in Tutankhamun's burial chamber. And an Egyptian prince called Ali Fahmy Bey was shot by his wife in the Savoy Hotel, also after visiting the tomb.'

There was a silence as the time travellers absorbed just how lucky they had been. 'Did anything else bad happen to the Carnarvon family?' asked Aidan anxiously.

'It seems they were OK,' replied the professor's hologram. 'The kids lived happily. Lady Evelyn married a baronet.'

Aidan looked at his boots. So Evelyn had become a marriage prize, just as she'd predicted.

'And the earl's widow, Lady Almina,' the professor went on, '*she* married again.' He gave a piercing whistle. 'Jiminy Cricket, she didn't wait long. She married a guy called Colonel Ian Dennistoun just eight months after Lord Carnarvon died.'

'Just like King Tut's widow,' said Luna, a little sadly.

'But what about the British Museum?' asked Mr Conan Doyle, getting the conversation back on track. 'Did it lose out on the mummy?'

'Well, I wouldn't *quite* say that,' the professor replied.

'You mean… you mean King Tut did end up there?' groaned Luna. 'And all this was for nothing?'

'Not King Tut, no. But they must've ended up with a helluva exhibition, because as of 1923 everybody started donating stuff.'

'What kind of stuff?' asked Aidan.

'Egyptian stuff,' said the hologram. 'Big stuff like mummies and sarcophagi. Funereal monuments and statues from people's gardens, and even some graveyards. Then the little stuff. Rings. Cups. Scarabs. Scrolls. Things that someone's father or grandfather had brought back from Egypt over the centuries, all robbed from tombs or chipped off temples. *All* of it was given to the museum, free of charge.'

'But… but,' stuttered Konstantin '… *why*?'

'People wanted nothing to do with it,' the professor replied. 'Didn't want it in their own houses, in their own gardens, in case the Mummy's Curse came for them or their kin.'

'Really?' said Mr Conan Doyle in a very interested voice, his moustaches working up and down as they always did when he was excited.

'Yessir. The biggest single period of donation since the British Museum opened. They had more Egyptian artefacts than they knew what to do with.'

'But the *actual* mummy of King Tut,' said Mr Conan Doyle, 'and the sarcophagus, and the death mask and all his treasures – they stayed in Egypt?'

'They did indeed,' confirmed the professor. 'He wasn't even moved as far as Luxor. They built a special museum around him just where he lay, and across the country street parties were held in celebration of the tomb being returned to the Egyptians.'

'God bless you, Monsieur Lacau,' said Konstantin to the starlit heavens.

'What's that, sport?'

'Nothing,' said Konstantin. 'But Professor, one more thing.' He took a deep breath, suspecting he wasn't going to like the answer. 'What can you tell us about the swastika, and a Mr Adolf Hitler?'

But Chronos's ruby eyes dimmed, his little head dipped, and the hologram stuttered and disappeared.

'*Verdammt!*' exclaimed Konstantin. 'If only he hadn't spent so much time on Mr Holmes!'

'It's always the way with Chronos,' soothed Aidan. 'But at least we got to know what we needed to know. King Tut… stayed put.' And then he grinned at his own rhyme. And when Aidan grinned, everyone else had to smile too; they just couldn't help it. 'Come on,' Aidan said, climbing into the cab of the Time Train. 'All aboard. Let's break the news to Mr Flinders Petrie and the Butterfly Club.'

THE ROYAL OBSERVATORY OBSERVATORY GREENWICH LONDON

25 JANUARY 1894

25 JANUARY 1894
7.30 p.m.

For just a moment, the time travellers sat still in the Time Train, partly waiting for the peculiar heavy sensation of time travel to pass, partly wondering what to do next.

The gentlemen and ladies of the Butterfly Club resolved into being, with their stovepipe hats for the men and bonnets for the ladies, and around all of their heads the whirling rainbow maelstrom of the butterflies, just beginning to calm down and settle on their cards on the walls, to spread their wings and be still. The blue lightning of the Time Train crackled and subsided, and at last the travellers felt able to speak.

Konstantin watched his father approach the Time Train, along with Luna's Aunt Grace and Professor Flinders

Petrie, the director of the British Museum, still clutching the original golden shabti from Tutankhamun's tomb.

'What shall we tell them?' he whispered nervously.

'The truth,' said Mr Conan Doyle. 'Or at least, a version of it.' The author unfolded his long body from the Time Train and the children got out too.

The Egyptologist's eyes were alight with hope. 'So? You found the tomb?'

'We did,' said Mr Conan Doyle. 'But...'

The hope died on Flinders Petrie's face.

'We have reason to believe the grave was robbed,' Conan Doyle went on. 'A platoon of German troops was seen inside the tomb, and that same night a sarcophagus was transported to Berlin, Germany. Isn't that right, Konstantin?'

Konstantin woke up. 'Er, yes. Yes, that's absolutely correct.' He blew on his fingertips, spreading them like a dandelion clock. 'Gone.'

'But who?' demanded Aunt Grace, her smile evaporating. 'Who took him?'

'My dear Grace,' said the author. 'It was Arthur John Priest.'

Luna looked about her. Arthur John Priest had been in the room when they left, but he was not there now.

Aunt Grace frowned. 'So allowing him to join our society did not work.'

'I warned you,' said Dr Tanius Kass testily. 'He has changed sides already.' He drove one fist into the palm of the other hand. 'I *told* you it was rash to invite him in, Grace.'

'I took a chance,' she shot back. 'And it was the only one we had.'

'My dear friends,' said Mr Conan Doyle, holding up both hands. 'Let us have unity. There is time enough to deal with Arthur John Priest.'

'Time is all we do have now,' grumbled Doctor Kass.

'Not so,' Aunt Grace snapped. 'We have Daniel.' Then, more softly, 'We have my brother.'

Professor Flinders Petrie looked utterly befuddled by all these names and coded statements shrouded in secrecy, so he attached himself to the only truth he knew. He clutched the golden shabti to his chest like a child and stuttered out a single, pitiful question.

'So… so… there is to be no exhibition at the British Museum after all?'

He sounded so sad, and so lost, that Luna felt sorry for him.

She was not the only one. Mr Conan Doyle approached his friend and dropped a consoling hand on his shoulder.

'My dear chap. I rather think there *will* be an exhibition.'

Professor Petrie looked up, the hope returning to his eyes.

'Have your commercial artists paint you a wonderful eye-catching poster of a mummy, announcing a great exhibition of Egyptology. Call it what you like, but make it seem mysterious and inviting. Opening date a fortnight from today. And one week from today, at 4.45 p.m. exactly, meet me on the steps of the British Museum. Children, you too. You shall have your exhibition, Mr Petrie, or I know nothing about the Great British Public.'

Mr Conan Doyle smiled so widely his moustaches lifted like the wings of a bird in flight. He bowed his head to the company then walked down the brass meridian line with rapid and lengthening strides.

'Where are you going?' demanded Aunt Grace.

Arthur Conan Doyle did not turn round as he opened the double clock door and walked through it. He merely called over his shoulder,

'To write.'

28 JANUARY 1894
8.30 a.m.

For the past few days Luna had been at home in the tall and skinny house in Kensington with the butterflies on the walls. And of course it seemed terribly dull without Konstantin and Aidan. Chilly drawing rooms and boring libraries were a poor substitute for the tombs and tents and temples of the Valley of the Kings.

Despite the failure of the latest Butterfly Mission Aunt Grace seemed friendly enough, and was interested in Luna's stories of her Egyptian adventures.

The one thing on which she would not be drawn was the subject of Papa. Over breakfast three days after her return, Luna tried to learn a little more about what had been said at the Butterfly Club, but Aunt Grace immediately shut her down.

'Daniel was always headstrong – even as a little boy. And clever as a college of foxes. You can be sure he knows what he's doing, even if we don't.'

So Luna changed the subject. 'You're not angry? That we didn't bring back King Tut?'

'It was never about the mummy. It was about the money,' Aunt Grace rhymed flippantly, but she seemed very serious. 'The Butterfly Club needs to fund itself, and we were due fifty per cent of the exhibition at the British Museum. But Mr Conan Doyle says there is still going to be one, so we must wait and trust.'

Luna thought about this. She had that odd squirmy feeling about the Butterfly Club that felt like a caterpillar twisting in her stomach. Aunt Grace had more or less confirmed what she'd begun to think in the Valley of the Kings – that the Butterfly Club was more about profit than progress – or even people. 'I suppose… I suppose you do trust that he can pull this off? Mr Conan Doyle, I mean?'

Aunt Grace nodded and buttered her toast at the same time. 'The butterfly tattoo is like a hallmark.'

'What's a hallmark?'

Aunt Grace lifted one of the silver spoons from the table. 'A hallmark is a series of marks struck into things that are wrought of metal. See?' Luna peered at the spoon and saw a series of symbols bordered by little squares. 'The hallmark is a symbol of quality. The butterfly tattoo is like that.'

Luna was confused. 'But Arthur John Priest has a butterfly tattoo now. I saw it in Egypt. And yet he acted against us.'

Aunt Grace sighed. 'Our newest member is what your friend Konstantin would call a loose cannon, it is true. But believe me when I tell you that we need him, for a very specific reason. Our club sometimes needs a person who is willing to do things which a... *gentleman*... would not.'

'So his purpose is to do the Butterfly Club's dirty work?'

Aunt Grace shrugged. 'If you like. He seems to be entirely motivated by money, and people like that are surprisingly easy to understand.'

It occurred to Luna that Aunt Grace was one of those people too, but she said nothing out loud.

'And there is another consideration. Did you ever hear the phrase "keep your friends close, and your enemies closer"?'

Luna shook her head.

'Our feeling is that if Arthur John Priest is a part of our club, we may be better able to monitor what he is about.'

Luna thought about this. 'But Aunt Grace...'

'Yes?' There was a warning in the caramel tones, as if Aunt Grace was reaching the end of her patience.

'Papa *doesn't* have a tattoo. Why?'

The shutters came down. 'Eat your egg.'

Luna dispiritedly bashed her egg with the hallmarked spoon and ate obediently and without appetite, staring, unseeing, at the breakfast mess of toast racks and napkins and newspapers.

Her unfocused eyes fastened on a headline and the words gradually resolved:

LOT NUMBER 249 - THE TERRIFYING NEW AND EXCLUSIVE STORY BY SHERLOCK HOLMES CREATOR, ARTHUR CONAN DOYLE

The sub-heading read:

You'll Never Sleep Again...

Luna picked up the paper and unfolded it. She looked up to see Aunt Grace watching her. 'See, what did I tell you?' she said, lips curling into a smile.

Luna gobbled her egg and gulped her tea as fast as she could. 'May I be excused?'

She took the newspaper to her favourite perch, the window seat where she'd first seen Mr Conan Doyle's carriage. She loved gazing out at the flower girls and butchers' boys and lamplighters, the chimney sweeps and chandlers, all of modern London life. But for the next hour she did not move, her eyes fixed on the newsprint, ignoring, for once, the hustle and bustle outside. She was utterly engrossed in the story, of an Oxford University student who shared his rooms with the sarcophagus of a mummy he had bought at auction – lot number 249. The mummy was described in a terrifying, but very familiar, way.

... a horrid, black, withered thing, like a charred head on a gnarled bush, was lying half out of the case, with its claw-like hand and bony forearm resting upon the table.

'It's Tut,' said Luna to herself, remembering the wizened form they had found in KV62. 'It's King Tut.' But Mr Conan Doyle had added a further dreadful dimension to his mummy:

... a lurid spark of vitality, some faint sign of consciousness in the little eyes which lurked in the depths of the mummy's hollow sockets.

She read on, heart beating faster, as the mummy in the story came to life and began to claim the lives of those who saw it walking abroad at night – stretching out its bony hands to choke the life out of its victims. Luna was rooted to the spot – so petrified that she was relieved when the story ended. When she was finished, she shoved the newspaper away from her, as if the evil of the mummy was contained within its pages.

She went about with a growing sense of unease for the next day or so, wondering what Mr Conan Doyle was up to. By the headlines in the papers it was clear the story was a sensation, but she could not for the life of her see how writing a scary story would get Flinders Petrie his exhibition.

And then, two days later, another story:

MR CONAN DOYLE'S NEW EGYPTIAN SENSATION: *THE RING OF THOTH*

This one told the tale of a young Englishman trapped overnight in the Louvre Museum in Paris.

The complete silence was impressive. Neither outside nor inside was there a creak or a murmur. He was alone with the dead men of a dead civilization.

But quite apart from this terrifying thought of being trapped in a museum at night, it got worse. The trapped student witnessed a mysterious Egyptian, a night cleaner in the museum, bringing a mummy back to life with the aid of a cursed ring.

The action of the air had already undone all the art of the embalmer,

she read.

The skin had fallen away, the eyes had sunk inwards, the discoloured lips had writhed away from the yellow teeth.

In the coming days Luna could see that *The Ring of Thoth* was as big a hit as *Lot Number 249* had been. Outside her favourite window she could see the urchins of London wrapped in dirty white bandages, taking it in turns to be 'the mummy' and chasing their fellows across the cobbled streets. She could hear the press boys shouting about 'the Mummy's Curse', using Mr Conan Doyle's stories to sell their newspapers. And when she ventured out with her ha'penny to buy a paper herself, the headlines she read screamed:

ARE *YOUR* EGYPTIAN ARTEFACTS *SAFE?*

COULD THOSE HEIRLOOMS AND TRINKETS BRING DOWN THE CURSE OF THE MUMMY ON *YOUR* FAMILY?

WILL YOU SLEEP SOUNDLY WITH THE TREASURES OF THE PHARAOH IN *YOUR* HOME?

Stories of 'real' curses of artefacts began to appear. The one that caused the greatest sensation was the tale of the 'Unlucky Mummy' – a five-foot coffin lid painted with the image of a female priestess of Amen-Ra. The story attached to this one was chilling. It involved five Oxford students who decided to celebrate their graduation with a trip to Egypt to sail down the Nile. To remember their travels, they bought a souvenir: the coffin lid of a priestess of Amen-Ra. On their way back from Egypt, two of the men died. A third went to Cairo and accidentally shot himself in the arm while quail hunting and had to have it amputated. Another member of the group, Arthur Wheeler, managed to make it back to England, only to lose his entire fortune gambling. He moved to America and lost his new fortune to both a flood and a fire. The coffin lid was then placed under the care of Wheeler's sister, who attempted to have it photographed. The photographer died, as did the porter who transported it. The man asked to translate the hieroglyphs on the lid committed suicide.

The coffin lid was declared to be cursed and, following the appearance of Mr Conan Doyle's stories in the press, Wheeler's sister donated it to the British Museum in an attempt to end the family's run of bad luck.

Luna read that last sentence again, aloud. '"Wheeler's sister donated it to the British Museum in an attempt to end the family's run of bad luck." Hmmm.' Luna suspected that it was no coincidence that this particular story had surfaced at that moment, and definitely sensed that it had something to do with Mr Conan Doyle.

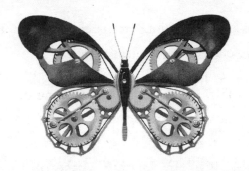

1 FEBRUARY 1894
4.45 p.m.

Twilight found Luna barrelling through London in a hansom cab.

After seven long days of Egyptian headlines it was, at last, time to meet Mr Conan Doyle and the other time-thieves at the British Museum as arranged. She couldn't wait to see Konstantin and Aidan again, and find out if Mr Conan Doyle's plan had worked. She was beginning to see, just as she had in 1922, the power of the press and how sensational stories could take hold in the public's mind.

At 4.45 on a January evening it was getting dark, and the sky was the colour of a Chalkhill Blue butterfly, but as Luna paid the cabbie and climbed down from the hansom cab it was still light enough to see the scene of utter chaos on the steps of the British Museum.

For a start, her own unfortunate cabbie could barely find a place to stop, so crowded was Great Russell Street. It seemed that every hansom cab and private coach in London had come to the British Museum. And every person that climbed from every conveyance was carrying something – a box, a carpet bag, a rolled parchment, or a wooden crate. And in each case the same thing happened – each package was unceremoniously dumped on the stone steps, the donor would get back in his waiting carriage, and then the horses would be whipped away at once, as if the plagues of ancient Egypt were after them. Then each carriage would be immediately replaced by another, and the process repeated.

It was a surprise to see this place, usually so noble and genteel, such a hive of activity. And now the lamplighters were lighting the gaslamps, Luna could see enormous posters hanging from the hoardings by the entrance. The posters, vividly coloured and cunningly realised, featured a face – one half a beautiful blue and gold death mask, and the other half the rotting countenance of a hollow-eyed mummy, complete with shredded bandages and missing teeth. The type screamed:

CURSED OBJECTS FROM THE MUMMY'S TOMB! NEW EXHIBITION COMING SOON!

It was so crowded, and the steps were such an obstacle course of artefacts, that it took Luna some time to spot Aidan, Konstantin and Mr Conan Doyle at the top of the stairs. It took her an even longer time to reach them once she did. She'd barely had a chance to greet them fondly before Professor Flinders Petrie threaded his way to their side, hopping over all the trunks and boxes.

'My *dear* fellow,' said the museum's director, grabbing Mr Conan Doyle's hand and working it up and down like the village pump. 'My *dear* young people. It's been like this all week. I've never *had* so many donations. I've had to take on more staff!' He turned to the author. 'Your stories *Lot Number 249* and *The Ring of Thoth* really worked their magic. The public are terrified – as, I expect, you planned?'

Conan Doyle smiled a satisfied smile beneath his woolly moustaches. 'I had a feeling that what had worked once in Egypt would work again in London. I just had to create another curse, but this time in our own era. So I wrote *Lot Number 249*. I decided if I could make the mummy truly scary, bring it back to life, so to speak, then it might capture the public imagination. And then, of course, it was child's play to place the story of the unfortunate Miss Wheeler and the Unlucky Mummy, to provide the Great British Public a solution of what to do with their own cursed artefacts. To avoid the Mummy's Curse, one simply had to give them to the British Museum.'

'Which they are doing in their droves,' chuckled Professor Petrie. 'Everyone's donating every single stone and trinket and won't take a penny for it. They're all following the example of your Miss Wheeler – they seem to think if they donate their artefacts to the nation it will turn the anger of the pharaohs. I'll wager we now own every Egyptian artefact in London, and the counties beyond.' He sighed happily. 'Of course, the donors' intention is that we return them to Egypt one day.'

'And will you?' asked Konstantin.

'In time, young man, in the fullness of time,' said Professor Petrie, not quite meeting anyone's eyes. 'But let's let the Great British Public have a look at them first.'

'There,' said Mr Conan Doyle, with a quite forgivable air of triumph. 'I told you, Petrie, that you would get your exhibition after all.'

'But Mr Conan Doyle, what if no one comes to see all these objects?' asked the museum director with a furrowed brow. 'Their owners clearly want nothing to do with them. What if the public are too terrified to view them, even behind a glass case?'

'My dear Petrie, I beg you not to trouble yourself,' soothed the author. 'What you suggest will never come to pass.'

'How can you be so sure?' asked Luna. The gentlemen dropping their artefacts on the steps clearly couldn't get away fast enough.

Mr Conan Doyle answered her question with another. 'Why did my story sell thousands of papers? Why have people gathered about their fireside for thousands of years – since Tut was alive and before – to hear ghost stories? It's elementary, my dear Luna. Shall I tell you the secret?'

He leant so close that his moustaches almost tickled Luna's ear. '*People. Like. Being. Scared.*' He turned to Professor Petrie. 'In fact, people don't just *like* being scared, they are willing to pay for it. And when your exhibition is the smash hit I predict it will be, don't forget our deal – fifty per cent to the Butterfly Club.'

Not even the reminder of this promise could dent Professor Petrie's joy. He shook on it gladly. 'A gentleman's word is his bond,' he said. 'And now, you must all excuse me. 'As you can see, I have much work to do.' He left them then, treading carefully through all the artefacts as he went.

Luna looked at all the objects, so numerous that you could hardly see the stone of the steps. 'What will happen to all this stuff?' she wondered. 'After the exhibition, I mean.'

'I sincerely hope it *will* be returned to Egypt,' said Mr Conan Doyle seriously, 'where it belongs. And now,' his tone lightened, 'I must leave you. For I have much work to do too.'

'Another ghost story?' asked Aidan.

'In a sense,' said the author. 'But this time, in place of a mummy, I am bringing someone else back from the dead. A certain Mr Sherlock Holmes.'

All three time-thieves turned to goggle at the author.

Luna frowned. 'But didn't Mr Holmes fall off a waterfall?'

'Well, I was thinking,' said Mr Conan Doyle consideringly, 'that as Professor Lorenz said, perhaps he *didn't* die after all. As that gentleman would doubtless tell me, all I have to do is to change *one small thing*…' And with a flourish of his opera cloak, he disappeared into the night.

'Where to now?' said Aidan as the time-thieves walked down the steps, dodging the artefacts.

A happy thought occurred to Luna. 'The Butterfly Club, of course,' she said. 'It starts at seven tonight.' She had had a long enough break from adventure.

'Of course. It's a Thursday,' said Konstantin, smiting his forehead with his palm.

'Wouldn't miss it,' grinned Aidan.

They had no trouble getting a hansom cab, as the carriages were still positively queuing to drop off members of the public with their donations. They scrambled into the nearest one to replace an anxious-looking gentleman who clearly couldn't wait to be rid of the Egyptian scrolls he held.

As the carriage door closed Luna looked out of the window, back at the British Museum. There, at the very top of the steps, quite, quite still among all the hubbub and the artefacts piling up, was a jackal, black as night, ears pricked up on the top of his sleek head.

He looked directly at Luna for a second with his amber eyes, then trotted off into the night.

UNTIL NEXT TIME . . .

A NOTE ABOUT THE PEOPLE AND THINGS IN THIS STORY

Although all the history books say that **Howard Carter** discovered the tomb of Tutankhamun, the 2020 exhibition at the Saatchi Gallery correctly credited a twelve-year-old boy with the most significant archaeological find of all time.

His name was **Hussein Abdel Rassoul**.

Howard Carter himself acknowledged that it was in fact Abdel who found the tomb, and gave the boy Tutankhamun's pectoral pendant as a reward. Abdel went on to open a coffee shop in Luxor. He donated the pendant to the Museum of Egyptology in Cairo.

Tutankhamun's dagger, which was found in the pharaoh's grave wrappings, was found to be a priceless artefact for a very interesting reason. Scientific investigation revealed that the iron from which it was made came from nowhere on earth. It was made of extra-terrestrial meteorite metals, so the dagger can truly be said to be out of this world.

Susie, Lord Carnarvon's dog, is said to have let out a heart-rending howl and died, at the very moment her master entered Tutankhamun's tomb.

Lord Carnarvon himself died in Egypt of an infected mosquito bite. He was laid to rest at Highclere Castle, now famously the setting for *Downton Abbey*. He was buried on a green hill overlooking his beloved home, and at his request there was no headstone or anything to mark his grave.

Lady Evelyn Almina Leonora Herbert was actually the first person in modern times to enter the burial chamber of Tutankhamun. Because of her small size, she preceded her father into the tomb, and so deserves her own place in history. The following year, Lady Evelyn returned to England, and married a baronet called Brograve Beauchamp. She never returned to Egypt, but she retained a lifelong interest in Egyptology, and survived to attend the 50th anniversary celebrations for Tutankhamun in 1972. She had one child – a girl.

Arthur Conan Doyle's Egyptian stories *Lot Number 249* and *The Ring of Thoth* were smash hits. *Lot Number 249* is thought to be the first appearance of the 'scary mummy' which has appeared in Hollywood movies ever since. Despite the success of these tales Conan Doyle abandoned historical subjects and instead brought his detective Sherlock Holmes back to life. He went on to write some of the most famous Holmes stories, including *The Hound of the Baskervilles*. Immortality was what the pharaohs sought, an afterlife better than the one that had ended, and arguably Sherlock Holmes was more successful *after* his death than before.

None of the multitude of Egyptian artefacts donated to the **British Museum** amid the scare stories of the Mummy's Curse have yet been returned to Egypt.

But **King Tutankhamun's** mummy never left his tomb. A museum was built around him and he still lies where he was buried, in the Valley of the Kings.

ACKNOWLEDGEMENTS

I feel extremely grateful to be releasing a book about Tutankhamun almost exactly 100 years after he was found. This is the bit where I say my thank yous, and they are as heartfelt as ever.

Thank you first and foremost to Jane Harris, Felicity Alexander and Teresa Chris who made this series happen.

I'm indebted to Emma Roberts and Jane Hammett for their forensic copyediting and proofreading.

Thanks to Inclusive Minds for introducing us to their network of Inclusion Ambassadors and a huge thank you once again to Charlie Castelletti for such a thoughtful and thorough early review.

Two wonderful artists, designer Thy Bui and illustrator David Dean, really brought this book to life with their wonderful cover and part titles.

Thank you to the entire team at Welbeck Flame for helping The Butterfly Club series to fly, with such dedicated hard work and enthusiasm.

The British Museum's Egyptian collection is certainly controversial, but it is also wonderful and comprehensive and was an excellent resource for this book. I heartily recommend a visit, and if you're brave enough you can see the fabled 'Unlucky Mummy.'

I couldn't write without reading, so thank you to (Sir) Arthur Conan Doyle for *Lot 249* and *The Ring of Thoth*, the short stories that sparked my interest in Egyptology. Oh, and thanks again to H. G. Wells for the Time Train.

For this book I also learned a lot from some excellent TV documentaries about Tutankhamun, most of which seemed to be on Channel 5. I can't recall specific names but they are all called juicy things like 'Who Killed Tutankhamun?' or 'The Curse of Tutankhamun' and I lapped them all up.

If you like tomb traps and puzzle chambers you can't do better than revisit the original Indiana Jones trilogy of films (1981-1989) which were a huge inspiration for this book.

Now some family. Thank you to Conrad and Ruby for knowing all the coolest butterfly names. My love of butterflies began in their company when they were little, in the caterpillar-shaped Butterfly House at London Zoo.

And last but never least, thank you to Sacha for always remembering to wind up my clockwork heart.

THE BUTTERFLY CLUB WILL RETURN IN THE MONA LISA MYSTERY...

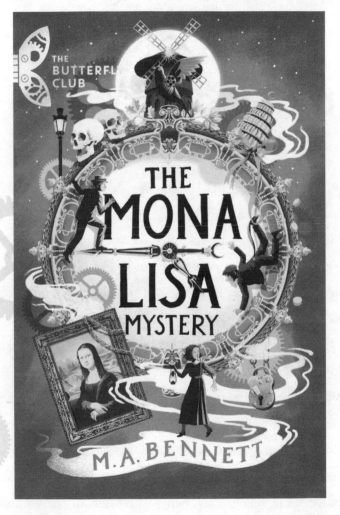

TURN THE PAGE FOR A PREVIEW

5 FEBRUARY 1894
9.15 a.m.

Aidan was the first to see the strange man walking down the railway track.

He was working with his father Michael and a whole gang of other navvies on a new railway snaking out of King's Cross Station – an iron way into the north which was to span rivers and burrow under mountains, a miracle of the modern age.

It was a bitter February morning. Aidan's breath smoked and his fingertips were numb, and as much as he loved the work, and the music of the steel picks sparking on the iron rails, he couldn't help just for a minute thinking of the arid sands and burning sun of Egypt. Even though to his father he'd been gone no time at all, in Aidan's timeline he'd spent months in the Valley of the Kings with Luna and Konstantin, following the historic discovery of the tomb of Tutankhamun.

Funny how, when he was there, he would have given anything to feel this cold, and now he would give the Crown Jewels to be warm again. Aidan stopped work to blow on his fingers, and that's when he caught sight of the man.

He was an odd-looking fellow; and a creature of contradictions. He was boxy and bow-legged and short in stature, but somehow impressive. He was wearing a frock coat and an opera cloak which bellied like a sail as he walked, as if he was moving unnaturally slowly; however, he seemed to cover the distance very swiftly. He seemed a man of importance, but as he came closer he appeared no more than twenty. He had that crinkly hair that refuses to do as it is told, which puffed out on either side of his head like a clown's, but his face was serious.

'It must be Christmastide already,' murmured Aidan's father, who always had a joke ready. 'The Pantomime's on.'

As Aidan and his father were working nearest to the station, the man arrived at them first and stopped. 'You are naffies?' he said in a strong accent which Aidan recognised, from his travels, as being from somewhere in the east of Europe.

'Navvies,' confirmed Michael O'Connell. 'Navigational engineers.'

'You haf chins?'

Instinctively Aidan put his hand to his face.

'Strong chins?'

It was an odd question. True, Aidan's jawline was not quite as masculine as he would like, but Da's chin was covered in a glorious black beard. 'I suppose so,' said Da, leaning on his pick, and pointing to his beard. 'One here and one there. We have cheeks and noses too.'

'No, no,' said the odd little man, with a chuckle dry as tinder. '*Chins.*' He performed a little mime, circling his forefinger and thumb on each hand and locking them together. Both Aidan and his father found themselves watching his hands. They were extraordinary – uncommonly white and delicate compared to their own rough working hands, and they moved in an exceptionally fluid way, graceful and swift. 'Chins,' the man said again. 'One link, two link, three link…'

'Oh, *chains*,' said Aidan, light dawning. 'You want chains.'

'Yes, zat is what I said,' said the man patiently. 'But they must be *strong* chins.'

As if he was addressing the village idiot, Michael O'Connell said, 'How long?' He spaced out his hands like a fisherman boasting of his catch.

'Oh, not long, not long,' said the man. 'Only long enough to tie pair of feet together and dangle a grown man over water tank.'

Aidan and his father exchanged their uncannily similar blue-eyed gaze. They were both, separately, convinced that this was, in fact, the village idiot.

'Come with me,' said Aidan to the stranger. Then, to his father, 'I'll show him the offcuts.'

He beckoned to the stranger, who followed Aidan, picking his way over the tracks in his shiny black-spat shoes. In an overgrown siding Aidan showed the little man various lengths of chain, left lying alongside the tracks. Some with links as big as a man's fist, some as small as a thumbnail.

The stranger looked down at them speculatively. 'Are they strong chins?'

'None stronger,' said Aidan. 'Good Sheffield steel. These large-gauge ones…' he pointed to the biggest, 'they can pull a locomotive.' He mimed the pistons of a train with his arms, and made the sound of a train's whistle for good measure.

The man nodded with satisfaction. 'I take those.' He pointed to the length of chain with the biggest links. Then he fished out his pocketbook. 'I pay you for chins.'

'No, no,' said Aidan, goggling rather at the sheaf of banknotes. 'These are offcuts. Scrap.'

The man looked confused.

'Chain too long for purpose,' said Aidan, doing a little mime to explain. 'Spare bits cut off. Throw away. You take.'

The man smiled for the first time, a rather charming expression which transformed his serious face. 'I am very much obliged to you.' He prepared to pick the chains up, first donning a pair of gloves to protect those exceptional hands. Aidan looked at him doubtfully – he didn't think his new friend had the muscle to carry the chains away.

'They're pretty heavy,' he said. 'I'll help you to carry them.' He coiled the chain expertly and heaved the bundle into his arms. The steel was so cold it leached the warmth from his body and burned his hands. He led the stranger back down the track and through the bustling concourse of King's Cross Station. The becloaked stranger and the young navvy carrying a huge serpent of chain caused the fine ladies in their crinolines and the city gentlemen in their bowler hats to stare. Outside on the street a hansom cab was waiting. The man got into the carriage and Aidan passed the chain up to the driver, to travel beside him on the box.

The stranger put his arm on the windowsill and leant out. 'You are very kind boy,' said the man. 'What is your name?'

'Aidan O'Connell,' Aidan replied.

The stranger looked at Aidan. His eyes were curiously intense, and seemed to have a light all of their own, almost as if they were made of mirrors. 'You come to the Egyptian Hall tonight. You know it?'

'*Do* I?' said Aidan. 'It's the big fancy theatre in Piccadilly.'

'The very one,' said the man. 'Come at 7 o'clock. Bring some friends. I put your name on door.' He reached behind Aidan's ear and brought out a shiny new sixpence. 'You will see quite a show.' Then he tapped on the roof to signal the driver to go.

Aidan stood for a moment, looking at the coin the strange man had dropped into his hand. Then he went back through the station and trudged back along the iron track to rejoin his father.

'What was all that about?' asked Michael O'Connell, when he had sight of him.

'He's in the theatre business, far's I can make out,' his son replied. 'Works at the Egyptian Hall. Maybe he needed the chains for security – lock the doors at night or something.' Aidan picked up his shovel. 'Must be doing well though. Feller had more money than sense. Pocketbook full of fivers he had.' He didn't mention the magic sixpence.

Michael O'Connell brought his pick down on the pinion with a ringing spark. 'Must be nice.'

Aidan shovelled some gravel to shore up the sleeper. 'He wants me to go to his play tonight, and to bring a couple of guests. You want to come?'

His father laughed. 'You know me, son. I'd rather be inside a coffin than a theatre. Besides,' the blue eyes twinkled, 'I can think of company you'd much better take – two young folks you've been panting to see again like a dog on a hot day.'